BLOOD RECKONING

Dan Waddell is the award-winning author of more than 20 works of fiction and non-fiction, among them the bestselling book which accompanied the BBC TV series Who Do You Think You Are? His first crime novel, the critically-acclaimed *The Blood Detective*, won the prestigious Prix Cezam Littéraire in France and was nominated for debut awards in the UK and USA. He lives in London with his family.

BLOOD RECKONING

DAN WADDELL

In memory of Jean-René Dastugue.

Prologue
The Northern Journal
Kenny Killing: Two Held

22 July 1992

*P*olice probing the brutal murder of retired miner Kenny Chester are questioning two schoolboys over the killing.

The boys, aged 10 and 9, were arrested at their homes last night, just days after the battered body of Mr Chester, 73, was found in a shallow grave on Dean Bank, a secluded beauty spot in Mackington, Northumberland.

It is believed they go to a primary school near where Mr Chester lived and close to the spot where he was murdered.

'We can't believe our own would do this,' Mrs Gladys Wrenshaw, a shopkeeper, said. 'Everyone is shocked. Kenny was a fine man. We all knew him and respected him. For him to be killed like an animal is awful. Whoever did it should fear for their lives. There are people here who would tear them limb from limb – and they'd deserve it.'

Three days ago, Britain was horrified when the body of Mr Chester, a widower, was found after his family reported him missing.

He had suffered multiple injuries. One senior detective told the Herald *he had been subjected to a 'frenzied attack'. His killers had apparently tried to hide his body by burying it.*

A police spokesman said: 'Two boys from Mackington are helping us with our inquiries.'

1

The cork snapped in the bottle's neck, such was his eagerness to get the damned thing out. He cursed. He fumbled through the drawer for a knife, a mess of cutlery, cooking implements and all manner of kitchen detritus, but found one eventually and used the tip to force it down into the red. Then from the same drawer he grabbed a metal sieve rusting from disuse, and through it poured two large glasses. He congratulated himself on his powers of recovery and took a deep breath.

This was never going to be easy. The place smelled of damp; he couldn't remember the last time he'd opened a window, never mind sprayed some air freshener. Why had he brought her here?

Stay in control, he told himself. *Stay in the moment.* Here was an opportunity he had thought he would never get. She had not run away screaming. Not yet. Squander it through cack-handed incompetence and his self-loathing would be limitless. He ran a sweat-slicked palm through his hair, used it to rub his face, drew a deep breath then picked up the glasses and went back out to the sitting room.

She was sitting at the table, pulling the takeaway cartons from the bag, taking care to lay them on the napkins the restaurant had provided. Her perfume was strong but pleasant. That and the smell of the food obliterated the odour of damp. He felt another flicker of anxiety. If he had known they were going to come back here on their first date he might have made more effort to tidy up. The living area wasn't too bad but he must keep her away from the kitchen. Dirty dishes were piling up in the sink and the older specimens were forming their own culture.

He handed her a glass, mercifully clean. She gave him a warm smile. She didn't seem put off. They took a sip. Another waft of curry from the table reached him, turning his stomach. He was too nervous. It had been so long. He wasn't so much out of practice as never in form. When she had suggested leaving the bar where they'd met, he'd agreed immediately, unable to believe his luck. He'd said how about a curry and she'd said sure, as long as they could take it away. Back to mine? he'd asked, almost certain she would say no. OK, she'd replied, and smiled. From that point on his breathing had been shallow, his hands sweaty, all of which he'd tried to keep hidden. Trying to appear normal. Whatever normal was.

Ten years ago he had paid a prostitute for sex. It had been a desultory, humiliating experience. Yet it was preferable to dating a woman who might want to get to know him. From then on, the prostitutes had become less humiliating and more dehumanizing. He made the decision to try and meet someone, his first choice a dating agency. At the last minute he'd pulled out of three arranged dates. Then only three weeks ago he'd met her at the bus stop in the pouring rain on the way to work. She was beautiful, tall, blonde, classy even, spoke well. She was there the next day. On the third day they spoke. She was eager, receptive, laughed at a weak joke of his. On the fourth he asked her out. She said yes. He wondered if there was a catch. She was working away for a week in the North but then they could meet. He asked what she did. Debt recovery, she answered. From that moment until this he had barely slept. He nearly hadn't shown up, but now he was glad he'd made the effort, as she smoothed down the front of her black dress and sat down.

He went to the plug-in CD player he kept on a bookshelf. Books, TV and games console provided his only forms of entertainment. He didn't have many CDs. But there was a Frank Sinatra album. He put it on and turned the volume down low in case she didn't like Sinatra. But he knew a background hum would be good. There was nothing worse than silence. He had spent years enduring silence.

He went back to the table, surveyed the cartons. 'What have we here?' he asked. He'd been so disoriented in the curry house he'd ordered in a daze. 'Chicken dhansak. Lamb bhuna. Which do you fancy?'

'The lamb,' she said decisively. 'There's lentils in the dhansak.' She shuddered. 'I can't stand lentils.'

Oh shit, he thought. A black mark. Why hadn't he asked? 'Luckily I love them,' he said. He handed her the carton of bhuna, pointed her to some aloo gobi and rice, and picked up a spoon, only then noticing that his hand was shaking. She gave him a sympathetic smile, seeming to sense his unease. He said nothing, sat down and dished out his own food.

She took a mouthful of her curry, started nodding her head. 'Hmm,' she said. 'Good choice.'

His head was pounding, mouth dry. He took a sip of wine, which didn't help with either. A deep rising sense of panic. *Eat*, he thought. *It might help maintain control.* He shovelled in some cauliflower. It was good. He felt better. He looked at her and smiled. 'Glad you like it.'

'I love curry,' she said. 'If I was told I could only eat one cuisine for the rest of my life, it'd be Indian.'

'Me too,' he said. He felt himself relaxing. He could do this.

'I'd miss pizza like crazy, though,' she said.

The way she said 'crazy' caught his attention, the stress on the last syllable, more of an 'ee' than an 'i' noise. Her voice had been free of any accent – but now there was a glimmer of recognition, although he couldn't quite place it.

'What's the music?' she asked.

'Frank Sinatra. Do you like him?'

She nodded eagerly. 'I love him. I quite like a bit of easy listenin'.'

Again, the dropped 'g' indicated an accent previously hidden. He didn't want to start prying, asking questions, because he didn't want to blow this. But curiosity and the need for small talk got the better of him.

'Where're you from?' he asked, putting a forkful of dhansak into his mouth. Then another. He was hungry.

'I moved to Leicester two years ago.'

'Before that?'

'I moved around a lot once I left school.'

'Originally, though. You have an accent. I can't place it.'

His own Geordie accent had faded. He'd not been home for two decades. There was no longer such a thing as 'home'. He fed himself more curry.

'Newcastle,' she said.

Shit, he thought. His heard started to pound, the panic returning. He felt a burn in his gut. 'Oh,' he said.

She laid down her knife and folded her arms. 'Near Mackington.' The accent had become far thicker.

He stopped eating. The discomfort in his stomach grew worse. He looked at her. Her face had changed. Grown harder, the eyes less soft. She started to nod. He saw something in that stare he recognised. Oh Jesus God no.

'That's right,' she said.

He stood up. Surely not?

'Who are you?'

'It doesn't matter, Craig.'

Craig? He'd stopped being Craig more than 20 years ago. The pain in his stomach grew more intense. 'What do you want from me?' He winced. It felt like a burning knife was being twisted deeper and deeper into his gut.

She shrugged. 'For you to die.'

He doubled over. Sweat began to pour from his brow. He vomited copiously, fell to his knees. He looked up. She was standing now. She'd got her handbag from the back of the chair. Another stab of intense pain seared across his stomach, making him gasp. He tried to speak but the pain was too concentrated. He fell on his side, curled up. His entire abdomen felt as if it was corroding, dissolving.

She kneeled over him. He hadn't noticed but she'd pulled a knife from her bag. The pain grew worse, making him twist, contort. He screamed out in agony. She remained still, smiling without mirth as his cries turned to a whimper.

'It will take some time for the poison to kill you, Craig,' she said softly. 'Yet every second will be absolute torture ...'

He didn't hear the rest. He squirmed as the fire consumed his belly and enveloped his whole being. He tried to sit up but the agony was too excruciating. He screamed once more, pitifully.

She held the knife to his heart. 'I could put you out of your misery,' she said.

He nodded. It was getting worse. Spittle bubbled at his lips. *Please*, he thought, *just end this pain. End it.* 'Yes,' he gasped.

'Fuck you,' she spat out venomously. 'You showed no mercy. You deserve no mercy.'

She put the knife back in her bag. Then she went to the wall and, grabbing her chair, pulled it over and sat down, leaning over him. 'I'm going to sit here and watch you die, just to make sure.'

2

Detective Chief Inspector Grant Foster could think of worse ways to spend the early hours of Sunday morning than attending the scene of a body in a burnt-out car.

He despised Saturday nights on call. They were awash with booze and its consequences. Of all the deaths he'd investigated in two decades of homicide work, he reckoned alcohol was a factor in well over a half of them. If it wasn't a bar fight turned bad, it was a drunk driver, or a smashed boyfriend who'd lost control and used something more deadly than his fists. Forget drugs; if they shut the pubs and off-licences of England tomorrow, the murder rate would shrink faster than a banker's bonus in a recession.

He'd be all right for a while if they did. He was working his way through his father's cellar of vintage red and there was still a year or two's worth of supply down there. Thinking about that did little to cheer him up. He could have been at home, asleep, after polishing off a bottle of 1970 Châteaux Lafite-Rothschild. But no, he was here on an affluent street in Chiswick, West London, cocooned in his car, the radio murmuring low, his air con blasting warm, recycled air.

The call had come from residents reporting a car on fire. Officers attending couldn't get near but once the fire brigade had doused the flames it was clear that someone was in the vehicle. There was little they could do initially. They needed to load the car onto the back of a truck, with the corpse, and let forensics have a look at both. In the meantime, it was his job to co-ordinate a door-knocking operation and hope a few curtain-twitchers might fill in the gaps.

He sat in his car, waiting for information on the vehicle's owner from its registration. It came through – David Stephen Lowell, thirty-five an address in Acton, West London, not too far from his own home. The man had owned the vehicle – a VW Golf – for three years. Foster checked his watch. Nearly 2 a.m. A bit late to be calling the Lowells to see if their car had been stolen. Or to make the first checks on whether the charred remains in the car were the owner's.

There was a knock at his windscreen. DS Heather Jenkins, bleary eyed and looking somewhat cold, despite it being unseasonably warm for November. He hit the button and the window fell.

'Warm, are we?' she said.

'Not as warm as him over there,' he said, gesturing towards the burnt-out wreck. 'But not too bad. I have an owner-male, thirty-five lives a mile or so around the corner.'

'Well, that figures,' she replied. 'We struck gold at number 16. Gnome-looking chap, lives on his own, the sort who seems to know the business of every person on the street. Chair of the neighbourhood watch. It was all I could to stop him setting up an incident room in his lounge.'

'Did he see something?'

'He says he noticed the car out there at 10.30 or so. Said it was still there an hour later. He could see someone sitting in the driver's seat, so he decided to take a walk, as you do. He passed the car, a black VW Golf, and said there was a young male approximately thirty, mousey hair, talking on a mobile phone and looking "agitated".'

'What constitutes agitated?'

'He said there were tears, shouting too. Said he thought he heard him repeat, "You can't do this to me!" with a few expletives thrown in.'

Once they had an ID they might be able to trace those calls.

'He says he saw no one else approach the car,' Heather continued. 'He was just going to bed, about 12.30, when it went up. He looked out. Saw no one running away. He called it in.'

'Was the engine running?'

'Apparently not. Not when he went for his walk, anyway.'

Foster's mobile rang. He answered. The control room. He said yes twice and ended the call.

'Jump in,' he said to Jenkins, starting the engine. 'Mrs Lowell called in a few minutes ago worried sick because her husband hasn't returned home.'

The house was a small terrace on a quiet side street, the type where the front door opened straight onto the street. Mrs Lowell answered the door, a timid woman in her late twenties, bags under her eyes. She explained in a whisper that their daughter was in bed as she ushered them in.

'How old?' Heather asked.

'Four,' she replied in the same hushed tone.

God, this morning is getting worse, Foster thought.

They went into a small sitting room, the TV a pale glow and low murmur in the corner.

'When did your husband go out, Mrs Lowell?'

'About five or six yesterday afternoon.'

'Did he say where he was going?'

'To the shops for a few things he needed. I didn't think much of it until it got late. He sometimes liked to get in the car and drive. Said it helped him relax, think a bit. Work's been tough for him recently. He's never been out this long, though.'

'Did you call him?'

'A few times, but only after about one. It went straight through to his voicemail. As I said, he sometimes needs his space.'

Heather cleared her throat. 'You said he was having a tough time at work. In what way?'

'He's in IT. They're talking of laying people off. He thought he might be in the firing line.'

'Was anything else bothering him?'

She fell silent as she thought. 'Nothing major I know of. He's often had periods of feeling low, ever since I met him. He always snaps out of it. He will this time. I just want him home. Can you help me find him?'

Foster took a deep breath. There was no point delaying her agony any longer. 'Mrs Lowell, your husband's car has been found on a street in Chiswick. It had been set on fire.' He paused. 'There was a person inside.'

'Are they hurt?'

'They're dead, Mrs Lowell.'

'Is it Davey?'

'We don't know,' he said; deep down, he did know. The only other possible explanations were that the car had been stolen and the thief was in it when it burnt. Or Lowell was faking his own death and the corpse in the car was some tramp or other. The first was improbable because car thieves tended not to park up on residential streets. The second stretched credulity to begin with but the eyewitness testimony of the nosy neighbour rendered it even more far-fetched. 'We need to carry out some tests.'

The woman began to cry. Heather went and sat beside her, putting a consoling arm around her. 'Is there anyone we can call?' she asked.

Foster took another deep breath and stood up. Suddenly the room felt too warm.

If Lowell's wife hadn't been on the phone to him before the car went up, then who was? He waited while she made a phone call to her mother.

'Had there been any problems with the car, anything mechanical, failures, that kind of thing?' he asked.

She shook her head. 'No, Davey took great care of it. Washed it every week inside and out. He liked fixing things.'

Foster turned to the mantelpiece. There were a few pictures of a child, presumably their kid, an angelic, smiling little girl with a mop of dark curls.

'Do you have a picture of your husband?' he asked.

'I do,' she said, almost hesitating. 'Not many though. He isn't one for having his picture taken.'

She crossed the room and opened a cupboard beneath a meagrely stocked bookcase. A few seconds later she emerged with small folder of pictures. She pulled a few out and started to sort through them. 'He didn't even let me put this up,' she explained. She found the picture she wanted. 'Here. Nearly four years ago. Outside Fulham Registry office. The couple with us were my parents. Dave didn't have any family.'

She handed the photo to Heather. She looked at it and smiled. 'You look beautiful,' she said. Mrs Lowell smiled, eyes filling with tears. Heather handed the photo on to Foster.

A sunny day. A happy couple. And a pair of pale blue eyes he'd not seen for almost two decades.

The picture fell from his grasp on to the floor.

Foster sat in his car unable, to take his eyes off the picture. He'd left Jenkins in there to comfort the woman until her mother or a WPC arrived. His excuse was that he needed to make a phone call. That was true, but he also needed some time to himself, to compose his thoughts.

Could it be who he thought it was? He'd asked Mrs Lowell all she knew about her husband, under the cover of potentially obtaining DNA from a blood relative. She'd said he was orphaned. An only child. He grew up in the north-east. Made his way to London at sixteen and had forged his own path since then. No family, not much of a past, she had said. It was a closed book. She knew David found it painful and didn't go there.

This time he didn't need a genealogist like Nigel Barnes to solve the riddles of the past. Barnes had helped him solve two series of murders with tangled bloodlines, but he could manage without him this time. Because if he was right, Foster knew this bloke's history almost better than he knew his own. He wound down his window and sucked in a few lungfuls of cold night air, wound it back and then grabbed his phone, willing it to ring. As soon as he got in the car he'd made himself monumentally unpopular by waking a contact at the Home Office, asking him to feed Lowell's name into the computer to see what came back. Eventually it rang.

Nothing. No red lights, warning bells, sirens.

He felt deflated. Maybe he had been mistaken. Heather appeared, climbed into the passenger seat.

'Mum's with her. WPC on her way.'

'What's wrong with you?' she asked, genuinely concerned, shifting her weight so she could face him. 'I've never seen you that thrown on a door-knock before. When you saw that picture it was as if you'd seen a ghost.'

'Maybe I did. Kind of.'

She raised her eyebrows. 'Being enigmatic doesn't suit you, Grant. You wear brusque better. You've come across David Lowell before, haven't you?'

'I think so.'

'Where?'

'A long time ago, in another life.'

3

Nigel Barnes was just rinsing the grounds of the previous morning's coffee from the pot in preparation for brewing a fresh one when the buzzer to his flat went. Sunday morning? Who could that be? Heather? But she had her own keys to come and go as she pleased. Unless she'd lost them. She had left in a hurry the night before when she was called to a scene in Chiswick, but they were attached to her car keys and she had driven.

'Hello,' he said into the intercom, not without irritation.

'Is that Nigel Barnes?' The voice was female, well-spoken, with a slight tremble to it.

'Yes?'

'I am so sorry to bother you on a Sunday,' the woman said. 'Especially so early. But I have been trying to call. My name is Lara Harrison.' He heard a child speak and she hushed it quiet. The name wasn't familiar. She sensed his hesitation. 'I read your column in this morning's *Herald*.'

Nigel had received some reaction from his weekly genealogy column in a Sunday newspaper, but mainly letters and emails, a few of them not very complimentary; but so far he'd not had people turning up on his doorstep a few hours after it went to press. But how had she found his address? He could worry about that later.

'I'm rather busy,' he lied. In his mind he scanned his piece for anything controversial or defamatory. He came up blank. It was an idiosyncratic article about the tendency for dates and events to repeat in families across generations. He told himself and his editor it was quirky, but deep down he knew it was born of desperation. His well of creativity had been dry for some time and his columns growing less inspired. It might soon be time to walk away. He wouldn't miss it. Though the money was welcome.

'Look, I'm sorry. I wouldn't be here if I wasn't desperate,' the woman said, interrupting his thoughts. She paused to quieten the child. She spoke again, even more plaintively. 'You have to help me.'

Nigel wasn't sure how, but if his article had prompted her to come and beg for his help then he felt indebted to let her in and listen. He found himself pressing the button to unlock the door and asking her to come to his flat, and hoping beyond hope she wasn't a psychopath who would walk in and tie him to a chair. A minute later there was a knock on the door.

He opened it. She was there, a little girl hanging on to her left hand. Her smile was embarrassed but grateful. In other circumstances Nigel could see she might be very attractive. Tall, slim, long brown hair, flawless skin, perhaps in her late twenties, early thirties...

But her hair was tangled and unwashed, her face was bleached of all colour, pale and drawn; circles like dark moons surrounded her eyes, which looked wild, unfocused.

'Thank...' she began to say before tears welled in her eyes and she bit her lip.

'Come in,' Nigel urged, thinking, *Please don't cry.*

He smiled at the little girl, blue-eyed, curly haired, who looked almost as tired as her mother.

'What's your name?' he asked.

'India and I'm four,' she said in a small voice.

'Are you?' he said, trying not to wince at the children's television presenter tone that had crept into his voice. 'Well, come in, India who's four.'

Ms Harrison had composed herself. Nigel took her coat. He turned on his television set, a recent purchase, the first he had owned in many years. Heather had insisted on it. She said she couldn't be at his flat without a TV because not having one was weird. He relented, like he had with so many other things. She had him wearing suit jackets rather than tweed blazers. Transforming him from a young fogey into a man of distinction, was the phrase she used. Before long she'd have him wearing trainers. He shuddered at the prospect.

'Do you have CBeebies?' India asked.

'Er...' Was it a disease? he wondered.

'Does the TV have Freeview?' her mother added, as if explaining a complicated subject to an imbecile. Which in a way she was.

'Satellite channels? Yes, I believe so.' He'd been quite excited at the prospect of documentaries, but then he watched one and saw they were mainly all about old machines or cars, presented by self-promoting contrarians.

'Channel 202' she said instantly. She smiled thinly. 'The TV's my co-parent.'

'Oh,' he said and flicked to the right channel. 'I was just making some coffee...'

'Yes please,' she said without allowing him to finish. She closed her eyes and put her hand to her head. 'Sorry, if you're offering, I would *love* some coffee. My manners have deserted me.' She bit her lip once more and he feared this time the tears would fall.

'Bad night?'

She took a deep breath. 'I haven't slept for more than two hours in a stretch for three years,' she said.

He didn't know how to respond.

'I'd better make it a strong one then.'

When he returned with the pot, she was sitting at the table with her head in her hands. The little girl was engrossed by the television. A sitcom actress he half-recognised was climbing into a spotted plane. He put the tray down and poured out two cups. It was only when the liquid hit the porcelain that she realised he was there.

They sat in silence, sipping the hot coffee, sound-tracked by the plinky-plink tunes of a children's show.

'Ms Harrison...'

'Lara,' she corrected.

'...Lara, how can I help?'

'My child doesn't sleep.'

He again began to wonder if she was mad. Had she mistaken him for someone else? 'I'm a genealogist,' he said.

'I know. I read your column. I know how you've helped the police catch killers.'

Nigel blushed. 'Only three times.' Only. A word that modestly dismissed three complicated, life-changing cases in one sentence. It often amused him how willing he was to downplay his achievements, but he felt it was vulgar to dwell on them. 'Most of my time is spent doing other things, tracing people's family trees and the like.'

'That's what I want you to do for me.' She stopped and shook her head. 'Actually, no, not for me, for India.'

'OK,' he said slowly. 'That shouldn't be a problem. However, forgive me if I'm poking my nose in where it's not required, but I fail to see what that has to do with your daughter's sleep issues.'

'Sorry,' she said for the umpteenth time. 'You must think I'm mad.'

'Not at all,' he lied.

'Well, I think I'm mad,' she said, and took another sip of coffee. 'I'm hoping something in her past might explain why she can't sleep.'

'I'm not sure insomnia is an inherited trait...'

'I'm not talking about insomnia.' She paused once more. He could see her fighting with every sinew not to snap. There was no doubt this woman was perched on the edge. 'She goes to sleep just fine. That isn't the problem. It's staying asleep. Every night, without fail, she wakes up within two hours of falling asleep, gasping for breath. She cries and cries, or at least tries to. Eventually she falls back to sleep, but within two hours the same thing happens. She wakes up saying she can't breathe, sometimes she says she's being pinned down. Every single night this has happened. For three terrible years.'

'Have you tried your GP?'

She snorted. 'Have I tried my GP? He says there's nothing wrong with her. I've tried psychotherapy. For both of us. I've tried craniosacral therapy. Homeopathy. Acupuncture. Zero balancing. Naturopathy. Healing. Massage. Aromatherapy. Hypnotherapy. Chinese medicine. Ayurvedic medicine. I've tried them all. There isn't a therapy, technique or New Age snake oil I haven't tried to make her sleep. My partner left because he couldn't handle it. My friends have abandoned me because they think I'm nuts. Only my parents are willing to help but they're old and live a long way away.

'This sounds really crazy, but frankly I don't care any more. For God's sake, I had her smeared with mud for a rebirthing ceremony because one practitioner told me she thought her entry into the world had been too stressful, so if she could be born again into a warm, safe environment it might help. Of course it didn't. Stupid bitch didn't have kids of her own, obviously. She charged me £200.' She sighed. 'Sorry, where was I?'

'Telling me why you think that researching your daughter's ancestry can help.'

'You wrote in your column this morning about things repeating themselves in families.'

'I did.'

'I found it very interesting.'

'Thank you.' Maybe he wasn't floundering in the world of journalism as badly as he imagined.

'Can you do it?' she interrupted, face tightening.

'Yes, I can do it, but…'

'How long will it take?'

'A couple of weeks, however…'

'I will pay more if you do it as soon as possible,' she said imploringly. 'I would give everything I own for just one decent night's sleep. Honestly, I will give you a grand a day if you do this for me.'

Nigel held his hand up, though the figure almost started them trembling. 'We'll talk fees another time.' He cleared his throat. Even after all this time he found it uncomfortable to talk about rates and payments, preferring to email that kind of information.

There was always something *vulgar* about discussing money, even if making it had become the only reason he still did this stuff. 'Just tell me one thing: how will tracing you and your daughter's ancestry help her sleep at night?'

'I think she's being haunted by an ancestor.'

4

By the time that Foster reached the post-mortem suite late on Sunday afternoon a few things had become clearer. Lowell was still missing. His mobile was a melted piece of plastic but his phone records showed there had been a series of received calls from a blocked number on the evening of his suspected death, including one that lasted for more than thirty minutes just before midnight. Lowell had also used his debit card at a petrol station that evening.

Foster had put a call into an old 'friend' who might help explain why Lowell's face was so familiar. He still hadn't got back to him.

Gareth Carlisle was waiting for him. Foster marvelled at the pathologist's appetite for work. He never seemed to be on holiday, always willing to come in at short notice. Foster could only guess that his home life was so miserable he'd rather be slicing and dicing the dead than having his feet up in front of the fire.

The corpse, blackened and unrecognisable, was laid out, or as close to laid out as a stiffened and contracted body could be. Despite the masking odour of disinfectant, the stench of smoke and burnt flesh still filled the room.

'Gareth,' Foster said, avoiding a long look at the body.

'Grant,' Carlisle replied, in his abrupt public-school tone. Many coppers found him too brusque but Foster appreciated the no-nonsense way he went about his work, and a parched sense of humour that the more precious missed.

'What do you reckon?'

'Were there any witnesses seen near the car or in it?'

'No, just a male at the wheel in the time leading up to the fire. Came from a neighbour. Though he didn't see it go up in flames, he saw it burning, can't have been too long after it started, and saw no one running away in either direction.'

Carlisle nodded. 'Interesting,' he said. 'I've had a look in the lungs and there's the presence of soot in there so I'd say he was alive when the fire started.'

'Maybe the car went up, caught him unawares? I'm assuming it's male.'

'Male, early-to mid-thirties at a guess. I'll come to that later. As for the car going up, perhaps, but unlikely. Look at the body. The head and upper torso are burnt much worse than the lower half of the body. Ninety per cent as opposed to fifty or sixty on the legs. I'd expect the opposite if the fire had started in the engine. You can't rule out some kind of bomb, I suppose, but given the overpowering stench of petrol I'd say that was your likely cause.'

'Self-immolation?'

'That's my hunch.' He wrinkled his nose in disgust, as if such a method of killing oneself was distinctly un-British. It was certainly rare, though Foster had encountered it before. For those dramatic souls for whom the hosepipe from the exhaust was simply too prosaic. Rather than going gently into the good night, they doused themselves in petrol and departed the world in excruciating pain.

'Trying to identify this wretched soul is more difficult. Or at least confirming identity. The name you supplied – Lowell, was it?'

'That's right.'

'Well, there's no dental records index we're aware of. The teeth are in ordinary condition, which suggests he had an aversion to the dentist in recent years. But there are a few fillings. Which could mean that this man isn't David Lowell.'

Or that isn't his real identity, thought Foster.

He left the post-mortem room, washed the stench of death from his hands and face, then walked outside, gathering his thoughts. Until Lowell was formally identified he couldn't be sure, and given the state of his body that could take some time.

He pondered his next move. He knew there was no way he could drop it now and walk away, even if stirring it all up once more was a daunting prospect. There were only two people who might know the answer he was seeking and be able to keep it quiet. The first, an old man, he wanted to forget. He would leave him until later. The second was the better option even though the prospect of contacting him made Foster feel sick. Still, he made his way to a public phone box. This was one call that he wanted to go untraced.

Age had not been kind to Harry Stokes since Foster had last seen him, outside Newcastle Crown Court, almost two decades ago. The mop of curly black hair had turned white and thinned. The cheeks had become ruddy and speckled with burst veins from the drink, the eyes deeper-set and yellow-tinged. But they still carried the same mischief; indeed, his wiry frame wore the pugilistic attitude his youthful career as an amateur boxer might suggest, even though he must have been nearing his mid-fifties. His face, as Foster wandered into a tattered south-east London pub, wore a look of amusement. A look that said if Foster was here after all this time, requesting a meeting, even though he hated Harry with a passion, it could only mean one thing. Foster saw Stokes' pint was full, ordered one for himself and pulled up a stool opposite. The pub was empty, save for a few hardened drinkers savouring a liquid Sunday lunch. It was the sort of pub he expected Stokes to frequent: shabby, frayed carpet; wobbling stools; ceilings still stained yellow from the days of smoking.

'Grant Foster,' Stokes said in his deep Glaswegian growl. 'Detective Chief Inspector, is it?'

'That's right, Harry.' He looked him over once more. A shiny grey suit that was two sizes too small, a maroon shirt and a yellow and black striped tie that clashed loudly. 'You just come from a GQ photoshoot?'

'Very funny.'

'Which rag are you on now?'

'The *Mail*, same as always. Of course things are a lot different now. Computers and shit, young Oxbridge graduates everywhere, the fucking Internet.' The last word was spoken as if mention of it would bring on a deadly disease. 'I barely leave the office. I'm like the Olympic torch. I never go out.'

'Pays the mortgage.'

'Aye, and the alimony.'

'You and Carol split?' Carol was another tabloid hack; together they had formed a hot-metal Bonnie and Clyde.

He snorted derisively. 'That mad old bitch? She had the good grace to drink herself to death after we split, bless her cotton socks. No, I'm talking about wives two and three.'

'You've been busy.'

'Well, a man has to have a hobby. Though macramé would have been less expensive. Anyway, Grant, this all very nice and cosy, meeting up and shooting the shit. But I know you think I'm a lowlife piece of scum so let's skip the bullshit, hypocritical, "how are you"s. I don't have to be nice to you because you obviously want something from me. What is it?'

'I still have dreams about it. Do you?'

Stokes said nothing, eyes narrowing. Then he sniffed and gave his head a small incredulous shake. 'What is this? You after some sort of therapy?'

'It didn't affect you?'

'Course it affected me. Ten weeks in that courtroom, hearing all that detail, looking at those two evil little bastards. Then getting slaughtered every night to try and forget about it enough to sleep. Ten weeks of that. It almost killed me. That's why Carol and me split. We lived that case. But who gives a shit? Stories like that come around once in a blue moon. This isn't why you're here, is it? You and I have seen and listened to all kinds of awful shit over the years, you more than me, I suspect. We deal with it. It's all part of the game, isn't it?'

'I think that's where you and I differ, Harry. I never see it as a game.'

'You always were a sanctimonious prick, Grant,' Stokes spat back, his cheeks reddening further. 'Some things never change.' He swigged hard at his beer, wiped his mouth with the back of his hand. 'But the way I see it, we've more in common than you might think. We're both becoming obsolete in this world. Don't tell me you don't know that.'

He had a point. Old school cop and old school hack were endangered species. He didn't expect people to weep over that fact.

'Come on,' Stokes added with growing impatience. 'What do you want to know?'

'Do you know where they are now?'

'Who?'

'Roy Rogers and Trigger. Who do you think?

'Dibb and Schofield?' Stokes' creased face wore a look of increasing bewilderment

'Yes, Dibb and Schofield.'

Stokes' demeanour became more wary. 'Surely that's information you know. Or you can at least find out?'

'Yes, I can,' Foster replied. Stokes' frown deepened. 'But I don't want to.'

'Why?'

'That's my business.'

'Sounds to me like you're making it mine.'

'Do you know where they are?'

'Yes.'

'What their new identities are?'

'Yes.'

Foster took another sip and paused. He looked at Stokes, a twinkle of joy in his rheumy eyes. This was always going to be the hardest bit. He girded himself. 'I know you don't hand over information without something in return, Harry,' he explained. 'Of course there will be a nice little exclusive for you. If I'm right.'

'Right about what?' Stokes leaned forward, nose scenting a scoop.

'What's Dibb's new identity?'

He slapped the edge of the table. The few solitary drinkers at the far end of the pub, who constituted the clientele, turned briefly to look before staring gloomily into their ale again. 'So it's Dibb,' Stokes hissed. 'What's he done? Killed someone?'

Foster shook his head. 'Let me know what he's called and then we'll play quid pro quo.'

'Well, I know it's him, so even if you do stiff me I can piece it together. He was called David Lowell. Lives in a two-up two-down in Acton...'

Foster drained his pint. 'Lived.'

'He's been offed?'

'Or offed himself. We found a body in a burnt-out wreck in Chiswick. It was his car.'

'No one with him?'

No. You may want to hedge your bets with the story. A few "believed to be"s or "a source claimed"s. It's not a hundred per cent confirmed it's him yet.'

'You think it is though.'

Foster nodded.

'Jesus.' Stokes' cheeks began to flush with excitement. Foster knew that this story would make him toast of the paper: Harry Stokes, grizzled newshound, last of the breed, the man they can't muzzle, rather than a booze-soaked relic of an age long gone.

What about Schofield?'

'What about him?'

'Where is he? What's he called?'

'What's in it for me?'

'Come on, Harry, I've just given you the best scoop you've had in years.'

He hesitated. 'You'll definitely let me know when it's confirmed about Dibb?' Foster nodded. Stokes pulled out a notepad from his pocket, scribbled on a page and handed it to him. 'New name and address. When you know more about what's behind this, suicide or not, will you give me a call?' he asked, slipping his jacket on.

'No,' Foster said. 'The flow of information between us begins and ends when I confirm about Dibb.'

Stokes shrugged his shoulders. 'No it doesn't.'

'Meaning?'

'Well, for a start, we probably know more than you lot about Dibb and his new life. We've got a dossier that thick.' He held thumb and forefinger four inches apart. 'Every cough, spit and fart since he was relocated. We've watched him every step of the way. Credit card history, job references, Internet browsing history, mobile phone records, mobile phone messages, emails, all kinds of shit. Maybe stuff in there you can use if he was done in.'

'None of it admissible because all of it was illegally obtained.'

'Maybe. Half of it from your lot.' Stokes smiled his rictus nicotine-stained grin. 'Just doing our job, protecting the public and its right to know, a responsibility the criminal justice system relinquished when that little animal was released back into the wild.'

'That was a politician's decision, Harry. You know that.' He didn't want to get into a moral debate with Harry Stokes.

'Perhaps.' Stokes pulled a cigarette from his pocket, in preparation for lighting as soon as he hit pavement. 'Plus, I know you thought there was more to it than came out in court.'

It was Foster's turn to narrow his eyes in distrust. 'Who told you that?'

'Doesn't matter. Jackie Corrigan tied it up. Jackie Corrigan liked a nice, tidy ending. But you and I know endings are rarely neat.' He jutted out his jaw. 'He's retired now.'

'I know.'

'Keep in touch?'

'None of your business.' They hadn't spoken since he left Newcastle to come back to London.

'Thought not. You should call him one time. Jackie thought highly of you. Very highly, I was told. Affected him when you swanned off like that.' He smiled, though it had the appearance of a sneer. 'Now, I'm going to light this,' he added, gesturing towards his cigarette. 'Want one?'

'No. I quit.'

The sneering smile again. 'Ah yes, the business with the nutter who was killing off the descendants of the guys who framed his ancestor.' He shook his head ruefully. 'Bloody great tale. Once in a lifetime you come across a story that good. Listen, if you ever wanted to talk about that, what it felt like, how you coped…'

'Save your breath, Harry.'

He nodded. 'Well, cheers for the scoop. I'll catch you round, Grant. We'll speak again. I'm sure of that.' He flipped the unlit cigarette into his mouth. 'Call it...an old hack's intuition,' he added through the side of his mouth.

I bloody hope not, Foster thought as he saw him dart out for his nicotine fix.

5

All the way up the M1 to Leicester, as dusk turned to night, the windscreen wipers flapped rhythmically back and forth as the rain beat insistently down on the windscreen. Recollections of that long summer wove in and out of Foster's head, hazy and indistinct, like a radio picking up a long-lost frequency. He lived almost exclusively in the present. The past was a closed book. But now, when he tried to snap it shut, livid memories leapt out.

He was twenty-four years old, trying to flee the capacious shadow of his father. He'd looked at a map of the UK and hunted for a region where being the son of Detective Chief Superintendent Roger Foster of Scotland Yard counted for nothing. A more difficult task than it sounded given his father's reputation. Newcastle looked far enough away. He applied and was hired there as a young detective after completing his training. It wasn't difficult. People were always willing to put in a word on his behalf. He might want to escape his father and his profile, but his name still opened doors. The plan was to get away from London, make his name somewhere else, then emigrate – the States, Australia, somewhere a background in British policing might help.

With his London accent and the knowledge of who his dad was, the local coppers didn't make it easy at first. In fact, the Geordies never made it easy, even if they respected him as a copper. He was 'Golden Bollocks', 'bagie 'eed', a 'soft, southern shandy-drinking shite'. But by keeping his head down, letting the piss-taking wash over him with a smile, working hard and buying his round, he slowly earned his colleagues' respect and some of their affection. Yet their grudging resistance was like a warm bath compared to the reception he got from the public. This was the aftermath of the miners' strike in a region that had fought the hardest; the police were the public, hated face of Maggie Thatcher's Britain. Many times on the doorstep or on the phone, the sound of his accent stopped people dead, the door slammed and the phone went silent, or he was told to 'gan and pelt shite'.

Despite the hostility, he enjoyed the job and the city, a grim, ramshackle, crumbling place stained with grime, yet with a stoic character and a gallows sense of humour he appreciated. He grew to love it. A senior detective, DCS Jackie Corrigan – an avuncular old-school copper in his late fifties with a soft lilting Geordie accent but hard as railway steel – took a liking to him, co-opted him as a junior partner and taught him all he knew about detective work in the real world and not the training room. He began to work all the best and most interesting cases in the region. He met a local lass – he even picked up some of the local lingo, like 'lass' – and reached the heady point of discussing moving in together. Life was good. Then July 1992 came and everything changed.

The details were etched into British criminal folklore. In a former mining village rendered a ghost town by the closure of the local colliery, two boys, Glen Dibb and Craig Schofield, one ten, the other nine, with the faces of cheeky urchins, had wagged school and were playing in a nearby copse, known officially as Dean Bank but to all the locals as simply 'the Dean'. Their game was interrupted by Kenneth Chester, a retired miner of forty-eight years' service. There was an argument, the substance of it still unknown, but Chester felt threatened enough to raise his stick at one of the boys. They pushed him over. Then a red mist descended on both and they attacked him. First with feet and fists, then with sticks and stones. Battered and broken, his seventy-three-year-old frame almost unrecognisable as a human being, they dug a crude shallow grave and tossed him in it. The pair then headed coolly back to school where they washed themselves clean in the toilets and made it in time for afternoon lessons.

It was a repellent and barbaric crime, matched by few others in the splenetic and violent outrage it awoke among the public, fuelled by the understandable bitterness of the old man's family and fomented by the tabloids, who descended on the village and camped out for weeks. Kenny Chester was revered, a hero. As a younger man, he had dug a group of his colleagues out of the rubble with his bare hands to prevent them being buried alive when the shaft they were working in collapsed. Which made the savage inhumanity of his death even worse for the public to bear and the irony of him being buried alive even more gruesome. In the days following his death, his deeds were recounted by the press, and his canonisation was complete. Dibb and Schofield had not just murdered an old man, but a paragon, a demigod, everything that had been good about this country, while they – both from broken homes, fathers absent – embodied all that was wrong.

Every time the boys were transported to court from their remand centre, vast crowds gathered, howling vitriol. The hunger for revenge was tangible. Within twenty-four hours of their arrest, an uncle of Dibb's, a ne'er do well with a criminal record, had been murdered, beaten to death on his way home from the pub. The culprit was never found, and while there were many suspects, given his past, few had any doubt it was linked to the public thirst for revenge. Had the boys been let loose, Foster never doubted they would have been torn apart like foxes by hounds.

He stopped for a tea at a soulless service station. As he stirred his brew, he called Nigel Barnes. The genealogist had helped Foster catch a killer and saved his life in the process. There was an irony in that, given how dismissive he had been of genealogy and the lessons of the past when he and Barnes first met. But now he was fully aware how the dark secrets of the past could invade the present. A belief this case would no doubt emphasise.

Barnes answered the phone in his precise, almost clipped voice. There was a hint of impatience.

'Have I picked a bad time to call, mate?' Foster asked.

'Oh, Grant. Hello. No, sorry – been a strange day.'

'Tell me about it,' Foster said.

'Yes, Heather phoned me. The man in the burning car. Seems a terrible business.'

Barnes and Heather had become an item. A sweet couple too, Foster thought, not that he'd admit such a treacly observation to either.

You don't know the half of it, he thought. 'Can you do a quick check for me?'

'Sure. What sort?'

'BMD.'

Barnes let out a small chuckle. 'You're learning the lingo, Grant.'

'Yeah, well, I've had you brainwashing me, haven't I?'

'Give me a second. Let me fire up the scamulator.'

For reasons Foster didn't know, Barnes always referred to his computer as a scamulator. The guy had his own way of viewing the world. He was just surprised he had a computer, and didn't still deal in paper, carbon copies and carrier pigeons.

'Right,' Barnes said. 'What's the name?'

'Wayne Schofield.'

'Date of birth?'

'I don't know. His brother Craig was born on 27th September 1981, though.'

'OK. Let me find him.'

He could hear Barnes hammering at his keyboard. He had learned to type on an old Olivetti, which meant he pounded away at a keyboard like it was a sworn enemy.

'Got him,' he said. 'Mother's maiden name is Smith. That'll narrow it down.'

'Dad's name is or was Winston.'

'Very grand.'

'They were a patriotic bunch. Lived in Mackington, Northumberland.'

'Got him. The one you want was called Wayne?'

'Yeah.'

'Born 1977, third quarter. Ah ...'

'He's dead, isn't he?'

'You knew? Yes, 1995, aged 27. I'll need the certificate for a cause.'

'Thanks. Call me when you do. No rush.'

Barnes would confirm it, but Foster had heard about Schofield's older brother. Now he knew it was more than just hearsay.

'Hang on,' Barnes said. 'We have other means.'

He heard him thumping away the keyboard. Foster took a slurp of his tea.

'Luckily for you, the newspaper database goes back to 1994. Would it be newsworthy?'

'Yes.'

'Right.' More pounding.

'Here we go.' Barnes paused. 'Jesus, he was the brother of one of the boys who murdered that old man. I knew I knew the name.'

'I told you it was newsworthy.'

'Is this linked to last night?'

'All will be revealed, Nigel.'

'Sure.'

'What happened to him?'

'The local rag says he was killed in a hit and run. An accident.'

'Yeah,' drawled Foster.

'You don't agree?'

'Who knows. Thanks for that, mate. Tell Heather I'll fill her in when I get chance.'

He hung up, left his tea and went back to his car. Wayne Schofield was a scumbag with a record the size of the Bible and a list of enemies which was twice as long as that. But Grant knew there was a link to the ill-feeling fomented in the aftermath of the Chester murder.

He got back on the road, casting his mind back once again. After the long trial ended and Schofield and Dibb were sentenced to eight and ten years respectively, provoking even more righteous fury. In the face of overwhelming public opposition and the plaintive pleas of the Chester family, the Home Secretary held his nerve and they were released after serving their time, to a backdrop of spluttering outrage, awarded new identities and relocated to try and live a semblance of a normal life.

Until yesterday evening.

It was dark when Foster pulled into a private car park near a purpose-built block of flats in an unlovely area on the outskirts of an unlovely town. The sort of drab, anonymous area where someone could blend in without notice. He got out of his car. The rain had stopped and the night was clear enough to see the few trees, bare and skeletal, outlined against the sky.

Foster tried the landline once more. No answer. He'd managed to obtain a mobile number via means Harry Stokes would have been proud of. He called. It rang countless times and then went through to an unpersonalised answer phone. He decided against it. He'd rather leave a written note if he was unable to see him.

He found the bell for the flat and rang it. There was no answer. He rang again. No response. This looked like it might be a wasted journey. He wondered what to do. Sit and wait? He could check whether Schofield was away. The local parole office or similar would still be monitoring him. Once he had clearance, they would tell him. But he wanted to keep this to himself for now. After all these years, it still felt like his case, and he didn't want a repeat of what had happened during the investigation of 1992.

He rang the bell of another flat. An elderly male voice answered the intercom.

'Yes?' he said.

'I'm after, er, John Samuel,' he said, for a second forgetting the new identity.

'He lives in number four.'

'I know. He's not in. I was wondering if you know where he might be?' Foster was shouting. The loud TV had been turned down but the distant dog was still yelping.

'No idea. He don't go out much.'

'Have you seen him today?'

There was a pause. 'Can't say I have.'

'When did you last see him?'

'A few days ago. Is he a friend of yours?'

'I'm a detective.'

'In trouble, is he?'

'No. I just need to speak to him. You said you haven't seen him for a few days?'

'No. But there's nothing strange about that. He's a private lad.'

'This last time you saw him, can you think of when it was?'

Another pause. 'Friday. He was dressed up smart.'

'Off to work?'

'No. He was a mechanic. It was the evening.'

Foster couldn't think of a reason to prolong the conversation. Looked like he had a straight choice between heading back or parking up in the car and waiting to see if he came back in the next few hours. Then he thought of another option.

'I wouldn't mind leaving him a note.'

'You can leave it with me if you want.'

'I'd prefer to push it under his door, make sure he gets it as soon as he gets back. Save you waiting up. You couldn't let me in, could you?'

The old gentleman hesitated but eventually the buzzer went and Foster was into the chilly, stark communal hallway. He spotted the light switch to the right. It was a on a timer; push it in and it slowly released and eventually switched itself off. He pushed it in. To the right was a grid of mailboxes. He headed up the stairs to the first floor and Schofield's flat. As he arrived on the landing, the old man's head appeared around the door. They nodded in recognition and Foster muttered thanks before he disappeared back inside. He pulled his notebook from his pocket, ripped a page from its binding and, using the wall to lean against, began to write.

Until the light went off.

In the dark, he immediately felt for the switch. He turned to look, first to his left, and then his right, waiting for his eyes to accustom and for the switch to hove into view.

It was then he saw the slit of light from under Schofield's door. *Odd*, he thought. Forgetting about the light switch, he went to the door and listened. Nothing. He knocked. No response or sound. He knocked again, this time more forcefully. Again, nothing.

Foster stroked his chin. Something didn't feel right. He reached for his phone and rang Schofield's mobile. There was a pause.

From inside the flat he could hear the trill of a mobile ringtone. It rang off.

He pushed the door gently. It gave slightly. It was on the Yale lock, not the deadbolt. *His insurers won't be happy*, he thought. Still, it made what he was about to do much easier. He got a plastic card from his wallet and dog-eared one corner. Then he manoeuvred the card between the door and frame and swiped it past the lock. It took a few attempts but there was a click and lock was broken.

He pushed the door open slowly. 'Hello,' he said softly, expectantly.

Nothing.

Except for the sight of Craig Schofield lying dead on the floor of his studio flat.

6

Foster crouched over Schofield's body. From the scent of decomposition, and the blue-black mottled complexion on his face, he reckoned he had been dead for more than a day, possibly two. Schofield, as depicted in a picture that had been widely used at the time of the murder and trial, and, he guessed, was about to be widely used once more, was an angelic-looking kid, all gap-toothed, wonky grin and twinkling brown eyes set beneath a mop of curls. That innocence had rendered the barbarity of his crime even more disturbing. Time had not been kind, however. He must have been two, possibly three stone overweight, and his hair had receded considerably. Death flattered no one, but he reckoned that even without its pall Schofield would have passed for at least five years older than his age of twenty-nine.

He looked back at the body. There was no sign of external injury, or any blood. Of course, it could be natural causes, or a drug overdose. But Dibb's death indicated otherwise. Poisoned or strangled, he guessed. He could smell vomit, as well as other effluvia, and there was a dried patch of some liquid on the carpet near his mouth.

He stood up and glanced around the small living room. There was another smell he recognised, along with those that accompanied death. Damp. It was clear, looking around, that Schofield wasn't house-proud. The place was uncluttered but a thick layer of dust coated the few objects in the room, while the carpet was stained and worn. At one end there was a sofa, a battered armchair and a TV. At the other a small, empty dining table, two chairs and a brimming bookcase. He had heard that Schofield had taken an interest in his education while inside. Those who argued that the pair had served their time, should no longer be punished for a crime committed when they were so young and were fit to take their place in society as men, cited this in support of their arguments. Foster shook his head. As if reading a book or two proved anything of the sort. His view on the pair had never wavered. They were two little savages. Their crime went beyond all bounds of human decency. It was not, as some bleeding hearts had suggested, a game gone wrong.

He browsed along the line of books. Classic novels mingled with bestsellers, but mainly non-fiction. One was an account of the Yorkshire Ripper's life and crimes. What answers had Schofield hoped to find inside those pages?

Not finding what he was looking for, he left the bookcase and drifted towards a small, dark hall area with three doors leading from it. Using the same handkerchief which had covered his mouth, to avoid transferring prints, he pushed open the one to his right. A bedroom, large enough to fit a double bed and little else. The smell was musty, mildly unpleasant. The sort you might expect from a bloke living alone. The bed was unmade. On the floor a battered clock radio blinked the time in red light. 21:45.

He tried the next door. A bathroom this time, from where the smell of damp originated. The sink tap dripped. The fittings were chipped and stained, a ring of grime around the bath perimeter. He closed the door, not wanting to spend more time in there than necessary.

The final door revealed a kitchenette. He walked in. The smell of damp faded behind him. He looked around. It was the cleanest room in the whole flat. The sides were clean and stain-free. The sink empty, its steel sparkling. He opened a cupboard above. The cleanliness was purely superficial. The glasses inside were streaked with dirt, the surface they sat on unclean. He closed the door and surveyed the kitchen once more. There was a built-in dishwasher. He opened the drawer. It was full and the wash had been run. Next to it was a unit housing a small bin.

He opened the door and slid out the bin. It was completely empty. No bag, no rubbish inside. He glanced around the room once again. How come the rest of Schofield's flat was sliding into squalor but his kitchen was pristine?

Still there was no sign of what he was looking for. Foster took in the room one more time. Then, at last, he spotted it. Behind the toaster, of all places. He moved the machine away, again using the handkerchief, to reveal a green button on the wall. A panic button. Pressing that would alert the local nick. It would have been installed when he moved in here, in case his identity was revealed and the vigilantes turned up at his door with pitchforks and burning torches. Either he had been too stricken to make it into the kitchen and hit the switch, or he had not felt the urge to do it.

Schofield and Dibb were dead. He knew it was not coincidence. It was directly linked to their crime … But who was responsible? Dibb, it appeared, had died after Schofield. Had he killed his friend and then destroyed himself? It was a possibility. It would explain his dramatic choice of ending. Yet there were no shortages of other suspects, of people who wished both men to pay the ultimate penalty for their crime.

He returned to the sitting room. Schofield's body lay there, on the surface unharmed, in direct contrast to the charred remains of the man with whom he would always be inextricably linked. He sighed.

Nigel Barnes was right. The past could not be denied.

7

The man unlocking the garage doors was so fat that Foster could not imagine him being able to fit in a car, never mind climb underneath and look at its workings. He wheezed as he waddled across the forecourt, legs wide to avoid his thighs colliding with each other, great sausage fingers working the keys in various locks, until all the doors were open. The ceremony over, Foster climbed from his car and uncurled his weary frame. He had not slept. Schofield still lay dead in the flat. He would make the call but he wanted to make his own enquiries first.

It was barely light, the sky a brooding grey, damp in the air along with the lingering earthy smell of engine and sump oil. The fat man had wandered into a small cabin and flicked on the light, which cast a wide beam across the front yard. Foster knocked on the open door before going in. The air was musty and thick with stale nicotine. The man lit a cigarette. From a room in the back he heard the sound of a kettle being filled.

'We're not open yet,' came a flat, gruff Midlands voice. 'Give me half an hour.'

Foster said nothing, just plunged his hands deep into his pockets and glanced around the walls. A wall planner, faded and unused. Two topless calendars, which had been updated to the right month. The fat man's head popped around the corner.

'Didn't you hear? I haven't had a cuppa yet. We're not open.'

'I'm not here to drop off or pick up a car,' he explained.

The face, all folds and wrinkles of flesh, like melting wax, the colour of bacon, darkened. 'Well, even more reason for you to fuck off and leave me alone, then.'

Foster shrugged. 'Sorry, I'm not going away.'

The piggy eyes narrowed further. 'You old bill?'

'Maybe.'

Now he was worried. *Probably owes more tax than an English lord*, Foster thought. He let him stew for a few seconds before ending his misery. 'I'm actually here to see John Samuel.'

The folds of fat seemed to sag further with relief. 'John? Not in yet.' He glanced at the clock on the wall which read just past 7 a.m. 'He usually gets in at seven thirty-ish. Cup of tea?'

'Yes please.'

'How d'you like it?'

Quite the host now, aren't we? he thought. He wondered how many dangerous wrecks were shipped out of here. 'Leave the bag in for at least five minutes. Splash of milk. Two sugars.'

He waddled off and returned in time, a cigarette draped from the corner of his mouth. 'Here you go,' he said, setting down the tea, which looked suitably strong. 'What's John done? I always thought there was something odd about him, I have to tell you.'

'I can't say. Just want to speak to him about a small matter.' He sipped the scalding hot tea. 'What do you mean by odd? Mr...?'

'Todd,' he said, extending a bulbous hand. 'Jim Todd.' Foster took it. Felt like cleaning his afterwards. 'He's a quiet boy. Barely talks. Good mechanic though. Can't imagine him being the sort to get in trouble with the law.'

'How long he been working for you?'

'Three years. No, hang on. More than that, four maybe? He's probably the best one I've got. Gets his head down, does his graft, doesn't piss around like some of others.'

'Does he have any friends?'

'Not here. Don't get me wrong, me and the other lads like him. But he's not that sort of bloke. We go off to the pub and he comes for one, but then goes home. It's like he doesn't like being out. If he has any friends he's kept them quiet.'

'Family?'

He thought, took a drag on his fag. 'Never heard him mention them either. Bit of a loner, all round. But he's a good kid. The other lads tease him a bit,

you know. Crack a few practical jokes and stuff.'
He began to laugh, or his face indicated a laugh,
though the noise was a dry wheeze, followed by a
couple of rasping croaks. 'First day they sent him
down to the butcher's, asked him to get a bag of
chicken lips.' His face had turned puce at the hilar-
ity of the memory. 'He only went and did it.' More
wheezing and croaking. Foster feared he might keel
over and die.

'They were at it last Friday,' he said, wiping his eye.
'Why?'
'I'm not sure. He had a date or something.' The
laugh rumbled to life once more. 'They ripped him
to pieces. "Do you know where to stick it?" "Is she
gonna bring her guide dog too?" "Does she have a
mate? We can double date down the kennels."'

There he lost the ability to speak. He waved his
hand in the air as apology as he regained his composure. 'Oh, we have a laugh.'

'Yeah,' Foster replied. 'Sounds like it... Do you
know who his date was with? A customer, maybe?'

He shook his head, wiped his eyes once more. 'No
idea. We'd know if it was someone who had come in
here. Unlikely though. John hides whenever someone
comes in. I never let him interact with the punters.'

'How about where they went?'

His eyes narrowed with suspicion again. 'What's
the interest? Has something happened to him? Or
her? God, he hasn't gone and done something fucking daft, has he?'

Foster realised he couldn't keep pushing this without giving something away. 'No. Not that I'm aware of. But it might be of use to what I'm looking into.'

Todd nodded. 'I do, actually. The Dove on Argyle Street. I know because the lads were gonna go along and have a look.' He looked like he was going to dissolve into laughter once more, but he reined it in. 'Some of them might have, actually. They'll be here soon. So will he. Why don't you ask him then?'

'I'll come back later,' he said, finishing the dregs of his cup. 'Somewhere else I need to be first. Cheers for the tea.'

The Dove was an anonymous grey terraced boozer on a small snaking road on the outskirts of the city centre. *This will have to be my last call before I phone this one in*, he thought. He had already pushed his luck way beyond its limits; there would be repercussions when it became known he had been striding around town asking questions, while a crime scene deteriorated with every second. The more information he had, the quicker he could try and piece the two crimes together, because once the local force got hold of it, there would be a mess of bureaucratic and procedural hoops.

Through the window, Foster could see the glow of bar-light. Which meant someone was in. He knocked on the door. After a few seconds, a tall bearded man, tired and bored-looking, unbolted the door and opened it.

'Yeah,' he said gruffly.

Foster flashed his badge. The man ushered him in wearily. Inside, the pub smelt of stale alcohol and furniture polish. It made for a surprisingly pleasant combination. The chairs were piled on the tables and a cleaner was at work. It was warm, inviting almost; Foster was tempted to sit at the bar and ask for a pint.

'How can I help?' the bearded man said.

'This your place?'

'I run it, yeah. The brewery own it.'

Foster glanced around the room. A quiet back-street alehouse. Not the sort of place to have fixed security cameras. 'Were you working Friday night?'

'Yes. It's our busiest night.'

'Full, was it?'

'At various times.'

'I'm trying to find out as much as I can about a guy who came here. He was on a date. I think.'

The landlord rolled his eyes. 'There were quite a few couples in here Friday. Do you have a picture?'

'No.'

'Well, not sure I can help you then. It was busy.' He nodded to the long wooden bar. 'Behind there you just get the drinks out. Unless they're a regular, or do something stupid, or start having a go, they all merge into one. Was he distinctive looking?'

Foster thought: mid-thirties, slightly receding hair, slightly overweight, no distinguishing features, was a child killer who stared out from every newspaper in the land twenty-five years ago. 'No.'

'Sorry,' the barman said with a shrug. He turned to walk away.

Foster knew this would be a long shot. 'He would have looked incredibly nervous. Really uncomfortable. I don't think he was used to being with a woman.'

The landlord turned back, face quizzical. 'Do you have a name?'

'Yes. John Samuel.'

He held up an index finger. 'Give me one minute.' He walked to the bar entrance, swung it up on the hinge and headed behind to the till. He opened a small tin and rifled through it, emerging with what looked like a bank card.

'He left his card.'

'On the table?'

'No. Behind the bar. He set up a tab. Then left without settling up. It happens. Usually because people get too pissed. They come back the next day to get the card and pay up. He hasn't been back.'

'How much is the tab, out of interest?'

The landlord checked a receipt. '£5.10.'

'Is that all?'

'Seems like it. One pint of lager and a gin and tonic.' He looked towards a table in the far corner. 'I remember them.' The beginnings of a smirk spread across his face.

Foster leaned on the bar. 'You do?'

The smirk became a smile. 'I certainly do. You're right, he was very nervous. But I'm not surprised.'

'Why's that?'

'Well, she was absolutely gorgeous. He was batting way out of his league. Johnny was on with me, and we had a joke about it. You know, he must have either had an enormous wallet or penis, because with the best will in the world, he was hardly George Clooney.'

Foster took out his notebook. 'Describe her to me.'

'Don't get me wrong, she wasn't movie-star looks. But she was a cut above the standard of women you usually get in here. Reasonably tall, slim, blonde hair, blue eyes, soft features. She was well into him too. Laughing at his jokes, lots of hair flicking, arm on his shoulder, all that kind of stuff. Lucky bastard. No wonder he scarpered without taking his card. Most of us would in his position.' The amusement vanished. 'What's he done?'

Foster wrote it down. 'Why do you assume it was something he did?'

He shrugged. 'Will I be getting my £5.10?'

Foster closed his notebook and slipped it inside his jacket pocket. 'I wouldn't bet on it,' he said.

Outside, on the street, he got into his car and made two phone calls. One was to the local nick reporting Samuel's death.

The second was to Harry Stokes.

8

Monday morning and Nigel found himself on an interminable bus journey to Chiswick. It would have taken him twenty minutes to walk there from Shepherd's Bush, but the rain was pouring in sheets and it was bitterly cold. Everyone else had been forced into cars and taxis and buses, so, coupled with the fact his journey coincided with the school run, the roads were at a standstill.

The number 94 eventually dropped him at Turnham Green Tube station. He walked a short distance around Acton Green, a small patch of common land of interest only to dog walkers by day and groups of eastern European immigrant drinkers at night. Nestled behind the railway lines that ran through Chiswick was a leafy enclave where the semi-wealthy with kids lived because of the good schools, a sort of Notting Hill lite: 'posh, no dosh' was how a friend of his had once described the residents. Lara Harrison's house was a huge Victorian semi at the southern end of a street that wound all the way up to Acton, growing less desirable the further north it went. Given the difference in size between her house and her neighbours', he guessed this must have been the house where the master builder of the street lived while the rest were built. Perk of the job to build the best and biggest place first and hole up in it.

He could only imagine what it must be like for Lara Harrison to live in a house so big with only a small daughter for company, He pictured her, wild eyed, roaming the rooms in the small hours, keening child in her arms, desperately trying to soothe her while struggling with the urge to pitch her out of the window, begging for the first watery signs of dawn light through the window to make her feel less alone. He felt again the pang of pity that had drawn him here, less than twenty-four hours after she had begged him to help. He hadn't got used to Heather's irregular working and sleeping times. If she was due to stay at his place, and was back late, he always waited up for her. Last night it was almost 2 a.m. She left again at 7.30.

The rain continued to fall, rolling down from his forehead into his eyes. His eyes were focused on the house. It was red-brick and sprawling, almost Gothic in the way it loomed over the lesser houses around it, though that may have been a consequence of the brooding grey sky. Nigel, realising he was getting soaked, pushed the gate open and rang the doorbell.

She answered the door before the ring even ended, an eager grin on her face. Not for the first time he wondered how a woman so attractive and seemingly intelligent had been reduced to such desperation. Was he really the only Prince Charming she had to turn to? He smiled and her eyes began to tear once more. She motioned for him to come in.

Inside a large hall, despite the space and high ceiling, the atmosphere felt oppressive, even claustrophobic. Kids' toys littered the side of the hall. These signs of homeliness appeared false. There was something about the place he simply didn't like.

'Lovely house,' he said.

'Yes,' she said, almost absent-mindedly. 'Yes, I suppose it is.' She took his coat. There was silence. She was washed out, leeched of all energy. 'It's too big. I should move. But that requires effort and energy.'

'How was last night?' he asked.

'The usual,' she sighed. 'A cup of tea?'

'Yes please,' he replied.

'Builder's or Earl Grey?'

He shrugged. 'Builder's tea.'

'I could do you coffee. I've had two already.'

'Tea's fine.'

He looked around the hall once more. What was it about the place he didn't like? It was the sort of house he'd love to live in, rather than his purpose-built, poky little flat. 'Was it the master builder's house?'

'Yes, it was,' she confirmed. She led him down the hall to a wide, open-plan kitchen, sparkling with chrome and every kind of appliance. The whole of the back wall was glass. She motioned to it. 'He obviously valued indoor space over outdoor.' He looked out. A small patch of grass, a rusting plastic child's bike on stabilisers, a plastic bubble car dripping wet in the middle and a ball decorated with dancing Barbie dolls. It was disproportionately small.

She filled the kettle from the tap.

'Your daughter?'

'At school.'

'How does she cope with the lack of sleep?'

'Better than me,' she said, and laughed mirthlessly. 'It's pretty much all India's ever known so she's used to it. Before she was born, I had thirty-three years of blissful, uninterrupted sleep. Then, bang!' She snapped her fingers. 'Nothing.' She attempted a smile. 'The school are very happy with her. I don't how she does it. It's all I can do to function normally.'

The kettle boiled and he was gratified to see her pour it into a warmed teapot. She collected two cups from a cupboard and placed them on a wooden island in the middle. She gestured to a stool. 'Take a seat.'

Nigel settled himself. Lara wrenched one of the sliding glass doors open, reached for a pack of cigarettes from a cupboard above a well-stocked shelf of cookbooks, and pulled an ashtray out from behind a digital radio. She pulled a stool across to fill the opening. 'Mind if I?' He shrugged. 'I need all the stimulants I can get.' She lit up and inhaled deeply, greedily, and exhaled with a sharp push of breath and with little discernible enjoyment, her finger tap-tapping on the stem.

'I'd never let India know I smoke,' she added. 'Crazy, isn't it? My four-year-old who never lets me sleep, and I'm appalled by the idea she might see me smoke. Sometimes I will leave her playing upstairs, or parked in front of the telly, and I'll come out into the garden for a fag.' She shook her head. 'Sometimes I'll say I'm off to weed the garden. I only realised until recently that she thought I was *weeing* in the garden.' This time she smiled genuinely, and it lit up her whole face, a glimpse of colour and life. 'She said to me, "Mummy, why don't you use the toilet like me?"' Again, the smile. It faded. She inhaled and exhaled again, barely keeping the smoke in her lungs. She reached behind the back of the digital radio once more, pulled out a pack of powerful mints. 'I even feel guilty about smelling of them.'

She plunged the half-smoked cigarette into the ashtray and twisted it with force to extinguish it. Then she took a deep breath, smoothed down the front of the loose dress she was wearing and poured the tea.

'So, what do we do?' she asked.

'You tell me everything you know about your family tree. And that of India's father.'

'That bastard.' It was a statement, not a question.

'Yes, well, we could always leave that...'

She waved her hand. 'No, no, I'll tell you what I know. Which isn't much.'

'Perhaps I could contact him?'

'No way. If I've sent you he'll tell you to piss off, frankly. He'll think the whole idea is crazy anyway.

He thinks I'm crazy. He's managed to convince himself that all of India's sleeping problems are down to me. That I've passed on this anxiety. He's managed to forget it all started when we were together and about as happy as we ever were.' She gazed past Nigel at the wall behind. 'God, that seems like forever ago.'

'Does he have contact with India?'

'The odd weekend. When he's not too "busy". Never overnight. Conveniently, his flat only has one bedroom, so he says it's not suitable, even though it has the square footage of most houses.' She paused. 'He's a selfish and immature little man. As soon as he realised how hard work it was raising India, he ran for the hills.'

She sighed. 'I'm sorry, Mr Barnes. When it comes to India's dad, I admit to being rather bitter. With some justification. I've given up everything to help her. My work has suffered, I have no social life, no chance of a love life because I have a four-year-old in my bed every night. I walk around like a zombie. He just doesn't care.' She bit her lip, gazed over his shoulder at the wall, eyes hollow shells. Nigel wondered what he would have done in her partner's shoes, faced with a sleepless child and a wife driven half-crazed. He hoped he would stay and help.

'I should have seen how he treated his mother,' she continued. 'He and his brothers speak to her like she's a piece of shit. That's exactly how he ended up speaking to me. The first lesson I'll teach India about men is to check how they treat their mum. If any man she's involved with treats his mum with disdain, I'd advise her not to go anywhere near, because you can bet any money that's how he'll treat her once the first flush of love or lust has worn off. How do you treat your mother?'

'I was a foster child.'

'You poor thing.'

'I did OK. It was all I knew. I was loved.'

Lara shook her head. 'I get so wrapped up in my own little sleepless world and I forget other people have it tough. I have a good home, a decent source of income.' Tears began to well. 'It's just being so *bloody* tired all the time drives you crazy, makes you lose sense.' She wiped her eyes. 'See, we were talking about you, and here I am crying again.'

'That's OK,' he said. He had pulled a pad and pen out of his bag. 'Do either you or your ex-husband know anything about your family tree?'

'I know a bit about mine. Xander, well, I'm sure his mummy has it all mapped out. Any rogues and villains will have been airbrushed out, for sure. If you do find anything strange in either of our pasts I'm betting it will be in his gene pool. It's very narrow. Lots of inbreeding. I'm joking.' He smiled back, thankfully. 'A bit, anyway.' She laughed quietly to herself. 'Sorry, I'm being bitter again. What do you need to know?'

He asked for as many dates as she could remember – parents' birthdays, wedding dates, known addresses. She recalled many from her own family, but unsurprisingly few from her ex-husband's. His birth date would be enough to get started with, Nigel assured her.

'What will you do with that information?' she asked.

'I'll use it to trace both your family trees, going back as far as I can. See what I can find.' His next question felt faintly embarrassing. 'Can you explain to me just what exactly it is your daughter experiences when she, er, has these episodes?'

'It's always the same. That's what makes it so disturbing. Lots of children have night terrors or nightmares, but often about different things. India's never changes. Within two or three hours of falling asleep, she wakes up gasping, or screaming.'

'Does she speak?'

'Not much, she can barely breathe. The first time this happened we took her to casualty. We were terrified. I was convinced she was dying. She came to in the car on the way there and she was fine. They've checked everything. She's very healthy.'

'Has she said anything about what she sees or experiences when these episodes happen?'

'Well, as I mentioned, all she says is that she can't breathe, or sometimes that something is pinning her down. She doesn't know what. But here's the strange thing, and it's why I sometimes use the word possessed – even if we've spoken in the night, when she's been fully awake, she has no recollection the next day. It's like something enters her body when she sleeps and leaves in the morning. When she wakes up in the morning, she gives me a big grin, says 'Morning mama' and wraps herself around me. I may have lain there, wide awake, like a human straitjacket, making her feel safe, cursing inwardly, for hours on end, wondering how my life got to this point, but none of that matters when she wakes up and gives me a hug. It's what I have to do for my little girl.'

Tears welled in her eyes. This time she didn't apologise. 'I just thought it would stop when she was three. Then it was when she was four. Now I just... feel like I have nothing left. I've been suffering chest pains. I've had a heart trace. I've been ill. Sometimes in the night when she's calm I can hear my heart thud against my chest and I feel certain I'm about to have a heart attack and then I get scared that she'll find me dead beside her... There are some days when I am so tired...' Tears were beginning to stream down her face. '... I'm so tired I just think, I can't do this, I don't want to do this, and I think of some awful, terrible, dark things. Then the next morning she pushes the curls out of her face, rubs her eyes and smiles and it just breaks my heart that I would think...'

She broke down completely, shoulders slumped, head lolling forward. Nigel spent a few seconds wondering what to do. Eventually he got up, went to the sideboard and fetched a box of tissues. He handed her a few and she wiped away the tears. Then took a deep breath.

'Thanks. You must think I'm crazy too,' she said.
'No,' he replied.

'I do,' she said forlornly. 'I never used to be. I can't take any more. You do believe me, don't you?'

Nigel believed every word she said about her exhaustion and what a mess her life had become. No one could be this convincing. But on what possessed the little girl he wasn't so sure. He was a man much happier with the truths of paper and records, and the safe distance of the past, than the caprices of the mind and the discomforts of the present.

'Of course,' he said, but he must have transmitted some hesitancy because he could see a wash of disappointment across Lara's face. It made his heart ache.

'Of course I do,' he repeated.

Her eyes were cast down to the floor. When she looked back at him he expected tears, but instead he saw resolution.

'Stay here.'

'I beg your pardon.'

'Stay here. One night. See what India does.'

'In the night?'

'Yes,' she replied, exasperated. 'God knows there are plenty of beds. But you will see and hear her. It may help your research. And it will let you see what I have to deal with.'

Nigel wasn't sure. For a start he could only imagine what Heather might say. But it was more than that. That distance thing again. He preferred to correspond with his clients. A phone call was often too much contact for his comfort. Yet here he was being offered a sleepover.

She was right, though. It could help. He knew it would help her.

'You're my last resort. If this doesn't help I don't know what I'll do.'

No pressure then. 'OK.' *Jesus, Barnes, you're such a soft touch*, he thought.

'Tonight?'

'Why not?'

9

The news of both Dibb's and Schofield's deaths was poised, ready to break like an enormous wave on a quiet shore. A silent few moments as the information was gathered and ingested, before a great roar as it crashed across every rolling news channel, online outlet and newspaper, then discussed in rooms, bars and offices across the land. Government departments would quietly release damning statistics and awkward news, while the PR industry would cease its endless promotion, all aware there was no spare newsprint or airtime to consume.

His ears deaf to the impending din, Grant Foster sat at his desk with a steaming mug of tea. The rain outside had turned to drizzle, while outside his office, a box within a box, the whole of his murder squad was gathering. A few had been working on the Dibb death when he was just David Lowell. Now he was one of Britain's most notorious killers they had called a three-line whip and every spare body had been hauled in.

There were four files in front of him. Two were official reports compiled by parole officers assigned to Dibb and Schofield, who reported to them after their releases with decreasing frequency. The other two were photocopied bundles couriered over to him only a few minutes before.

Heather popped her head around the door. She looked as exhausted as he did. Neither of them would be given any chance to catch up on sleep in the days ahead.

'They're all in, sir,' she said.

He nodded. It was their task to crawl over the Dibb death. East Midlands would handle Schofield's. If there was any sign that the two investigations would clash, or tread the same paths, then they might come together, but for now the plan was to treat each case as separate, then meet up and join the dots.

Foster picked up the parole files, left the others and wandered out into the modern, soulless incident room. The only objects apart from desks, computers, phones, chairs and lights were whiteboards. On one of them someone had taped a picture of David Lowell's wedding photograph. Next to it was the urchin schoolboy shot that had smirked from the front page of every newspaper more than two decades before.

Foster glanced around the assembled detectives. Usually at such times there was a charge in the air, a crackle of energy, a group of professionals eager to be let loose to do their job of catching bad guys. Not here. They lolled against desks, arms folded, yawning and scratching their arses. For many of them, he reasoned, the bad guy was already dead. All of them were old enough to remember the Kenny Chester killing. Foster knew he would have his work cut out. He looked around and they slowly started to come to attention.

'Before we get on with the business part of this briefing, I want to say a few things. For those of you who don't already know, I worked on the Kenny Chester murder.'

There was a murmur of surprise around the room. Now he really had their attention.

'I saw his body. I interviewed the suspects. I liaised with the family. Believe me, I lived every fucking minute of that case. It almost killed me.'

The room was quiet. He could only hear the hum of the strip lights, each turned on to ward off the gloom, even though it was only the middle of the afternoon.

'So, when I say that I think Dibb and Schofield were two little animals who deserved to rot in a jail for the rest of their lives, I mean it. The decision to release them was a political one. I didn't agree with it. In fact, I knew something like this would happen. Did they have it coming to them? I don't know. I don't believe in karma or what goes around comes around. I believe in police work and I believe in doing a job properly.'

He cleared his throat.

'Which means we do all we can to find out what really happened to Dibb and who killed him. The public might be dancing in the streets to know he's dead, but they also expect us to carry out every murder investigation with the same efficiency and professionalism. Because a few of us don't think Dibb should have been at large doesn't mean we won't be as thorough and as methodical as we usually are. Actually, if we believe in what we do, then we should go the extra yard to try and find out who did this. It's our job to carry out justice, not some vigilante. If we allow people to get away with this kind of shit then our job becomes infinitely harder. The eyes of the country, and much of the world, will be on this case – so let's give it our best shot.'

He looked around the room. They were hardly punching the air with agreement, but he could see his argument had got through.

'Isn't it just suicide, sir?' a young detective asked. 'We're going to find that he killed Schofield and then did himself in, aren't we? If anyone had a reason for topping themselves like this, and you would need a good reason, then Dibb had one. He killed Schofield and didn't want to go back to jail. Probably wanted to go out in a blaze of glory.'

There was faint snigger from a few of those present.

'The phone call was probably to the wife, or a lover. No wonder he was agitated. He was about to burn himself to death and he'd just killed someone,' another detective added.

'Fair enough,' Foster said. 'We have to accept suicide is still a compelling explanation. I don't go for it, though.'

'Why not?' The question came from the same young cop who had asked the original question.

'Gut instinct, mainly. But let's look at it dispassionately. What motive would he have had for killing Schofield? His life was good, so it seemed. He'd moved on.'

'Maybe Schofield had been in touch with him. Maybe he was trying to blackmail him or something.'

Foster shook his head. 'I've seen Schofield's body. It's not our case, but he was poisoned. If Dibb wanted to kill him, I doubt he would have chosen that method.'

DI Drinkwater piped up, a chiselled, intelligent cop for whom Foster had a great deal of time. 'Maybe he killed himself because he knew Schofield was dead and he was next.'

'Perhaps. If one of their covers was blown, then the other might have been too. But kill himself like this? Why not go to the authorities and tell them there had been a breach? He must have thought a terrible fate was waiting for him to take a course of action this extreme.'

He paused. 'These are all valid theories but let's look at the facts that we know.' He went through the timeline since Dibb had been found in his car on Saturday night. Then he started assigning tasks. To DS Khan, a jokey yet talented cop with a good knowledge of modern technology, he gave the job of trying to work out who Dibb might have been speaking to on the phone.

'Ordering a flame-grilled whopper,' he said, and there was the odd laugh and a few groans. Foster ignored them.

He picked up the parole file and handed it to Heather, sitting next to a young shaven-headed detective in glasses who was the source of a great deal of ribbing. 'Jenkins and Kojak, you'll be in charge of his life. Here's a file from the parole service that goes into the life he had built as David Lowell. It appears he assimilated himself much better than Schofield ever did. He worked in IT, had been promoted several times. I'm told he was very proud of the new life he had built, and believed in his independence so ferociously he was willing to forego any protection. He didn't even have a panic button in his house. I want you to speak to his work colleagues, any friends he might have had. Go through his accounts and see if there were any money problems, or an affair of any kind. Once we're done come into my office because I may have some more for you.'

He turned back to the group. 'I want the rest of you to go and knock on the door of every house on the road in Chiswick where the car was found. Did anyone see or hear anything?'

Thinking he'd finished, they began to rise and move, and a few of them started to talk.

'One final thing,' he added. 'I've got a bit of a roving brief on this one, given I was involved back in the day. Andy is going to coordinate the investigation from here, conduct the daily briefings if I'm not around and generally keep you in order.' He gestured towards DI Drinkwater.

The briefing over, he headed back into his office followed by Heather and Kojak.

He sat down and tossed towards them the huge photocopied bundles he'd had couriered over.

'You haven't seen that,' he said.

'What is it?' Heather said, curiously thumbing through the pages.

'That, my dear, is the file held by one of our bestselling newspapers about Glen Dibb.' In return for tipping him off about Schofield's death, Stokes had agreed to share a copy of their files on the men.

She pulled a face. 'Ugh,' she added.

'It's massive,' Kojak said. 'Twice the size of this.' He held up the rather meagre parole file.

'Well, the *Mail* have invested rather more time and resources prying into the life of Glen Dibb than the parole service have.'

Heather was unimpressed as she leafed through. 'None of it's admissible because half of it has been obtained illegally, and when I say half, I'm being charitable.'

'Agreed. However, it's damned useful. I've only had a quick glance and it told me more about him in five seconds than the other file did in five turgid minutes. The press may be scumbags, but they're highly efficient scumbags. Almost every corner and cranny of these men's lives was being monitored, surveyed and inspected, for the day when their true identities could be revealed and the world could know how they had lived.'

'Men's?' Heather looked nonplussed.

'Oh, I have Schofield's too.'

Her face turned quizzical.

'Best if you don't ask how. But his life was a miserable, cheap affair. His bank details showed he was a regular user of Internet pornography. He had signed up with several online dating agencies. Schofield smoked heavily, drank moderately, gambled occasionally, usually on the horses. Beyond that, there was little to report. He had no friends and little social life.

'But our man Dibb's is far more substantial. It's clear which of the two the *Mail* believed was most likely to be the subject of a news story first, and who would make the best copy. Dibb threw himself into it. There are allegations of drug abuse. A classic tabloid sting. Dibb was offered cocaine, which he bought, and the reporter was wired. It wasn't taken any further. Probably not newsworthy enough to risk the wrath of the Home Office. There's also further allegations of promiscuity, other drug use, even homosexual activity.'

'Who do these allegations come from?' Kojak asked.

'Many are anonymous. But there was an account of him having to be moved from a town in Surrey when someone twigged who he was, and started sending him hate mail. I've cross-referenced it with the official file. No mention of it in there. No change of identity. Just a request to move to London.'

'If Dibb felt threatened enough to move to London, then why didn't he tell his protectors about the threats?' Heather asked.

Foster shrugged. 'He must have told someone, hence its inclusion in the file. But the, er, contact who provided the file has been very careful to purge it of any names that might reveal his sources. However, there's one thing he must have missed. A reference to a report written by a man named Levine.'

'What do you want us to do with it?' Kojak asked, handling the bundle which Heather had given him.

'Gut it for anything that might interest us and then drop it back on my desk. Nothing will be said about it again.'

Heather's hands were on her hips, lips pursed. Foster could tell she didn't approve of using the press's illicitly gained information. 'There may be a few watchdogs or press industry inquiries we can pass it on to. They might be interested to know what they've been up to.'

'That won't be happening, Heather.'

She shrugged. 'What about this Levine character?'

Foster knew who that might be. 'Leave him to me.'

10

The ample woman who opened the door to Foster was the same one he had met at a police function or two more than a decade before. Her face was pink and she seemed flustered and irritated.

'Shirley?' he said.

Her eyes narrowed, then twinkled with recognition. 'Roger,' she shouted, tilting her head back behind the door to speak to someone he couldn't see. She turned back to him. 'Grant Foster! Come in, come in.'

'I'm parked on the street, is that...?'

'Fine, fine,' she said, grabbing his shoulder and almost dragging him into an immaculately kept hallway. 'We have understanding neighbours.'

Foster had been guilty in the past of London parking, sticking his car in the first available spot, forgetting that convention was often different in the suburbs; people did not take kindly to strangers parking outside their house. The drive in front of the house had been unavailable, filled as it was with three cars. A small run-around, a sleek new Jaguar and a fuel-guzzling 4x4. Foster wondered what kind of off-roading people did in Thames Ditton, a sterile Surrey enclave where newspaper executives and ex-coppers went to die.

The whole house was alive with the sound of ringing phones. From behind a door, a tanned face with a hooked nose and a shock of grey hair appeared. He looked angry.

'What?' he said to his wife.

She pointed to Foster. His gaze shifted and the anger subsided. 'Fuck me! Look what the cat dragged in! Grant shitting Foster!'

'Roger!' his wife admonished.

'Charming as ever, I see, Roger,' Foster said. Roger Levine emerged from the room and started to pump Foster's hand with a tight grip. He must have been in his late fifties now, but he was still tall, broad-shouldered. In the background, the chorus of phones continued to sing.

'Sounds like you're busy,' he added.

Levine rolled his eyes pantomime-style. 'You don't know the half of it, mate. It's gone absolutely bonkers since about mid-afternoon.' He paused, scratched his chin. 'But you probably know why, don't you? In fact, I'm guessing that's why you're here. Schofield and Dibb.'

'Sharp as ever.'

'Can't say I'm losing any sleep over those two scroats getting their comeuppance.' He rubbed his hands. 'In fact, suits me fine. I'm making a killing.'

He turned to his wife, who was still standing beaming in the hall. 'Go and give the girls a hand with those phones, love. Tell them I'm in a meeting and I'll get back. Follow me, Grant.'

'Girls? Got staff, have you, Roger?' Foster asked as they wandered down a thickly carpeted corridor. On the walls were various pictures of Levine from points in his career: a young cop in uniform; a detective clad in suit and sideburns; another with a group of greying old hands at some retirement drinks, possibly his own. Foster recognised several familiar faces.

'Not really,' Levine said, unlocking the door to a small office. 'Those are my daughters. I rope them in when the phones get hot. I'm a big believer in keeping it in the family.' He opened a small cupboard filled with bottles of liquor. 'Scotch?'

'A small one. I'm in the car.'

Levine ignored him and poured two gigantic measures. Foster let it slide and took the glass, accepting his host's offer of cheers.

'It's been a while.'

Foster nodded. They had worked in murder squad together for a few years; Foster as a young addition to the team, Levine as an old hand. 'It must be twenty years?'

'And six months, and twenty-seven days. Every one of them a joy. You want to try leaving too, Grant.' He took a slug of whisky. 'Best thing I did, taking the shilling to leave. Bloody hefty payoff too. Not sure they slip you that kind of cash on the way out now.'

'You went off sick, didn't you?'

Levine winked. 'It took its toll in the end. Or at least that's what I told the daft young twat who they hired to speak to me about it.'

'It' was a rather sordid case of the death of a drug dealer. The details were hazy, given the time that had passed, but Foster wasn't sure if they'd been any less murky back then. There was talk that armed police had not been acting in self-defence when they pumped four bullets into the dealer. No one was charged and before anyone kicked up too much of a fuss the main protagonists were offered early retirement. One of them was Levine.

Foster sipped his drink. It was good single malt, smooth and peaty. Very expensive. 'Well, gathering from the wheels on your drive and the contents of this glass, life's been pretty good to you.'

'Very, very good, Grant,' he agreed, nodding vigorously. 'I mean it, you should give it a go. I'm probably going to pack in soon anyway and clear off to Spain. We've got a place there. Murcia. Lovely. None of this shit winter weather. Plenty of good golf courses.'

Foster despised golf. Too much walking and too much bad knitwear.

'Anyway, once I've gone there'll be a big gap in the market,' Levine added. 'Not that it's that much fun any more. People have got cold feet about using us these days. That doesn't mean there's not a few quid to be made.'

Do me a favour, he thought. *A private detective? Sleazing around in the garbage of the rich and famous, doing the bidding and dirty work for the reptiles of the press, trying to catch out the workshy and malingering. No thanks,* thought Foster.

'You know me, Roger. A company man through and through.'

Levine shook his head. 'I admire your loyalty to it all, mate. I couldn't do it. All the red tape, the pen-pushing, the politically correct rules and regulations, all those slimy bastards who climb to the top to get their faces in the trough and on TV. It's not about putting bad guys away any more, is it? It's about meeting targets and crap like that.' He sipped once more. 'You're more than welcome to it.'

Foster shrugged. 'Someone has to do it.'

There was a pause, during which the sound of ringing phones permeated along the hall, jolting a sudden impatience into Levine. Foster always remembered him as the kind of bloke who acted as if he were your best friend, clapping you on the back, laughing at your jokes, but only if you were of use to him. If not, he couldn't get away soon enough. Now he sensed the warm glow of nostalgia had cooled and Levine wanted to get back to what he loved most of all – making money. He glanced at his watch.

'Most of your work come from the papers, does it?'

'Most of it? Nearly all of it. Though for how much longer, God knows. There's another industry on its arse. Not surprised, though, the lazy bastards.

Honestly, I wonder what actual work these journalists do, other than pick up the phone and ask me to find it out for them. Still, I'm not complaining, am I?' He looked at his watch once again. 'So, I take it you want some of the inside info about Dibb?'

'Both of them, if you have it.'

Levine shook his head. 'They hired another private dick to run the rule over Schofield. One in the Midlands.' He smiled. 'I got the best deal. Dibb was quite the little bastard when he came out. Drinking, drugging, shagging, shouting his mouth off, all kinds of shite.'

'Were you just trading this information with journalists?'

'As far as I'm aware, yeah.'

'No one came to you and asked for it who you thought was suspicious?'

Levine was becoming defensive. 'Not that I know of. This isn't the sort of info I would spread around to any old punter. You know that. This was for good clients.'

'Well, I'm going to need a list of those clients, Roger. All of them. I don't care how good they are. I need to speak to them. Lowell's old identity leaked somehow, and we all know how indiscreet most hacks are.' *And most coppers*, he thought but didn't say.

Now Levine was beginning to ooze resentment. 'That would seriously put me at a disservice, Grant. There is a certain confidentiality in this business.'

'I couldn't give a shit, Roger. There was more than a certain confidentiality to Dibb's new identity. But now he's dead. All bets are off. I need that info and you'll give it to me.'

For a few seconds the pair stared at each other, the atmosphere thick with hostility. Their relationship had always been testy. Time had done little to temper that. Levine eventually left the room. A minute or so later he returned. 'Shirl's putting together the stuff you want,' he hissed.

'Thanks. I appreciate it.'

'What's the big deal anyway? He killed himself, didn't he? Set himself on fire. Probably after killing his old mate. Pretty dramatic way to go, but no indication someone did him in, is there?'

Foster spread his arms wide. 'Who knows? But even if he did, the question is why?'

A sneer appeared on his florid face. 'More like, "Who cares?"'

'Maybe,' he replied, unwilling to be dragged into an argument.

'You been following him since he got out?'

He sighed. 'Just about, yeah. He was living quite near here to begin with.'

'Then he got the death threats.'

'That's right. You're obviously clued up. Especially when you consider he didn't take those threats to the cops or the parole board. Who made them?'

Levine said nothing for a few seconds, again resentful of the intrusion. 'I have no idea. Never found that out. Truth be told I never saw any threats. Just got proof of Dibb talking about them. Between you, me and the lamp post, it could have been he was lying. He was full of crap, you know. Proper Charlie Big Potatoes. Always bragging, shooting his mouth off. It was always going to catch up with him someday.'

'One thing puzzles me, Roger.'

Levine drained his glass, set it down on the side and stuck both hands on his hips, eyes narrowed. 'What's that?'

'Who cosied up to him? He's telling this person stuff he didn't tell his parole officer. He blew his own cover to tell them about the death threats, for God's sake. He must have trusted them.'

'We have our means, Grant. You know that.'

Foster waved his hand to dismiss him. 'Not that kind of stuff. I mean transcripts of conversations. One on ones. Going back years. The sort of stuff you can only obtain when you've got someone close to the subject. Someone so close that he was willing to break his own cover. Now you're the last person I need to tell, that that's someone I have to speak to. Who was it?'

'You know I can't tell you that, Grant,' Levine replied wearily.

'Oh, I think you can. And you know it. Otherwise the next time we speak it'll be in an interview room. And all the stuff I've seen in Dibb's file – the transcription of answerphone messages and emails you've hacked into, the mail you've intercepted, the credit card records and so on – all of that will be on the table.' He paused for effect. 'Could be a pretty long stretch, all that. All in your court, too. You know they'll never have the minerals to go after the journalists who paid for the info. Just the bent cop who provided them with it …'

Levine's eyes burned with fury. Foster noticed his hands were clenched into fists. He had witnessed his temper in the past. A few suspects had suffered at the hands of it, too. 'You always were a sanctimonious fucking prick, Grant,' he said, spittle bursting on his lips. That was the second time he'd been called that in the week. Maybe there was something in it. But he could live with being called names by the likes of Levine and Stokes. 'Only way you got as far as you did was because of your old man.'

It had been a long day. Foster was in no mood to be handed a lecture by a discredited old cop who had long since sold his soul. In his mind, breaking the law as Levine was doing now, for the sake of some squalid tabloid, put him on a level with all the corrupt cops he'd come across.

'Save me the anger, Roger. I really couldn't give a crap. Who was feeding you all this stuff? Let me know now. Or Spain, Murcia, all that golf, this nice little family industry you have here, built on the sludge and shit of the press, will all come crumbling down.'

Levine did nothing for a few seconds but stare, chin tilted upwards, boring holes of hate into Foster.

He didn't let his eye contact slip. 'Tell me, Roger.'

They continued to stare. The phones were still going mad off the hook. Journalists from every newspaper, highbrow and low, all wanting and willing to pay to get their hands on the information Levine had spent years collecting, waiting for a day like this when it could be sold ten times over. Now, on this biggest of pay days, Foster had arrived to ruin the mood. He could understand his resentment.

'Tell me.'

Levine finally looked away and shook his head. Foster knew he had him. Levine was not principled enough to die in a ditch for the sake of a source. In two weeks' time, the invoices for this day collected and cashed, Levine would be in a lemon Pringle sweater at the nineteenth hole sipping a gin, somewhere in central Spain, moaning without a hint of irony or self-awareness about bloody immigrants back in Blighty.

'Who is it, Roger?'

He gave Foster a look of pure malevolence. Then he spoke.

'His wife.'

11

The evening had passed at a crawl. Nigel had arrived just before Lara put India to bed. While he sat at the granite kitchen counter, with a large glass of wine Lara had poured for him, Lara brought India in her pyjamas, clutching a teddy bear under an arm, her face flushed with tiredness. Not that Nigel was an expert, but she seemed like any other child about to go to sleep. Lara told her to wave goodnight to Nigel.

'Why are you here?' she asked.

Nigel was left speechless for a few seconds. Lara saved his blushes.

'He's a friend of mummy's and he's staying the night.'

Nigel shifted uncomfortably. He'd only been able to leave a message for Heather on her mobile about why he wouldn't be home that evening. Heaven knew what she'd make of it.

Lara then disappeared upstairs with India. A few minutes later, as Nigel sat in silence wondering what he was doing, she returned.

'That was quick.'

'Oh yes,' she said, as she went straight to the bottle of white wine in the fridge to top up her glass. 'The ultimate irony of my daughter's night terrors is that when it comes to bedtime I can put her down in her bed and leave her there wide awake and she drifts peacefully into sleep without a murmur. She just never stays in that state.'

They spent the next couple of hours chatting in her sitting room, but Nigel could tell that Lara, running her hand through her hair and blinking furiously, was a strung-out mixture of exhaustion and wariness.

'Why don't you go to bed?' he said.

She sighed. 'Would you mind?'

'Not at all. I have a book...'

Lara nodded. 'I usually go to bed at the same time as India because between then and her waking is the only unbroken sleep I get. I put her down about nine, so at least I enjoy a bit of an evening. It's late for a kid her age but if she goes down any earlier she wakes up more, and I can't go to bed at seven p.m. even though I'm shattered.

'Does the same thing when she sleeps somewhere else?'

She smiled. 'It's been so long since we've slept elsewhere I can't remember.'

'Does she always sleep with you?'

'Yes, the episodes are worse if I'm not there. I hear them and react immediately and she goes back to sleep quicker.'

'What time does she usually wake up?'

'Depends. Between eleven and one a.m. normally, depending on when she falls asleep. I've made you up a bed.'

He held his hand up. 'I'll be OK. I'm here to see and not to sleep.'

'What are you going to do until then?'

'Read. Do some work… unlike you, I'm not short of sleep.'

'OK, if you're sure.' She got up and walked over to a baby monitor and switched it on. 'I'll go and switch it on in her room. It will help in case you fall asleep, though…' She didn't complete the sentence. 'Good night. Help yourself to anything you want, from the fridge, wine, tea…' Her voice tailed away. She smiled, her face pale, as if she might pass out. Then she left the room.

He watched her go and then checked the clock on the wall. It was only 9.30 p.m. He reached inside his bag and found his book: a detailed history of the 1936 Olympic Games. A client believed an ancestor of theirs had been a competitor, and before he knew it the story of how a previously sceptical Hitler had hijacked the Games and used it as a means of spreading Nazi propaganda had captured him, despite the fact that any sport bar cricket usually left him cold.

He read, stopping to think, mainly about what might be happening upstairs. The house was silent apart from the occasional creak. He got up to get a glass of water then returned to his book. The sofa was soft and comfortable and he let his head fall back, the open book on his chest...

The yell that woke him sounded like a screaming animal. It was high-pitched and wild; the sound of someone in great pain. Nigel sat up, stabbed with adrenaline, the book falling to the floor.

The scream again. Guttural, primeval almost. He looked to the right and the monitor. It was loud and distorted, the red lights indicating full volume. Across the floor above he heard pounding footsteps. The light on the DVD player blinked 00.57.

He heard Lara call his name, almost drowned out by screaming. He went to the stairs and ran up them. The light was on in Lara's room. He went in. Lara was holding her daughter close, but India's arms and legs were flailing. Her eyes were shut and she continued to cry out. Lara must have sensed his disquiet.

'It's OK,' she shouted above the din. 'She's not in pain. This is normal.'

Jesus, he thought.

India's screams were subsiding. Instead she had started to gasp, as if she was choking. The rattle in the back of her throat made it a gurgle. He could see she had become hot, her face turning puce. It was like she was drowning. Lara continued to hold her close, curled up, her limbs absorbing the blows from the child's flailing arms and legs.

Lara had closed her eyes too, and lay still, as if that would transmit itself to her daughter. But the girl's eyes were open now, wide and bulging. They seemed to be looking at Nigel without seeing him. Her mouth continued to suck in air, as if it needed it every ounce for survival.

'No!' she said. The voice was different to the one that had bid him goodnight earlier. Lower in pitch, urgent and panicked.

'No!' she repeated, still flailing.

The sounds stopped. Then she closed her eyes. Soon she was still and asleep. Her chest rose and fall calmly. It was like the previous two minutes had never happened. Lara said nothing. Just lay there. Nigel, shaken, went back downstairs.

By the time he left to walk home at 7 a.m. the next morning, India had suffered three more episodes, almost identical in nature. This time her mother was there to hold her as they started. Each time there was the same awful scream that froze his blood. As he left, he felt uneasy. But he also felt emboldened. He didn't know how he would help Lara Harrison, but he knew right then he wouldn't be able to walk away until her troubles were ended and that little girl could sleep.

12

The media had set up camp overnight outside her Acton home, eager to picture and interrogate the woman who had been blissfully unaware she had married one of Britain's most notorious killers. The siege had been anticipated once Lowell's true identity had been confirmed, and Jenny Lowell spirited away to her sister's house in Teddington. Yet it was only a temporary respite; it wouldn't be long before the press pack realised they had been sold a dummy and tracked her down.

There was not a reporter to be seen as Foster and Heather arrived at the house, a neat terrace on an unassuming back street. Jenny Lowell was in the kitchen, sipping tea with her sister. The atmosphere as they entered was hushed, the silence oppressive; Mrs Lowell might have been able to talk freely, even smile, surrounded by family, but the detectives' presence was an immediate, sombre reminder of her husband's violent death.

They asked to speak to her alone; she nodded and her sister slipped out, claiming she needed to visit the shops. Foster sat opposite across a small pine table, while Heather sat next to Jenny. She asked how their daughter was bearing up.

'She doesn't understand,' Jenny whispered softly. 'I've tried to explain that daddy's gone, but I think she thinks he's just gone away to a place called heaven and he'll be back. The sad thing is, so do I.'

Foster thought of all those tabloid headlines and letters and leaders pontificating about where Dibb would now be rotting. The conclusion was that it wouldn't be heaven. He then wondered how this woman would ever broach the subject of her father's crime with his little girl. It may be necessary to give them both a new identity, a new start, free of the stigma.

'Is she here?'

'No, she's with my mum for a few days. I was told to expect some press and thought it best. She likes it there.'

Some press? Foster guessed the world and his wife with a long lens would soon be at their door.

'Were she and … her dad close?'

'Davey, I called him Davey,' she answered, sensing Heather's hesitancy. 'Yes, they were. He doted on her. Very protective. Too much, sometimes. She's a very headstrong, very independent little girl, and I think that scared him. He saw demons and danger every-where.' She let out a small laugh. 'The other day she walked back from school. He was horrified.'

'On her own?'

'Yes. I went to get her but was running a few minutes late. It's only around the corner and you get a bit lax. Anyway, when I got there, she'd gone, they said. I almost died right there and then. I looked around the playground and didn't see anything. I walked back home. I felt sick. I was going to ring David and see if he'd picked her up for some reason, but my phone was at home. I got back and there she was, on the doorstep, waiting.'

'That must have been terrifying.'

'It was. I told David. He went white. The next few days, Thursday and Friday of last week, he left work early and was there waiting at school as soon as they let them out. He was a good dad.' She looked down at her hands, which she was wringing.

Foster explained they needed to go over a few facts. 'How did you meet your husband, Mrs Lowell?'

'In a bar. I was with a friend...'

'Where was that?'

'In the middle of town. A pub called The Polar Bear, near Leicester Square.'

'When?'

She was remarkably composed. She puffed out her cheeks. '2002? It was in the run up to Christmas. We married in 2005.'

'And you knew him only as David Lowell?'

'Yes. The first I heard of all... that business, was when one of your colleagues came around yesterday to tell me, and to get out of my house because it was going to be a very big story.'

Heather interrupted. 'Didn't they offer you some counselling?'

'They did. I refused.'

'Why?' she asked.

'It hasn't sunk in. It's too unreal. I expect him to walk back in through the door. Now I'm being told he was someone else, and not just someone else, but somebody who did a truly horrible thing. It's like I'm watching it happen, not actually experiencing it.' She sighed. 'It's difficult to explain. I just want time to get my head round it all before I start talking to counsellors and people like that, you know?'

'He never told you?' Foster asked.

'About the murder? No, never. He was always very quiet about his past. Never talked about it and made it clear he never wanted to. I saw it was a no-go area and I never pushed him on it.'

That was enough for Foster. He snapped. 'Why are you lying to us, Jenny?'

Her eyes were wide, as if she were shocked, almost dazed. 'Lie about what?' she muttered. 'I don't know what you mean.'

She continued to stare at him like a wounded deer. *This woman is one hell of an actress*, he thought. A few nights had passed without any decent sleep, and he was irritable and impatient, but he had to remind himself that, however much she lied, and whatever he had done, Jenny Lowell had still lost her husband and the father of their young child.

'Jenny, I know. You can drop the pretence.' She continued to give him a simpering look. He softened his tone. 'No more lies, no more stories. We're going to wind back to the start and this time, I want the full story. OK?'

She looked at her hands, wrapped around an empty mug of tea. From the corner of her eye, Heather flicked Foster a brief look of concern. Probably worried that Jenny Lowell had built an edifice of lies and delusion in order to deal with her terrible secret, and that it would come crashing to the ground once she admitted it was all a facade. But a hunch told Foster she was more calculated than that; he had seen what she had told Levine. There was no epic deceit here. Just a front that gave her the ability to interact with the outside world free of disapproval.

The tears came. Her shoulders began to heave. Heather instinctively threw an arm around them. Foster had expected this. The cynic in him said this was just a diversion. That was why Heather was so useful to him. She provided the empathy and sympathy he often failed to muster. He waited for Mrs Lowell to dissolve into sobs, but she soon regained her composure and looked back up at Foster, wiping her eyes.

She spoke. 'I'm sorry. It's just that I've got so used to living like this. Telling someone about it feels strange.'

Foster waited, deciding to pass up the urge to enquire how this strange feeling she spoke of tallied with her singing like a canary to Roger Levine. Once a few seconds had elapsed, and Heather, aka his conscience, nodded her approval, he spoke.

'So, how did you actually meet?'

She wiped her eyes. 'It depends on what you mean by "meet"?'

'I don't really want to play word games, Jenny.'

'Sorry. I suppose you could say we met before we physically met. We'd been corresponding for a few years.' She paused. 'When he was Glen.'

'Inside? You wrote to him while he was in prison?'

They were interrupted by the phone ringing in the hall. By now the press would have the details of her family. That might be them. Soon the doorbell would be ringing. They waited for it to stop.

'Yes.'

'For how long?'

'Seven years.'

'You must have been, what, twelve?

'I was thirteen. Look, I know it sounds weird. It *is* weird. But I just remember reading something about it a year or so after the crime.' She looked at Heather. 'You were a teenage girl once. You know about crushes. It was a very difficult time. I saw his picture and I got a bit ... obsessed. My life was always very safe, very cloistered. I wrote to him one day. All this stuff came pouring out. Stream of consciousness stuff. I sent it to the prison. I didn't expect to get a reply. But I did. That was it from then on. We wrote to each other all the time. I didn't think it was possible to fall in love with someone through a letter, but that's what happened. We fell in love. He was a very sensitive, intelligent boy. Yes, he got involved in something truly wicked but not a day of his life went by where he didn't regret it. I offered him forgiveness. Few others did. Not even his own family. They never went to see him. The day after he was arrested, his uncle was killed walking home from the pub. They all loved him, and while he wasn't short of enemies, the family all thought it was because of what Glen did. His mother never really forgave him. He was about as alone as a kid could be. It was like double jeopardy. Punished by losing his freedom. Punished again by losing all the people he loved.'

'Then what?' Foster asked.

'He was released. We hadn't written about or discussed what might happen then. I think he was a bit apprehensive and I wasn't sure how to broach it. I knew it was coming-you couldn't open a paper without reading about it, but I didn't know what it meant for us. It was a few months maybe. But one day the phone rang and it was him.'

Heather spoke this time. 'And it felt the same way, meeting him in the flesh, as it did in print?'

She nodded, smiling at the memory. 'Even more, if that was possible. We didn't exchange one or two letters; it must have been nearly a hundred. There were very few things we didn't know about each other. Of course, I was a bit uncertain when it came to meeting him. But I sort of knew what I was meeting, if that makes sense.'

'You started going out? Foster asked.

'Yes. To everyone who knew me, he was just a boyfriend. He had moved nearby. We didn't need to speak about the past because we'd covered it. Everything was geared to the future. It was taken for granted we would share it together. I loved him, wholly and utterly.' As the last words left her lips, she began to weep, head drooping. She started to sob.

They waited a few minutes for her to recover, Heather once again helping comfort her. Meanwhile, in the background the phone continued to trill incessantly. He left them and unplugged it from the wall. He walked through to a small sitting room and checked through the window. No sign of any press outside. Yet.

Back in the kitchen, Heather was making tea while Mrs Lowell dabbed at her eyes with some tissues. 'Sorry,' she said as Foster returned.

He waved his hand as if to dismiss her apology. A weak morning sun had risen. Foster watched a few particles of dust dance in the shaft cast across the room from a crack in the blinds. Heather came back with three steaming mugs.

'Was his cover ever rumbled?' Foster asked, before blowing across the rim of his cup to cool it.

She took some time over her answer. 'Once,' she said.

'When? Recently?'

She shook her head. 'It was shortly after he was released.'

'How?'

'He got recognised. A friend of his sister's from back home, he said. We never knew for sure but he always suspected his family tried to keep tabs on him. They were so ashamed they probably wanted him banged back up or killed. He saw this girl. Then he got a letter, threatening him. He decided then and there he needed to get out of a small town and lose himself in a big city like London. So we moved here together.'

'But he didn't tell any of this to the parole board or the local police?'

'No,' she replied. 'He valued his independence. The chance to make another life under another identity. He said to me he didn't want to keep running, keep changing his name. "I'd rather die than live on the run." It would have meant me changing my name, maybe leaving behind family and friends, and he wouldn't have wanted to make me do that. So he kept it to himself. He figured they wouldn't be able to track him down in London. And they were right. That was the only time he'd ever felt threatened.'

'There were no threats in the days and weeks before his death?'

'None that I knew of,' she said. She jutted out her jaw defiantly and folded her arms across her chest. 'If there had been, he would have told me. I'm certain.'

Foster looked to the wall, stroked his chin.

'And, presumably, you would have told Roger Levine?'

He could sense Heather bridle at the way he had introduced her duplicity. But Jenny did not seem to register any sense of shock or disquiet. She uncurled her fingers from around her tea mug and inspected them for a few seconds. Then she looked directly at Foster, her eyes red-ringed and tired, yet brimming with conviction.

'He knew.'

'Glen?'

Her nostrils flared, her eyes wide and alive. 'You don't honestly think I would have gone behind his back, do you?'

'I don't think anything, Jenny. I'm here to find things out.'

'Glen knew the press would be skulking around. He knew they would find him wherever he went because someone, somewhere – probably a police-man – would tip them off. He also knew there would be some wild and lurid allegations made about him. If it ever reached the day when they decided to ignore the banning order and write a story, he wanted to make sure they had their facts right, or at least some of them. He also thought, if they were willing to pay for this information, then it was only right some of that money should be coming to him. Plus he knew what these people would stoop to. They would find the information, even if we didn't give it to them. Glen was burgled within a few days of being released, at a house that was supposed to be safe. He knew it was someone rooting about to try and snitch to the press, a private detective. They're willing to go to any lengths. So, this way, we were in control.'

'You were paid?'

'Quite handsomely.'

Foster tried but failed to repress a smirk. Here were these newspapers, champions of law and order, inadvertently and indirectly handing their money over to the wife of a convicted murderer.

'That guy you mentioned, Levine, I met him in a bar. Or he came across to me. Absolute creep. Glen wasn't there. Gave me his card. Said we might want to talk. Next week he was there again. That was when he made the offer. I initially told him to shove it. But that was before I talked it over with Glen. So I called him back and we spoke. We've spoken irregularly ever since. I've always made sure I did it from another phone, as if it was some big horrible secret. He lapped it up.' She shuddered. 'He made my skin crawl. Out of this whole horrible mess, the only thing I'm glad of is that I'll never have to speak to him again.'

It was rare that Foster was lost for words, but for a few seconds he was. They had played Levine and the press like a Stradivarius. He almost admired Dibb for it.

Jenny Lowell was warming to her subject. 'Glen was right too. Here we are, he's dead, and the newspapers are going to be full of stuff about his life. Because of what we told Levine, at least his side of the story is out there, the true way he lived his life. Yes, I know there's going to be all kinds of stuff, lies and innuendo. But the truth – how he held down a job, got promoted, got married, had a kid – is out there.' Her vehemence subsided, her reddened cheeks began to pale once more. Her eyes flickered and fell downcast. She shook her head. 'It's as if Glen knew this day would come and he was preparing for it.'

'Do you believe that?' Heather asked

'I do,' she replied, her voice a cracked whisper. 'I do. I think he always thought something or someone would catch up with him.'

'He said that?' Foster asked.

'Not in as many words. It's just something I felt, from the way he spoke sometimes, the way he looked and the things he did.' She flung her arms up in frustration. 'It's too, well, it's too difficult for me to explain.' Her eyes began to moisten once more.

'Any idea who the person or people might be who caught up with him? His family, perhaps?' Heather questioned.

She shook her head.

'The family of the old man?' Foster asked.

'Maybe. I ... I don't know. It was just a feeling.' She went quiet.

Foster sensed it was time to start wrapping things up. 'Did he ever mention Schofield?'

'Rarely. Never, really. I remember one time. He was always proud of the way he had bounced back and built a new life. It required strength, he said, as well as my support. "I couldn't have done it without you," he would tell me. He said that often. One day, he said, "Craig will always struggle." It took a while for me to work out who he meant. By then, he'd moved on. That was about the only time I remember him mentioning his name.'

'Did he ever talk about that day, Jenny?'

'What day?'

'The day of the old man's murder.'

The last word made her wince. Foster guessed her mind had done all that it could to scrub from her mind the idea that the man she loved had been capable of killing a defenceless pensioner. Her head began to shake.

'No. Never. That day was the one place he would never go. I never pushed him on it either. I think that was tied in with his fear.'

'That something or someone would catch up with him?'

She nodded. 'I remember him mentioning it once. There had been a programme on TV when it just came up, in passing, unexpected. Usually we avoided any sort of show where it might be discussed or mentioned. But it flashed up. He went silent. I can't remember what the voiceover said but it was the usual stuff, about it being brutal and callous, the shock it caused, amazing that kids were capable of such evil and all that bullshit. I didn't know what to say. He said, "If only they knew." I asked him what he meant. "If only they knew the truth," he said. Then I asked him what it was and he shook his head. "I can't tell you," he said. I urged him to but he refused. "One day," he said. I must have been a bit put out, because I said "Yeah, when hell freezes over." It was a bit petulant of me. He gave me a smile and said, "I would do then. Because when hell freezes over it means the devil's dead." Then he said, "Which might be sooner than you think." I didn't know what he meant. We never spoke about it again.'

There was a pause. The shaft of light was now cast across her pale face, causing her to squint. Tears were rolling down her cheeks. 'And now I'll never know.'

13

Researching the family histories of Lara Harrison and her ex-husband was an insight into how the other half had lived. As he tended to do on most jobs, to see if it provided any interesting lines of research, Nigel searched the Internet under both their names. They worked in the PR industry. Xander Harrison, it turned out, was one of the most influential men in that business, with a string of clients including newspapers, broadcasters and television and music stars that even Nigel had heard of. He even found a gossipy report in a PR journal of their wedding; their union was as close to a royal wedding as the industry had experienced. The best man's speech contained a lame joke boasting about how bride and groom each knew half of London, so that they were now uniting the entire city.

He recalled the haunted, hunted woman he had recently met and how it contrasted with the vivacious party girl who shone out from what he had read. Whatever distaste he might have for her choice of work, to have been cast from this nexus of influence and plunged into a solitary, sleepless world of single motherhood must have been a profound shock. No surprise that her grip on sanity seemed slight.

Both were descendants of wealthy and notable bloodlines. Xander boasted a politician and successful businessmen, even one with a title, while Lara's ancestry was less decorated but featured a long line of professional men, doctors, lawyers and brokers. They even shared a glint of scandal: Xander's great-great grandfather was accused of bigamy, though he escaped charges, while her great-grandfather, a doctor, was accused of murdering a patient, also escaping charge.

Yet, however close Nigel peered, any detail that might explain her daughter's night terrors proved elusive. He went through every single child born to each family. Because of their wealth, only two had died before reaching adulthood, one from influenza, the other during childbirth. The influenza victim had been twelve, a boy. He noted down the details to present to Lara but knew it was not the solution she was craving. History was history and the facts could not be shaped to suit people's wishes; he felt like a fraud for charging the poor woman for such a desultory return, and for being no nearer helping her achieve the peace she sought.

Rather than go back to her with bad news, he gave it a day or two while he pondered other avenues his research could follow. He was unable to shake the memory of the large, brooding house she lived in and its oppressive atmosphere. It gave him an idea.

The first stop was the title deeds. The property had been built in 1898. As he suspected, the first signatory was a John Arthur Rankin, a builder by trade, and the man responsible for laying out the whole street, which was completed in 1902. Those at one end of the street had Victorian houses, while the others were Edwardian. Rankin owned the freehold and the 1901 census revealed that he lived there with his wife and four children.

Nigel went to the 1911 census, the most recent available. The Rankin family had gone. The property was empty. Nigel checked the neighbouring houses. They were all occupied. Maybe it had been sold and the purchasers were yet to move in? Or the Rankins had decided to rent it out and it was between tenants? There was no further census so the riddle was left hanging, tantalisingly so.

That evening, it gnawed away at him. Why was such an impressive property empty? Unexplained omissions or quirks of the past were common in his work. History left many puzzles, some impossible to solve. Experience had taught him that when there was a solution, even the most impenetrable riddles had the simplest explanations. Occasionally, he got an inkling, an intuition almost, that there was more to a story than he first thought. This was one such occasion. When that happened, the reason he might be looking for an answer, the point of it all, became secondary; all that mattered was finding the answer.

The River Thames flowed nearby and he knew the area surrounding Lara Harrison's house was at risk from flooding. He checked the weather for the period leading up to census night 1911. No records of heavy rain. The next morning he was in the local history section of Chiswick library. No reports of a flood in any of the source material. With water all but ruled out, he turned his attention to that other destructive element: fire. There were copies of the local newspaper going back to the mid-Victorian period available on microfilm, so he set up himself up, requested the appropriate reels and began his search.

It did not take long. When the answer came, it was an act of God, a particularly cruel and harsh one.

The Rankins were gone. A family named the Bathursts were the new occupants, also with four children. Christopher Bathurst, the head of the family, was a lawyer. His wife, Esme, had live-in help with the children and keeping the house, an eighteen-year-old girl named Yvette Franklin. Bathurst had been at work, his wife on an unspecified social engagement. She had returned one cold early December afternoon to find Franklin sitting on the front doorstep in tears. The youngest of their children, Esther, aged fifteen months, had been put down for her nap. When Franklin went in to wake her she found the child dead.

Nigel read on. The pathologist concluded the little girl had died of natural causes. She had been feeling unwell for some days before and had exhibited flu-like symptoms. The family accepted the finding and the case, tragic but not uncommon, had been closed.

However, a few days later the servant girl was arrested. The family had changed their mind. One of the other children had reported that she had heard Franklin become frustrated with Esther, whose illness had made her irritable and whingy. She was also reported to have said she would do 'anything to hush the child'. She was then charged with murder, accused of having smothered the child with a pillow.

It came as a shock to all. What had been her motive? Surely, the question was asked, she wouldn't murder a child because it was irritable? She had been employed by the family for only a few months and everyone spoke well of her, while others who spoke to reporters testified how well she got on with the little girl and her three older siblings. Perhaps, it was suggested, she was in the grip of some mania.

A second post-mortem was held, which backed up the conclusions of the first: no outward signs of injury, yet stated clearly that the child's body was also in keeping with being smothered by a soft object such as a pillow.

Franklin refused to accept her guilt. The hiatus between charge and trial caused a vacuum which the newspaper filled with all manner of lurid stories about her private life and mental state. A further report spoke of her receiving psychiatric treatment at a mental hospital as a young girl. The Bathurst family had moved elsewhere, and while they found a purchaser and a new place in which to rebuild their lives, the house had lain empty, harbouring too many ghosts and painful memories for them to return.

The case eventually came to trial and the newspaper was there to report it. Four main people gave evidence before a jury: Esme Bathurst, 'demure, yet dignified under the weight of her obvious grief'; the pathologist who carried out the second post-mortem; a senior policeman, whose evidence was rather glossed over, and Yvette Franklin, who took to the witness box 'frail, her wild eyes a testament to the tempestuous feelings within', in sharp contrast to her more considered former employer.

The mother gave evidence that her youngest daughter had been running a high temperature, as well as showing signs of having laboured breathing. Yet she was in decent spirits, still acted 'good in herself'. She could think of no reason as to why Yvette Franklin would harm her baby. The doctor had been called, an insignificant fever noted and bed rest prescribed. On the morning of her death, as her mother left to attend a luncheon for the local temperance association, she noted more colour had returned to the child's cheeks, and believed this meant she was on the road to recovery.

Franklin spoke through stifled sobs and frequent pauses with which to gather herself. She had taken the child to her bed in the nursery room on the first floor of the house at the front and 'read her a story to prepare her for a nap'. As the child drifted off towards unconsciousness, the maid stroked her hair and whispered 'peaceful entreaties' into her ear. The girl had fallen asleep, she had left, and it was only on her return that she found her dead, when it was time to wake her. Under cross-examination, it was reported, the teenager 'crumbled'. She agreed to having frequently lost her temper with the children, and admitted that she was temperamentally unsuited to looking after small children. Despite that she claimed to have loved the infant. Her barrister claimed that such was her grief and anguish at her wrongful arrest, she had twice attempted suicide. This appears to have been taken as some form of admission of guilt, as the jury recorded a verdict of guilty. The judge took into account her age, her remorse despite the fact she had refused to accept her guilt, and said he would not be asking for the death sentence. Instead he sentenced Franklin to life imprisonment. Interviewed outside court, Esme Bathurst recorded her satisfaction at the verdict. They were not believers in the death penalty. 'The death of Yvette Franklin will not bring back our daughter, nor would it alleviate our grief. No human act could.'

The reports strewn in front of him, Nigel took off his glasses and rubbed the bridge of his nose. *What an extraordinary case,* he thought. Something troubled him about it. More pressingly, he wondered if there was any relevance to the sufferings of Lara Harrison's daughter. Nigel subscribed to the theory of psycho-geography; the belief that places carry the stains and traces of past events, of a special atmosphere which no amount of rebuilding or gentrification or demolition could erase. He had witnessed it time and time again; areas where events recurred, or where, despite years having passed, an aura from tragic episodes was left behind. Yet his belief was in something ineffable, intangible. This case, and the idea that the death of the little girl was having some bearing on the life of another little girl in the present, veered far closer to the world of the paranormal than he was comfortable with. Nigel believed in the power of the past; he did not believe in ghosts, apparitions and ghouls. No, people could be haunted by events unspoken and secrets long buried, but not by things that went bump in the night.

Yet it deserved further investigation. There was a chance that the past had not been buried here; that justice had not been done. Could that have some effect? It was improbable. But it might be a good idea for him to let Heather look over the facts of the case and offer a professional verdict before he took it to Lara Harrison.

He ran a weary eye over future editions of the newspaper, in search of any more morsels about the Bathurst case. There were none. Until he reached the edition of the first anniversary of the little girl's death.

Yvette Franklin had hanged herself in her prison cell.

14

Foster had been sent a copy of Schofield's post-mortem and toxicology report. Schofield had been dead for forty-eight hours before Foster found him. As suspected, he had been poisoned. The toxin was nicotine, introduced in its purest form to the curry he was eating and later found undigested in his gastrointestinal tract. Its efficacy was rivalled by few other toxins, apart from cyanide. Within a few seconds the dose would have caused a crippling burning sensation in Schofield's mouth, throat and stomach. Unable to scream or call for any help, he would have vomited and soiled himself before his muscles entered paralysis, including the diaphragm. Slowly, tortuously, in the most excruciating agony imaginable, the blessed relief of death would have come from respiratory failure. Schofield was a heavy smoker, so his tolerance to the lethal dose would have been higher, prolonging the torment.

The killer knew that, Foster was sure. For him, this was confirmation that the same person was involved in both killings: both men had endured extreme pain in the seconds before they died. Much like the old man. Someone wanted them to be aware of their impending death and experience a grotesque suffering in those final moments. It was all about revenge.

He knew most of the detectives in his team still clung to the theory that Dibb had killed Schofield and then himself, and it was a matter of trying to prove he could be in Leicester. He left it to Drinkwater to urge them to drop their preconceptions. In the meantime, it had been agreed that someone should approach the surviving family of the old man, and his experience of the case and familiarity with them made Foster the best candidate.

So it was on a cold Wednesday morning that he found himself on a train from King's Cross to Newcastle, returning to the city for the first time since he had left, only a few weeks after Dibb and Schofield had been sentenced.

Twenty-five years had passed since he'd been on a train crossing the dirty old Tyne, pulling out from the city with a pang of regret at what he was leaving behind and what the future held. On this morning, the sky as slate grey as the bridge itself, he felt apprehensive and nervous. There were a few ghosts to confront; not all related to Dibb, Schofield and the murder of the old man.

As he got off the train, even the air was familiar; colder, thicker. The clean air act had long been passed, yet when he'd been here few people paid heed, and the enormously comforting, sweetly acrid smell of burning coal reminded him of his time there, each dense breath a rush of memory. London was his home, but, denied a university education or the opportunity to travel, Newcastle had been the place where he had first truly lived.

As he passed through the ticket barriers he saw a stubbled man in a sharp grey suit, holding a small placard bearing his name. He was smoking a cigarette. Some sort of copper's communion meant they recognised each other without any sign or greeting. The man – Foster pegged him to his early thirties – tipped his fag to the floor, crushed it under a heel and thrust out a hand.

'Detective Sergeant Derek Whelan,' he said, in a Geordie lilt. That was another thing Foster hadn't realised he'd missed. The coarse music of the northeast accent. 'Canny trip?'

'Aye,' Foster found himself replying, without thinking, as he often had done when he worked up there. 'It was all right,' he added, quickly, in his own London accent, in case Whelan thought he was taking the piss.

'I'm parked over there,' he said, nodding to a Ford Scorpio in an illegal bay. They made their way over, Foster pulling his jacket against his chest to protect himself from a fiercely cold blast of wind.

'Bit nippy out,' he said.

'Aye. It's a teeth rattler today,' the detective agreed.

The car was warm and Foster was thankful for it. Maybe nostalgia had its limits. There was the faint whiff of tobacco smoke. He buckled up. 'What's the plan?' he asked.

'You're the boss,' Whelan replied. 'I've been told to assist you in any way possible.'

He spoke the last sentence as if in quotes, which told Foster that he might not be too happy with having to play chauffeur to a London cop swinging in to do a job a Geordie could have done with ease. *Better to confront any bad feeling now rather than let it fester,* he thought.

'You do know why they sent me up, don't you?'

'Aye. You worked the case back then and you know the family.' He glanced over at Foster from the corner of an eye. 'It's not a problem.'

'Good. I've had some experience of out-of-towners coming in to tread on my toes, so I know it can be a pain. Hopefully I won't be.'

'Where to?'

'No point pissing about. Take me to Barry Chester's house.'

Barry Chester was the old man's eldest son.

A light rain started to fall as they drove through the town centre, slicking the buildings and making the roof slates glisten. It was clear to Foster that much had changed since he'd left. Then the city was mired in a depression, resentful, inward-looking. Less so now. New office blocks, converted buildings, bars and redevelopments suggested a city with renewed confidence and purpose. Another reason to love the place: resilience.

'When did you leave?' Whelan asked, breaking his thoughts.

'1992. Things have changed a bit since then, by the looks.'

'They have, that,' Whelan agreed. 'Still the same gritty city underneath though. Don't be fooled by the fancy bars and art galleries. Just window dressing, that, like.'

'I'm glad to hear it.' He meant it. All the clichés he'd been told about the North prior to moving up here, about the cold weather and darker winters and rain, but also about the sense of community, the friendliness, the warmth of the people, had turned out to be true. Not for a second had he missed London. Had he taken a few different turns and made some other decisions, he might well have settled here.

Foster had always been terrible at keeping in touch with anyone from his past. Unless they were part of your present, he failed to see the point. Life moved on and people did too; the hooks and burdens of history were an obstacle to progress. What mattered to him was the here and now. That said, he found himself watching the rain drops run their crazy paths down the passenger window and thinking of a few of his former colleagues.

'Jimmy Ashcroft still on the force?'

Whelan paused. 'Nah,' he said. 'He died.'

'What?'

'Aye. Forty-seven. Pancreatic cancer.'

'Fuck me. He was married, wasn't he?'

'Three kids.'

'Jesus.' *Another reason why it was never a good idea to go back*, he thought. *Often what you found broke your heart.* 'How about Andy Colborne?'

Whelan emitted a mirthless laugh. 'He died too. Car accident a few years back.'

'Fuck me,' he repeated. The two best blokes he knew, guys he worked with, drank with, laughed with, local boys who accepted him, took him home to meet their wives, families, their friends. Both dead before they hit fifty.

'I didn't know them that well,' Whelan said. 'I came to this a bit late. But they were respected blokes. Good coppers.'

'Great coppers,' Foster corrected. On the train, watching the lines by the side of the track swoop up and down as he hurtled north, he had contemplated giving them a call when he arrived to fix up a pint, relive past glories, reminisce. Not now. There were no others he was interested in seeing. Just two he would like to avoid.

'I bet Sharon Carter is still alive,' he muttered.

Whelan laughed, this time genuinely. 'You're kidding, right?'

'Why?'

'She's our Detective Super. You knew that?'

Talk about there being no justice, he thought. 'No, that's news to me.' He shouldn't be surprised. Sharon had always had the drive, the ambition and the political nous to work her way up the greasiest pole and through the hardest glass ceilings. She was one to inspire admiration rather than affection, and reaching a position like that in an old-school force like the Newcastle one, with all its inherent sexism, was an impressive achievement.

'Busts your balls, does she?' he asked.

'Like you wouldn't fucking believe,' Whelan said emphatically.

That left only one more to check on. 'How about Jackie Corrigan?'

A flush of energy lit Whelan's face. 'Jackie's still going strong.'

Of course he is, Foster thought.

'He was eighty the other week. They had a grand old do for him. He pops in every now and then, has a chat. Great bloke. Never worked under him but they say he was one of the best.'

Foster fell silent; he sensed that Whelan was anticipating a stream of stories testifying to Jackie's skills as a detective.

'They don't make them like that any more, do they?' Whelan asked, as if urging him on.

'One of a kind.' The word 'thankfully' he kept silent.

Whelan began to rattle off a list of Jackie Corrigan anecdotes. One aspect of the north-east culture he never warmed to was the desire to canonise people. Even when those men or women least deserved it. Not that anyone knew the truth about Jackie Corrigan. Certainly not Derek Whelan, who was still recounting Corrigan tales as they left Newcastle behind and headed north towards Morpeth, and the small former pit village of Mackington, the home of Kenneth Chester and the scene of his awful murder.

15

As they drove into the village, Foster could see much had changed since his last visit. The pub was now a drop-in centre, advertising aerobics classes, clinics on stopping smoking, and Internet and IT workshops. The image of former miners, who had spent their lives performing arduous and dangerous manual work, now learning how to use Google and set out an Excel spreadsheet flashed across his mind. It didn't seem right. Most of the shops on the main parade were still boarded up. Mackington would always look wistfully over its shoulder to a time when the clank and churn of the pit provided the soundtrack to a place at ease, not the silence which followed and came as a reproach. Foster looked east, to where the pit head once stood, though the seams the miners worked were two miles out beneath the North Sea. It was gone. The only sign that there had once been a thriving pit were the slagheaps, now grassed and verdant; the only signs of renewal he could detect.

They passed a small church, then turned left onto a long avenue of terraced houses he remembered so well. On the right was where Kenny Chester had lived. Kenny had been a widower, angina having claimed his wife, Jean, a little more than two years before his own violent end. Once Kenny had died the rest of the family moved in, as if wishing to preserve it in his memory.

Whelan pulled the car up outside number 77. Foster climbed out and stretched, cracking his knuckles, drawing in a deep breath as if to summon sinew and gird himself. Never go back, that was his mantra. Yet here he was near the scene of the crime he remembered most vividly of all his cases and always would. He looked at the door, set back at the end of a long, narrow front garden, like all the others on the street. There were no back gardens to speak of, just yards were once the residents kept their coal and their crap. Even in the late 1980s and 90s some of them still had outdoor toilet. Beyond the house, and the street at the back, was the Dean, the locals' name for a wooded bank and a small river, and the place where Kenny Chester met his brutal end.

Foster opened the gate and let it close behind him and Whelan on the catch. He thought he saw a net curtain twitch at the window. The garden was overgrown and strewn with weeds, not like the last time he had seen it, with vegetables sown in ordered lines. The old man had been renowned for the growing the best leeks in the area. As they reached the front door, he could see a large plastic tub, filled with piles of empty bottles of beer and other booze.

The door opened and there stood the large, billowing figure of Barry Chester. A giant of a man, at six feet six, an inch taller than Foster himself, and wider at the waist and shoulders. His hair, once jet black, had turned silver, but he looked well, considering his drinker's face showed the sign of years of what the locals called heavy gargling.

'Detective Grant Foster,' he said in a deep smoker's growl. His smile creased his whole face.

'Detective Chief Inspector now, Barry,' he said, extending his hand and feeling a large, rough palm wrap around it and give it a tight squeeze. Barry was a carpenter, a successful one, or had been at least; Kenny, who spent forty-eight years in the pit, was adamant that none of his children would follow him down.

Barry nodded at Whelan and beckoned them inside. Vince, Barry's younger brother, stood at the door of the sitting room stood. Quiet, terse, Foster had never heard him utter anything other than a murmured greeting. He conformed to type by nodding and offering a limper handshake than his brother. Barry's glamorous wife, Dawn, pottered around behind him, layered in make-up. 'Hello again,' she said, when Barry introduced him.

Foster looked around. They had done much with the place, knocking through so that sitting room and kitchen were one. Through some folding glass doors at the back of the kitchen he could see that the cree, the shed which had once held the coal, had been removed and the whole surface had been decked with wood. It was as modern as a former colliery house got.

'How come you're still living here?' Foster asked. He thought he saw Dawn roll her eyes.

'It's home.' The word was spoken to rhyme with 'worm'. Barry's accent, like most north of Newcastle, was even thicker. 'I own three more places, like, but we choose to live here.'

Foster understood. He lived in the house he had grown up in, moving back when his father was ill. There were ghosts and memories, but it was a place he loved and he didn't want to leave.

'How's business?'

'Aye. Canny,' he replied. 'Take a seat.' He nodded towards an armchair. Foster took it. Whelan grabbed the sofa, squeezing next to Vince, who was running to fat, unlike his older brother, who was the right side of bulky. Barry took the other chair. 'Stick the kettle on, pet,' he called to the kitchen. He sighed, looked at Foster. 'You've not changed much.'

'Thanks,' he said.

'Though you had a bit more hair, like, the last time you saw us.'

'That's life in London for you,' he said, smiling.

Barry wrinkled his nose. 'Don't know how you do it. Can't stand the place meself. Stinks of rat piss, eh?'

Foster shrugged. 'You know what they say: in London you're never more than four metres from a rat. But it's home. How are the kids?'

'Grand. Kenny senior's in Newcastle, working as an architect. Married a bonny lass, for a Mackem anyway, two kids of his own. Helen's, well, she's doing her own thing. The youngest is at uni.'

'You had another?'

'Aye – all clever buggers too,' he said, with obvious pride.

'And grandkids, eh?'

'Cannae beat having them. All the fun with none of the pain. How about you? You got kids?'

'No. Never been married.' It was a lie; he had a daughter, one he had never seen.

'Your loss,' Barry said. 'Best thing a man can do, have a family.'

'I'm sure it is.'

'So, what brings you back to Mackington?' The glimmer in his eyes gave away that he knew exactly why Foster was there, and why he had been on the doorstep waiting, the house behind him spotless and immaculate.

'That tub full of empty booze bottles outside. Don't suppose you've been celebrating anything, have you?'

'What have we got to celebrate, Detective? Sorry, Detective Chief Inspector.' The eyes continued to gleam. He was enjoying this.

'I don't know, Barry. You tell me.'

He held out his hands. 'Don't know what to say. Just an average night's drinking. We like a drop, don't we, Vince?' Vince nodded.

'What about you, Vince?' Foster asked. 'Married, kids?'

Barry snorted with derision. 'Haddaway, man. What lass is gonna gan near that soppy shite? Nah, he's single till the day he dies, that one. If patter were water he'd not fill a thimble. Good worker, mind.'

Vince said nothing, just a simple smile. Foster had forgotten how people spoke about him as if he wasn't there.

Dawn brought a pot of tea, some mugs and a plate of biscuits. She poured out four cups. He took the steaming mug gratefully. She went back to the kitchen and came back with a can of Coke, which she threw rather than handed to Vince. Foster guessed he spent rather more time in their company than she might have expected, given they were both past fifty and Vince was only four or five years younger.

'Where were we?' Foster asked.

'You were making oot that we were a bunch of drunks,' Barry shot back, eyes still agleam.

Foster decided to stop dawdling and get to the crux of the matter. 'Where were you when you were told that Dibb and Schofield were dead?'

The light in his eyes dimmed. 'Here. Yer man there phoned us Monday,' he added, nodding at Whelan. 'The press were outside. We said a few words. Yes, we had a gargle or two. I hope those two fucking bastards rot in hell for eternity. I'm no hypocrite, you know that. If we'd had our way this day woulda come sooner. I'm glad they're dead.'

'I didn't see any quotes from you in the press saying that.'

'That's because all we said was that we were thinking of me dad, and honouring his memory.'

'Very noble of you, Barry.' Foster was beginning to think he'd make a mistake coming here. Should have left it to the local force, only speaking to the family if the evidence led them in that direction. Travelling half the country on an extended fishing trip suddenly seemed pointless. All he was going to do was dredge up bad feeling. He didn't think these people had killed Dibb and Schofield. They had their flaws but they were good, honest working folk.

'Aye, well ...' Barry's voice tailed away. 'Let's just say I'm not too fond of the press for some of their actions back when me dad was murdered. I'd rather keep me counsel than give them what they want.'

'Other than Derek here, has anyone filled you in on what happened?'

Barry took a sip from his mug of tea. Then he looked at the assortment of biscuits, picking one up and dunking it in the mug. He took a bite and washed it down with another swig. All the time he looked at Foster, as if studying him. It was as if a million things were being left unsaid. Foster had forgotten Barry Chester's lively intelligence and sharp wit; how he revelled in others' discomfort. He had also witnessed his capacity for rage. Anger simmered perpetually beneath the calm surface.

'Aye,' he said simply.

'Who? Derek?'

'No.' He took a long pause, another sip, another dunk. 'Jackie Corrigan.'

'Jackie?' His response was almost reflexive. Barry sensed his bewilderment.

'He stayed in touch,' he explained. The inference being that Foster hadn't. They had spent a great deal of time with the family during the investigation, keeping them up to date and as involved as possible, because of their understandable anger, yet also because both saw it as right and just. The family had suffered a grievous loss, the press were attempting to whip them into a vengeful frenzy; they needed to make sure the investigation into their father's murder was carried out with transparency and rigour.

However, while they had established a bond, it was still a case. Detectives moved on to the next one. They were not an arm of the care industry. Remaining a part of the victims' family lives was not an option. Or at least Foster thought that way. Perhaps Jackie Corrigan didn't.

'Did he?'

'Aye. Every year on the anniversary of me dad's death he'd call, or come by the house, see how we were. He's a good fella. One of us. His dad and my dad were pitmen at the same colliery. I know you lot down in London don't give a fuck for community and solidarity, but we do here. Whenever something new happened, you know, like when those two little bastards got released, Jackie'd be there to keep us posted. Let us know the details.'

'What sort of details?'

'Not the ones you're thinking of,' Barry said

'What was I thinking of, Barry?'

The amiable features swiftly contorted into anger. 'Insinuating Jackie gave us the identities of them two.' Those last two words were spat with tremendous venom. The intervening years had done nothing to dissipate his anger towards the boys who had killed his father. Nor, it appeared, had their deaths.

'I did nothing of the sort,' Foster replied, keeping his voice calm. 'But seeing as you mention it, did he give you their identities?'

'No.' His stare was cold, unyielding.

Foster nodded. 'So you never knew their new names?'

'No.'

'And I suppose you have alibis for last weekend?'

'I told Jackie exactly where we all were.'

Foster ran his hand over his shaven head. 'The problem with that, Barry, is that Jackie is retired. Now I know I can't stop him coming to see you, that's his prerogative. But whatever he told you and you told him, well, that was a private conversation and nothing to do with police business.'

'He said he'd pass it on. So as we wouldn't be bothered, dredge up the past and bad memories and that.'

Out of the corner of his eye he could see Derek Whelan, legs apart, a hint of a smirk on his face.

'Well, sorry to make you do just that, but nobody has passed these alibis on to me. So…'

'You think we killed them?'

'Did I say that?'

But something made him uneasy. The same thing that had drawn him back here.

Barry was shaking his head in exasperation. 'I don't believe it. One of them fellers poured petrol over his own head and set himself on fire. You think we had owt to do with that?'

'I never said that. Come on, you're not naive. Dibb and Schofield show up dead. They were guilty of a crime in their past. It's the only thing still connecting the two. I'm not accusing you of anything. You've told me you didn't know their new identities. Now tell me your alibis and I'll check them out and we can move on and try and find those responsible, yes?'

'You could always speak to Jackie?'

'Why? When I can ask you?'

A smile played on Barry's lips. 'Sorry, I forgot, you don't speak to him any more, do you?'

'Tell me where you were last weekend,' Foster said impatiently. 'Then I'm done, we can go and you can go back to the rest of your lives.'

'We were here. At home.'

'OK. Who can corroborate that for me?'

'Dawn can. Vince can.'

'Anyone who wasn't a family member?'

Barry shrugged. 'Don't know.'

'Did you go out, meet anyone?'

Another shrug. 'Paper shop on Saturday morning. Supermarket in the afternoon.'

'That's it?'

'Quiet weekend. What can I say? I like to let the grass grow under my feet these days.'

Foster sighed. He could carry on trying to squeeze blood from a stone here, or he could go elsewhere. Even better, he could get a train back down south. He took his notebook from his pocket and threw it so it landed in Barry's lap. 'Jot down the contact details of all your kids and kids-in-law. Mobile is fine.'

'What do you need to bother me kids for?'

'Find out where they were.' Barry stared at the notebook, saying nothing. 'I don't know why you're being so obstructive, Barry. I've done nothing but be good to you. I almost killed myself working my balls off on your dad's case. Why the hostility? If you've got nothing to do with the death of these two, then you've got no reason to resent me coming here.'

Barry continued to stare at the notebook. He didn't speak. 'Get me a pen, love,' he said to Dawn. She found him one and he began to scrawl onto the page in a large, laborious hand. When he finished, he threw the notebook across the room. He fixed Foster with another of his baleful looks.

'You know why I don't want you here,' he said, utterly devoid of emotion.

'I do?'

'Yes. You wouldn't let it lie. Now get the fuck out of my house.'

They left, Foster striding ahead purposefully down the path, not once glancing back, though he could hear Whelan trying to keep pace. At the gate he turned left, walking around twenty yards, until he reached Whelan's parked car. There was a beep as it was unlocked remotely but he carried on walking. The light was draining from the day, giving way to a grim, grey dusk, lit by intermittent street lamps. The air had grown colder and the wind even more brutal. The place had once felt charmingly out of time; now it felt oppressively small and run-down.

He reached a school, the same primary that Dibb and Schofield had attended. The playground at the front was empty though a few lights in the building pierced the gloaming. Foster took a left, doubling back on himself, down a wide snicket that ran between the school and the street the Chesters lived on. He could hear Whelan behind, still struggling to keep up, his long stride keeping him ahead. The snicket reached a narrow backstreet, onto which the houses of this and the next street backed. Barely wide enough for a car. Not that many ventured down here. It was where you often found drying washing strung across the street, women talking at their back-yard doors, the occasional fish or grocer's van making their rounds, and kids playing football, chase, tag. Not now though. The whole gloomily lit alley was deserted.

He crossed over, carried on along the snicket until it opened out into a further street. The houses here were newer, bigger, more ambitious, some even semi-detached. The street was empty and he crossed, reaching the mouth to another snicket, leading past the houses and on to the Dean. The place where Kenny Chester had met his death.

He strode along the path, ignoring the soft mud that clung to his shoes. There were perhaps twenty minutes of daylight left and he had just passed the last street lamp. The wide path gave way to a narrower one, winding down away from him. Despite the gloom he could see the trees at the top of the bank, before the ground gave way. Another twenty or thirty feet beneath that lay the water; on the far side another bank rose away and became woodland.

The small path forked and he knew to take the right, treading carefully because the mud made the going slippery. The grass was overgrown, bushes lay in clumps. He continued towards the bank edge, to an opening between two large horse chestnut trees; the Dean made rich pickings in autumn for kids hunting conkers.

The opening was dark but he made his way through. He had just passed through what for weeks had been the perimeter of the crime scene. He was in a small clearing, about thirty feet square, ringed by trees, dark looming presences against the blackening sky.

In the centre, a grey marble monument stood protected by a high spiked painted metal fence. In the exact place where Kenny Chester had been tossed into a shallow grave. Foster walked forwards for a closer look. The monument carried an inscription: *In loving memory of Kenny Chester. May his soul rest in eternal peace.* Short, pithy, to the point and free of sentimentality. As he thought it should be. He looked at the monument, a plain column topped with a cross, dignified and proud. Then he turned around and surveyed the scene before the light closed in. The ground around had returned to normal; nature as blithe and blind as ever to the atrocities perpetrated on her soil. It was peaceful; perhaps Nigel Barnes and his psycho-geographic gobbledegook was wrong: places did not always carry the stain of evil carried out there.

'You can shift, I'll give you that,' Whelan said, appearing at his side, breathing heavily. Foster ignored him, continuing to look around. The last time he'd been here it was a glorious summer; it had been hard to believe such a wild, resplendent place could ever bear witness to such cruelty.

'Why the hell didn't you tell me that Jackie Corrigan had been to see them?'

'Whoah there. You never asked.'

'You didn't think it was relevant?' He shook his head in amazement. 'God knows what he told them.'

'He paid them a visit out of courtesy, to tell them in person and warn them. Good detective work if you ask me.'

'He's not a detective any more. He's retired.'

'Aye, but that doesn't mean he's on the scrapheap. He's still a well-respected man. By some, anyway...'

Foster finally turned to face the young detective. The implicit criticism hung in the air. 'I don't mean to be patronising but you never worked with Jackie. I don't care how much you all worship him; I don't care if he's been given the Freedom of fucking Newcastle, he's no longer active and he shouldn't be playing any part in this investigation. None of you should. It's got fuck all to do with Newcastle police any more.' It was this kind of parochial bullshit he had dreaded on the train up that morning. 'Did you know he took alibis?'

'I didn't. I just know he popped in to see them. Saw nowt wrong with that, to be honest.'

'Yeah, well...'

Foster failed to finish the sentence, instead staring out into the growing darkness, attempting to contain his anger.

'What was Barry Chester going on about, you not speaking to him any more?'

'None of his business. None of fucking yours, either.'

'Fair dos,' Whelan said. 'Care to tell me where you want to go next? Back to headquarters? Or to your hotel? Which one did they book you into?'

'Bollocks to that,' he said, setting off back towards the opening. 'Take me to see Jackie Corrigan.'

16

Foster stared out of the window, seeing nothing save the occasional smudge of street light as Whelan bleated and whinged behind the wheel. He was insisting that calling cold on Jackie Corrigan's doorstep was verging on blasphemy. Foster ignored him, his mind far from the present, instead curling back to late 1988 when he'd first encountered the man he'd considered his mentor. All manner of thoughts and memories collided and coalesced as they drove to Corrigan's remote, sprawling home, near the headland overlooking the wild untamed shores of the Northumbrian coast.

The house stood on its own, a few hundred yards from any other, at the end of a gravel road. Little of it could be seen from the main road, just a distant glimpse of soft light though towering boundary hedges. Foster had visited several times: once asked to drive by and pick up Corrigan for a leaving dinner; an honour, he was told, though it felt like a nuisance because he expected to be driven home, and a night spent avoiding alcohol while the rest of the company

drowned their livers fit to float was never his idea
of fun. Then, as he spent more time in the city and
the force, Corrigan asked him back a few times for
a cooked dinner – tea, they called it up here – by
his wife, Pauline, a red-faced woman, natural mother
and homemaker. Delighted to be fed such decent
wholesome food – his own repertoire involved opening a tin or slamming a packet in a microwave – he
accepted every subsequent invite. A few nights, usually after sinking too much Scotch with Jackie until
well into the night, he crashed in one of the many
spare bedrooms.

Since those days, large metal gates had been
installed. Electronic. It never occurred to him at the
time, but now it did – Jackie had been well paid, but
not enough to fund this kind of lifestyle. Where had
all the money come from?

Whelan insisted on staying in the car when Foster
got out to press the call button on the intercom at the
gate, clearly trying to avoid being questioned about
bringing him here unannounced. Foster snapped.

'Just piss off,' he said.

'But how will you get back?'

'I'll phone a cab.'

'It's miles ...'

'It's on expenses. You don't want to be here; this
way you can save your sorry arse any trouble.'

Foster could see the dilemma play out on his
face. Stay, and risk any fallout from Foster's unannounced visit to the most respected living alumnus

of Newcastle metropolitan police force. Leave, and chance retribution for deserting the detective he was supposed to be chaperoning in the middle of nowhere in the dead of evening.

'Look,' Foster added, trying to help, 'I'll tell them it was my idea. I released you. Go home to your wife. Thanks for the ride.'

'What if he's not in?'

'Just clear off, Derek.'

There was a split second of further indecision until he stuck the car in reverse, pulled back onto the main road and started to drive away, holding a half-hearted hand up to say goodbye. Foster nodded and watched as his tail lights faded to black.

It was only then, on the dark and deserted street in a place he no longer knew, buffeted by a biting wind, that the thought crossed his mind that he might have been rash. Whelan was a pain, but he had wheels. What *if* Jackie wasn't in? He checked his mobile. He had a signal. All wasn't lost.

In the gloom he located the intercom to the side of the gates. He pressed the button and waited, the cold seeping into his bones.

A voice, familiar if slightly diminished by time, crackled through the speaker. 'Hello.'

'Jackie Corrigan?'

'Aye,' it said suspiciously. 'Who's this?'

He paused. 'Grant Foster.'

The pause that came in return was heavy and pro-longed. For a second Foster thought that he needed to press something else, do something, say anything. Then he remembered those long silences that everyone made the mistake of leaping into; crooks and coppers alike.

'Well, you'd better come in,' he said amiably, as if he was inviting him over the threshold for a cup of tea.

The gates swung open. Only then could Foster see he still had another two-hundred-and-fifty yards of drive to navigate before reaching the front door; memory had shrunk its distance in his mind to a short walk. When he'd got about a hundred yards, the door opened and a tall, wiry grey frame filled the entrance. Foster looked around. The grounds were immaculate, professionally kept no doubt. It looked like an extra wing or two had been added to the house. There was a parking bay in front of the doors where Corrigan stood. A huge silver Bentley took pride of place. The old man liked his classic cars, he remembered. On a small, round island in front was a flagpole, on which a flag flapped in the cold breeze. Foster smiled. It had been put up by another detective, a creep seeking advancement.

Foster reached the door. Up close, he could see the years had been kind to his old boss. He was older, greyer, but no stouter, and he could have passed easily for someone ten years junior. His creased face wore a look of mild puzzlement.

'You've never walked, have you?'

Foster shrugged. 'Needed the air.'

A broad smile broke out on Corrigan's face. He offered a hand. Foster accepted it. 'Ya bugger,' he said, clasping his hand tight. He let go and stepped back. 'You've put on weight, mind. And you'll be unbalanced cos you've lost more than a bit up top,' he added, looking at his shaven head.

'Cheers, Jack,' he said. 'Can't say the same, though; you look exactly the same.'

'Aye, well, been blessed with good genes, haven't I? Come in.'

He closed the door behind him, took Foster's coat. The house was warm, well-lit, spotless. Little had changed. 'Pauline not in?'

Jackie raised his eyebrows. 'She died, son.'

He felt his heart flutter. *Shit*, he thought. 'I'm sorry to hear that,' he mumbled. 'They never told me.'

'Five years ago. God rest her soul.'

'She was a lovely woman.'

'Aye, she was that.'

Foster wondered about him rattling around in this huge house on his own. All his kids had flown. It conjured a sorry image. Jackie, as was his way, sensed the direction Foster's thoughts were going.

'I have a housekeeper,' he explained. 'It's her night off, though. And the kids come back a lot. I've got eleven grandkids and they all live reasonably near. I don't go short for company.'

'Good,' Foster said, still feeling a twang of guilt. One he quickly dismissed. *Don't be such a hypocrite*, he thought.

'Do you have any yourself, Grant?'

'What? Grandkids? Nah.'

'No, I meant kids.'

'I don't have those either. Not the marrying kind.' He found himself saying that phrase a great deal recently.

'You didn't carry on seeing that bonny lass you were with while you were up here? What was her name … Cathy, was it?'

'Caitlin,' he corrected. 'No, we lost touch.'

'Aye, well,' he replied, followed by a long, awkward silence. 'Come on through.'

He turned and Foster followed him through to a large, warm sitting room, immaculately kept as before, though it had been redecorated. It was here they had talked and drunk long and hard, deep into the night. He noticed Jackie was wearing slippers, which was incongruous given that he was wearing smartly pressed grey slacks, a blue V-neck jumper and tie underneath. But he was of that generation that would never dream of dressing casually, even in their own home.

'A drink?'

'Go on,' Foster said.

'Scotch?'

'Got something lighter? A beer, maybe?'

'A Broon OK?'

Foster nodded. Corrigan left, returning with a large bottle of Newcastle Brown Ale and a glass. It had been a while since Foster had had one.

'It's not chilled. I never chill it. I was in the States a few years back and in this one bar they had it in the fridge. Why, I said to them, it should be served warm. They looked at us as if I was mad.' He shook his head. 'There they are, most powerful country in the world, all that technology and economic power, and they don't realise that ale should be served warm.'

'Sacrilege,' Foster said, flipping the cap and pouring the foaming brown liquid into the glass. Corrigan, meanwhile, disappeared off to a corner of the room to his drinks cabinet and returned with a generous slug of Scotch.

'Cheers,' he said, raising his crystal tumbler. Foster lifted his pint pot in return.

'Like old times,' Jackie said, before taking a sip and letting out an inaudible gasp of satisfaction. 'How's life been treating you, son?'

'Can't complain. Yourself?'

'Aye, canny. Retirement has its benefits, I suppose.' He sighed gently. Foster guessed he felt the drawbacks more profoundly.

'Really, what are those, then?'

'My golf handicap is coming down.' He paused, smiled ruefully. 'Give us time. I'll think of some others.'

Despite the slippers, the sedate, elderly aura, Foster found it difficult to imagine him spending his days on the golf course rather than patrolling a crime scene, hands behind his ramrod-straight back, or at the head of a meeting, saying little yet commanding absolute respect, or delivering a quiet bollocking to some hapless detective who had not followed the Corrigan code of conduct.

'You still get involved?'

'What do you mean?'

'On cases. Do they still call you up, ask for advice?'

'Aye. Sometimes. They've been good. I nip in quite a lot, for a chat. Help out. If they need it, that is.'

'Good,' Foster said, nodding. 'Good. I hear Sharon Carter is in charge now.'

Jackie's old pale blue eyes sparkled with mischief. 'Sharon, that's right. Bloody good she is too. Not everyone's cup of tea but she knows that to run things successfully you don't have to be liked, you have to be respected. We speak a lot.' He took another sip of his whisky. 'I'm surprised you haven't moved further up the ranks, Grant.'

He shrugged. 'Not the political kind.'

'Aye, it seems there's many things you're insisting you're not. Tell you what, though, you were a bloody good detective. The best kid I ever worked with. Your modern coppers can't detect shit on a white blanket.'

Foster casually flicked a hand, as if to shoo away the compliment. Praise always sat uncomfortably with him. Corrigan had always given it and after a while Foster didn't know what to do with it. His father had never once said a good word about him, or at least his abilities as a detective, until he was on his death bed.

'You haven't asked why I'm here.'

'I know exactly why you're here, son.'

'Really?'

'Aye. You've been sent up to look into the deaths of those two lads, speak to the family. You went there today. You learned I've been round there before you. So you came straight here.'

'Barry Chester called you?'

'Maybe. He never told us you were coming here afterwards. I just knew you would.'

'I'm that predictable?'

'No. I just know how you operate. We worked together very closely, though maybe you've forgotten that.'

Foster looked at his glass. He anticipated being put on a guilt trip. 'No, I haven't, Jackie. I'm not one for wallowing in the past. Life moves on and I move on with it. Doesn't mean that I'm not grateful for all you did for me.'

Jackie nodded, took another sip. The aura of authority, of certainty and self-containment, had become diluted by a tinge of melancholy. 'Nice of you to say, son. You just took off. It was difficult for some of us to take. Had us thinking we'd done something wrong.'

'Yeah, well, it was time to move on, like I said.'

'If you say so. A goodbye might have been nice. Not just me either. I had that lass, Caitlin, calling us up and seeking you. You never told her you were away, did you?'

Foster was keen to drag the conversation away from the past and into the present. 'It was a sudden decision. I had to get away.'

'Aye, well, you left us in the shit. But I reckon you must have had your reasons.'

The words hung heavy in the air. Foster mulled them over in his mind. Jackie looked at him, as if expecting an answer.

Yes, Foster thought. *I discovered that you and several of my colleagues, whom I respected, turned out to be cowards in thrall to money and power, and I couldn't stomach looking you in the eye again.*

'I suppose I did,' he agreed.

This wasn't the time or place to confront Jackie and dredge up the final case they had worked on. That could wait. For now, there were other issues that were more important. 'You knew I'd come here, then?'

Jackie took a languorous sip of his drink. 'You think I passed on the details of Dibb and Schofield's new identities to the Chesters.' He paused once more. 'They didn't have anything to do with their deaths, Grant.'

'And how do you know that?'

'They have alibis that stand up.'

'So I'm told. Listen, I know you've obviously become close to them ...'

'I keep them informed. It's the very least they deserve.' A hint of his old irascibility was returning.

'Informed about what?'

'What do you think? What was happening to Dibb and Schofield. But I never, ever told them the new identities and I never gave them any information that would have led to them tracking them down. Quite honestly, the idea that I would is bloody insulting.'

'But the alibis. You're retired, Jack. It simply isn't your place to get involved like that.'

'I knew someone would be coming round. I knew they weren't involved. To make sure, I asked what their alibis were, because I knew they'd be asked. They told me.' He raised a finger. 'That was my case. Always has been. Always will be.'

'They told you or you helped them tell you?'

'What the fuck is that supposed to mean?'

'Come off it, Jackie. You going round there and talking to them about alibis. It smells a bit suspicious to me. Not saying it is, but if you were in my shoes then you'd feel the same.'

'Piss off with the high horse shit, Grant,' he shot back.

He was leaning forwards in his chair, now, his face reddening, warming to his theme. 'The decision to release those two was taken without any consultation with the family. They were left out of the whole process. Rather than have them read about it in the papers, I took it upon myself to visit them, answer what questions I could and offer them whatever solace I could provide. Which wasn't much. But never forget they were the victims here, not those two little pricks.'

He sat back, breathing deeply, clearly agitated.

Foster allowed him to calm and settle; for all his sins, he didn't want Jackie dropping dead on him.

'They had nothing to do with the deaths of Dibb and Schofield, Grant,' he repeated.

'Maybe. But someone did.'

'Aye. But there's no shortage of people who would have done them in given half the chance.' He sniffed. 'You know what, I wouldn't blame them. Nor would you, would you? We saw that poor old bastard's body. We saw what they did to him. He was about the same age as me now. Frail, his body falling apart, eyesight gannin', all the other indignities of age, and those two little fuckin' animals beat him like a rag doll and buried him alive. You saw it too and I know you felt the same. Animals, and they needed treating like mad animals.'

Time had lent some perspective, but Foster agreed; his trip to the scene had brought back the awful images of the bloodied and battered old man. 'Yes, Jackie, but it's one thing to feel and another to act. You and I worked to uphold the law. You can't just have people handing out their own justice.'

'Aye, but don't ask me to weep for those boys. They stole an old man away from his grandkids, and from him a chance to enjoy the last few years of his life in peace, with his family, and a dignified death. I hope they rot in whatever hell awaits them.' He drained the remnants of his glass, sat back and jutted out his jaw, as if daring Foster to suggest they were bound for any other place.

'Who else might have done this, then? Not sure how much you've caught up with the reports of how they died, but they suffered a heck of a lot of pain before they died. Schofield was poisoned by nicotine; Dibb set fire to himself.'

'You consulting me, Grant?'

'Suppose I am.'

'Sorry, I'm retired.' He winked. 'But, for old time's sake, I'd look in their lives now. I think someone found out. They were obviously going to out Dibb, which is why he torched hisself.'

'His wife knew.'

'Knew what?'

'Who he was. What he did.'

'Well, that's interesting. She knew? Maybe it's worth looking at her. You know as well as I do that most murders are committed by people closest to the victims.'

Foster shook his head. 'She didn't do it. I'm as sure of that as you are that Barry Chester didn't. What about extended family? The kids. I remember them taking it hard.'

Jackie coughed, cleared his throat. 'They all took it hard.'

'Do they have alibis?'

'The kids? I dunno. I'm sure they weren't involved, Grant.'

'I'll need to check it out, or get someone to. The youngest is at uni in Birmingham, isn't he?'

'Think so. Bright lad, I know that. Go easy on him, eh?'

'There is no way that the Chesters could have found out where Dibb and Schofield were?'

'I can't say for definite, can I? All I can say is that I never told them. To be honest, I don't even know myself. Never asked. Wouldn't have trusted myself not to tell them if they asked, so thought it best I never knew.'

The head on the beer had died and gone flat. Foster wasn't sure how much he believed Jackie Corrigan. It was time to leave. He had not eaten since breakfast, and the empty stomach and strong ale were combining to stir deep, buried resentment. Then there was a flash of memory.

'Do you remember the letter?' he asked

'What letter?' Corrigan said, yawning.

'The one we got before the trial. The parents of the lad in Mackington, said he'd been acting oddly since the crime.'

'He wasn't the only one. It affected the whole community, the whole region. We got all kinds of letters, if I remember.'

'True. But there was something about it that chimed. You told me to leave it.'

'I did? Well, we were on the way to sewing the case up. There seemed little point.'

'Maybe,' Foster muttered. 'I always thought there was more to the case than we found.'

He'd wanted to pursue the letter. It echoed a feeling he'd had, based on what one of the boys had said, that there might be a witness to the crime. But it was only a week or so before the case went to court and no one wanted to miss that date, least of all Jackie. The world's media was about to descend on them to hear the verdict and sentencing.

'Yes, well, you always thought there was more to every case, if I remember rightly,' Corrigan added, a chuckle in his voice.

Foster felt another flash of anger. Definitely time to go. He stood up. 'Well, I'll be off. Thanks for the beer, Jackie.'

The old man rose and followed him out of the room. 'Thanks for coming by,' he said, as they reached the front door. 'Hope I've been a help.'

Foster nodded. There followed another awkward silence. 'How will you be getting to where you're going now?'

'Good point.' In his haste to leave he had forgotten he had no mode of transport.

'I'll call you a cab if you want. I would drive but that was my second whisky...'

'Was that a pub I saw back down the road?'

'The Mill? Aye. It's still a mile or so, though.'

'I need the walk.'

'Divven't be daft, man ... Let me get you a cab.'

'Jackie, no. It's fine. I'll walk.'

'If you say so, son.' He watched as Foster put on his coat and fastened it. 'You left because we didn't go after Lord Patrick, didn't you?'

He didn't stop doing the buttons, said nothing.

'I know you did, Grant. You thought we bottled it. We were scared.' He let out a deep sigh. 'Detectives have to compromise, Grant. I hope you realise that now.'

'Compromise?' Foster snarled, unable to contain his anger. 'You capitulated. The case I built was solid. But you and the rest ran when he bared his fangs.'

'It wasn't that simple,' he said, eyes closed, shaking his head. 'Surely experience has taught you that much.'

'Experience has taught me never to cower in the face of power.' He could feel years of frustration and betrayal building in him. 'You turned out to be everything I thought you weren't.'

He opened the door.

'Grant…'

But he was crunching his way back down the drive and the old detective's words faded on the wind.

17

It took Foster twenty minutes to walk to the pub, head bowed against the blasting north wind. The warmth as he stepped inside was such a contrast it made his eyes water. The place was half-empty. Most people were eating. A couple of lone drinkers sat at stools at the bar. He joined them and ordered a pint and a Scotch to go with it, which he downed quickly, feeling the heat of it catch his throat and permeate down. He went to lift his pint and saw his hand still shaking.

He had thought he'd never see Jackie Corrigan again. He'd never wanted to, even if his face and words had flitted in and out of his mind over the years. There would always be a part of him that was grateful for the education he had received, but a greater part which resented that a man he'd idolised turned out to be made of straw. The first cut was always the deepest.

He ordered another Scotch, seeking to take the edge off some more. He looked around the boozer again. It used to be an old-fashioned dive, used by fishermen, the few locals that lived nearby, and the odd lost and thirsty traveller. Now, looking at the stripped floorboards and hand-typed menus, it had become a destination pub, a place you came to eat on special occasions. The locals had probably been driven out to make the place more appealing to tourists.

The Scotch came and he threw it back. Then ordered another pint. The alcohol initially brought him peace but now started to act like a stick, stirring the thick mud of the past which had long since settled in his memory.

Two cases, two very different memories of Jackie Corrigan ran across his mind.

There had been an attempted killing, a young girl stabbed outside a nightclub in South Shields. She lived but her injuries changed her life for ever. The prime suspect was the son of a successful local businessman and, perhaps more significantly, a member of a prominent Masonic lodge that featured several high-ranking coppers among its number. An alibi was dutifully provided for the suspect; whispers behind hushed hands said that witnesses had been bought off. It would have been easy to mark the case down as unsolved. Foster would not have it, though. The evidence against the local scion was compelling and undeniable. The girl lay half-dead in a hospital bed, her lung punctured, her aorta split, her face scarred. She deserved better than a sordid cover-up. Foster hauled the objectionable, violent, arrogant young kid in who thought his father's name could shroud his crime and, when he crumbled under questioning and his alibi fell apart, charged him with attempted murder.

The whole department held its breath, waiting to see what the consequences would be when news filtered upwards, and the tall, swaggering cockney was upbraided for his insolence. Foster spent a few sleepless nights planning his next move; out of the police force if necessary. Eventually, he was summoned to see Detective Superintendent Jackie Corrigan, a man he had only glimpsed and heard mentioned in awestruck dispatches. As he entered his office, thick with cigarette smoke, he had been surprised to find not some irascible martinet behind the oak desk but a whippet-thin and wiry gent, with rheumy blue eyes and a soft-spoken Geordie lilt. He exuded authority, though; the feeling, Foster thought, of a man who remembered all, said little, heard everything and had utmost belief in his own talents and judgements.

Foster shuffled though the door. Corrigan offered him a fag, which he took, puffing nervously. Nothing was said for at least two minutes, a silence so deep that Foster wished to dive headlong in, to explain and justify. Yet the words of his father, a man with an economical approach to speech of any kind, came to him: 'Never speak first. Let the other bugger flinch.'

Corrigan had looked at him, one eye half-closed, though a fug of nicotine, the outline of a smile on his thin lips. 'So,' he said eventually. 'You're sure of this are you, son?'

'Yes, sir. I am.' His voice was cracking, higher, reedier than usual.

'Grand,' Corrigan said. 'Grand. And you're sure this will stand up in court?'

He sensed a trap, not one he was going to fall into. 'Certain.'

To have admitted any doubt would have shown weakness, and given Corrigan the out he might have been looking for. Foster wasn't sure he was looking for an out.

'Good,' he replied, nodding. 'I've always wanted to lock this spoilt little prick up and if you've done your job right, you've cured us of a mighty headache. Good work, lad.'

He went back to the papers on his desk, placing his cig end on the edge of a large glass ashtray. Foster stood like a wallflower for a few seconds, then realised he was expected to leave.

'You're doing well, y'knaa,' Corrigan added.

He turned. The old man was still peering at his papers. 'Thanks,' he said, and he meant it. 'I've learned a lot.'

'Still a lot to learn, son,' Corrigan corrected. 'Still a lot to learn.'

He walked away feeling both ten feet tall, buoyed by praise, and terrified in case some uncrossed 't' caused the case against to collapse.

The verdict two months later was guilty. He only received a three-year sentence; the prosecution were looking for at least ten. The judge, it transpired, was a member of the same Masonic lodge. Corrigan bought Foster endless Scotches that evening to help ease his anger at the sentence. It worked. From that moment on, whenever he had any concerns, when a case caused him any consternation or bemusement, he turned to Corrigan for counsel; in turn, the old man often sought him out, saw how he was settling into the department and the town. A few other detectives resented the blessings the great man bestowed upon him, while for others it conferred an air of the oil anointed; Foster, they all agreed, had *it*, if only because Jackie Corrigan said he did.

There could not have been a starker contrast with his last memory of Jackie Corrigan, the final case he had investigated in Newcastle. The Lord Patrick whom Jackie had referred to at the end of their meeting.

He was Patrick Hardcastle, a Conservative MP for Northumbria North, the only Tory for miles around in a left-wing stronghold. His family had been in the area for years, landowners, and their bloodline and altruism afforded them a deference few other nobility could expect. Lord Patrick was the runt of the litter, a nasty mean-minded, sexually incontinent maverick, who traded on his notoriety and blunt-speaking, but was loved for it. A cad and a bounder, people said, but in an indulgent way. Foster cared little for his politics but he did care that he flouted the law regularly and people were happy to turn a blind eye. Still, as a murder detective, Lord Patrick wasn't his problem.

Until one evening, when his Jaguar sports car left a deserted country road not far from where he was drinking now, burst through a hedge and somersaulted for around fifty yards into a field. The female companion in the car died from her injuries. Lord Patrick was scratched and bruised but relatively unscathed, though found to be way over the legal limit. He admitted to being drunk, but said that was the reason his 'friend' was driving, and, not used to the car's speed and thrust, she had misjudged a corner, lost control and the car left the road. Everyone had been too willing to accept Patrick's version. Foster believed otherwise. Unbeknown to Corrigan and everyone else, he conducted his own inquiry. He found a drinker in the pub where they had stopped who saw Patrick climb into the driver's seat in the car park. There was a friend of the dead girl who said that, while she had a licence, she loathed driving and would have refused to get behind the wheel of such a powerful car. To back that up, he found a taxi firm who remembered taking a call from Patrick from the pub. He'd asked for a cab only to be told it would take an hour to get there. All this helped build a case against but was hardly conclusive. Then Foster found what he believed to be the gilding piece of evidence: a photograph of the now buried corpse of the girl, which he showed to a pathologist, who confirmed that the marks from the seatbelt caused during the accident could only have come from her having sat in the passenger side. Believing he had all he needed to prove that Patrick was guilty of at least manslaughter, he went to Corrigan and presented his argument for the case to be opened and charges brought against Patrick.

Corrigan refused to re-open the case. When asked why, he said the case was closed. No more explanation. Patrick was never charged, and while his political career was in ruins, he was free to live his life of luxury and prestige, while the family of the young woman killed by his drunk driving were denied justice. It made Foster sick to his stomach. The next morning he had emptied his flat and got a train back to London. It took three months before he could even contemplate rejoining the force. *Sometimes a detective has to compromise*, he thought to himself darkly, as he ordered another Scotch. On that journey back to London he vowed never to be warned off a case again, never to back down for fear of upsetting someone in power; he would rather be sacked or resign than do so. Which might explain why he still languished as Detective Chief Inspector. Since that day, he had followed every hunch, every instinct, regardless of what he was told or ordered to do. Even when it seemed point-less and superfluous.

Then he remembered the letter from the parents of the boy who had been so affected by the Kenny Chester murder. That was an early compromise, done on the say-so of Corrigan, despite his desire to pursue it. He downed his Scotch, the cold now a distant memory, a new determination flooding his veins along with the booze.

It might have taken twenty-five years, but in the morning he would eventually get round to following that hunch.

18

Nigel could tell from the dark rings under Heather's red-rimmed eyes as she kissed him that she had been working hard on the murder case. Her insane hours sometimes worried him, but she was always adept at shaking off the troubles of work when she was at home, and at times of stress made sure she booked them both a holiday at a point in the future when the workload would have subsided.

'I could murder a glass of wine,' she said.

Nigel went to the kitchen, poured her a large glass and brought it back to her. He often marvelled at the burden detectives were placed under and how they coped. Of course, some didn't. Heather was made of stern stuff; a larger than average glass of white wine after a brutal day or a double espresso after a night of work was as far as it went.

She was on the sofa, curling her legs underneath herself as she often did. She put the television on; she often sought diversion from the harshness of work in soap operas, delighted to turn off her brain and soak up something involving yet inconsequential.

'Nothing on,' she said irritably, after flicking across a few channels. She sighed. 'Tell me about what you've been up to.'

'You don't want to know,' he said, mindful that she could do without the burden.

'Come on,' she said, letting her hair down, placing the bobble between her teeth, winding her curls back up and retying. 'I need distracting: what's the latest on the little girl who won't sleep, Sir Galahad?'

He smiled. 'It's not very uplifting either.'

'I still want to know.'

He filled her in. She listened and then read through the newspaper reports. When she wondered if there might be a copy of the coroner's report he explained that such records, sadly, rarely lasted the test of time and the reporter's account was the best they could hope for. Once she had finished reading, she stretched and yawned.

'Well?' he asked.

'On the one hand it sounds entirely plausible,' she replied.

'What?'

'The official reason given for her death. I'm no pathologist and I don't know how efficient and conclusive their reports were back then, but nothing jumps out at me. Apart from, well…' She paused.

'Go on,' he urged.

'It has all the hallmarks of cot death. No outward signs, no real explanation. Of course, she might have suffocated her, but it seems, in the absence of any evidence proving she *didn't* do it, that she has been found guilty because the idea that the little girl could have died in her sleep from Sudden Infant Death Syndrome wouldn't have occurred to them for a second.'

How tragic, Nigel thought. His first feeling was sympathy for the nanny, accused of a murder she didn't commit, for which she later took her life, when it might just have been a catastrophic accident.

'What time of year did this happen?' The question was rhetorical. She scanned the newspapers. 'March. And the report of the trial mentions what the little girl was wearing for her nap.' She sifted through the copies and found the one she needed. 'Here we go: "Franklin told the court she put Esther into her bed dressed in her usual sleep time attire of night-dress, bed socks, shawl and swaddling blankets." That seems a lot of clothing to wear in bed in March. I'm not sure what they mean by swaddling blankets, whether she was swaddled and couldn't move, or just blankets used for swaddling which were laid on her. We also don't know whether she was asleep on her front or her back. But she had been ill, was wearing a lot of clothes, under blankets. What I can tell you is that if that happened today then one of the first theories you would pursue would be cot death.'

She paused, mulling over another report. 'Then again, there are cases of what have been put down as cot death where it's turned out the mother or whoever has smothered the kid with a blanket or a pillow.' She sat back and spread her arms. 'So, the short answer is I don't know. But there's a good chance that the nanny was sentenced for a crime she didn't commit.'

'Thanks,' Nigel said, thinking about what she'd said. Sudden Infant Death Syndrome was a modern phenomenon, or at least acknowledgement of its existence was. He had never once seen it on a death certificate. Yet while its incidence may have become more commonly known, he knew that children had died unexplained deaths in their sleep for hundreds of years. He wondered how many others – nannies, mothers, fathers and siblings – might have been labelled a murderer for what were rare, tragic accidents, or attributed to a 'visitation from God', which he had seen on many early Victorian certificates under cause of death, it being the only explanation plausible to the pre-scientific mind.

'Who's this for, anyway?' Heather asked.

'Oh,' he said, switching back to the present. 'Lara Harrison.'

'The mum with the kid who doesn't sleep?'

'Yes, that one.'

'This is one of her ancestors?'

'No. Not at all.'

'What's the relevance?'

'It happened in the house she lives in.'

Heather's eyes narrowed. 'The one she lives in now?'

'Yes.'

She sighed, again deeply, with more exasperation. 'Where are you going with this, Nigel?'

'What do you mean?'

'You know exactly what I mean. She asked you to trace her ancestry to see if there was anything there that could explain why her little girl gets the screaming heebie-jeebies every night. I presume you didn't find anything. So you start researching the ancestry of her house ...'

'Strictly speaking a house doesn't have anc—'

'You know what I mean. You've gone a bit beyond your remit.'

'Not exactly,' he answered. 'I mean, she asked me to find out something, anything that might help her solve the problem of her daughter's sleeplessness. I've done that.'

'Now you believe that because someone died in that house you have might have an explanation. Let me tell you something: all sorts of people have died in everyone's houses. If you have an old house, then the likelihood that someone passed away there at some point is pretty damned high.'

'I agree,' he said, trying not to sound aggrieved, because she was tired and he knew if this turned into an argument and not a discussion she would end it and clear off to bed. 'And even though I believe in the fact that places can bear an imprint or a memory of the past, I'd say it was far-fetched. But you have to admit there is something uncanny here; an infant girl, round about the age Lara Harrison's daughter was when the episodes began, episodes which involve feelings of choking or being suffocated, dies in somewhat mysterious circumstances and a nanny is punished for the crime despite maintaining her innocence. There might be something there. I definitely think it's something I should inform her about, don't you?'

'Maybe.' Her face took on a mock-demonic look. 'Then what, though? She performs an exorcism to rid her house of the ghost of the little girl who has possessed her daughter? Here's another shocking idea – she could move house!'

'I'm not sure you're taking this altogether seriously. I don't suppose there's anything that could be done in the house. Could you do anything on the body?'

Heather shook her head. 'That's not an option because it's nearly a hundred years ago. There will be nothing left of a body to dig up and test. And even if there was, I doubt anyone's going to licence an exhumation based on what you have.'

He nodded.

'Children are very receptive,' she said. 'Perhaps the little girl has picked up a sense of something sad or grievous?'

'I think I'm going to have to dig a little bit more.'

19

There were no spare desks at the nick, so Whelan had to relinquish his to Foster. Which might have explained why he unceremoniously dumped seven thick files on it, all dating from the Kenny Chester case, his face tightened by anger. Foster thanked him. There was no acknowledgement. He knew he was now officially pushing his luck.

He settled down to read through them. Each one trailed a host of recollections: there were pictures of the hideously disfigured body of Kenny Chester, close-ups of his injuries, his face swollen and distorted beyond all recognition, and his pale white body a patchwork of welts and bruises. There were more pictures from the post-mortem which he wasted no time passing over, and reams and reams of the crime scene.

He wasn't looking for photographs. All he had to do at night was close his eyes and he could recall the state of Chester's face and body. Those images would never leave him. What he was searching for lay among two thick files which contained the transcripts of interviews with the two boys.

There were hundreds of pages; the result of scores of interviews, each limited to a maximum of half an hour because of the boys' ages. Reading through it reinforced what he had always believed, and what eventually transpired once they were freed and their lives unfolded: Schofield was inarticulate, morose even, struggling to express himself, yet seeking to do the right thing. Dibb was more eloquent, craftier, responding to humour and the kindness of those present, whereas his mate registered little.

The interviews took place over the course of a few weeks. The boys had been swift to admit their role in the murder in the initial interviews conducted by Corrigan. These had been informal affairs – 'fact-finding', he called it, all off the record. Then Foster and a few others became involved, piecing together the details; understandably each blamed the other, and claimed to be only a witness to the violence and not a participant. Schofield rarely cried but was inconsolable for several hours when it did happen. Dibb, in contrast, could turn the waterworks on and off, and those conducting the interviews recognised he often did so to create a diversion when he was asked to address anything awkward, or came under repeat questioning when he was being less than truthful. Most of all, what sang from the pages was something which had escaped him at the time: they were kids; they spoke like them, and acted like them. At the time, the images of Chester's ragdoll body fresh in his mind, he had seen them as part-monsters. Even at their most childlike, when they cried, or asked for their mothers, he saw killers, just young ones. Now, time having erased some of the searing horror of their act, he could see in their words the bewilderment of kids who had committed a terrible act and just wanted the forgiveness of the grown-ups who were judging them.

'I'm going to go to sleep tonight and wake up tomorrow and all this won't have happened,' Dibb said plaintively in one interview, words he remembered him uttering at the time and had thought little of. Yet twenty-five years later he found them strangely moving. As if he could magically rewrite the course of his life, in the same way he thought the sickening injuries he and Schofield had inflicted on Kenny Chester could be erased. There was no concept of the permanence of their act; no comprehension that any amount of apologies could reverse the hideous finality of what they had done. It was still a form of make-believe, the idea that things can be undone. There was no one day when it suddenly occurred to them that they would have to live with this awful act for their rest of their lives; just a gradual dawning, a slow puncture of innocence and youth.

For the first time he wondered if a child could ever be tried for a crime in the same way as an adult, and if children should feel the full weight of adult law for the senseless cruelty for which most are capable but thankfully learn to rein in. Before then it had always been his belief that if you knew what you were doing was wrong or wicked, and failed to stop, then you were culpable and should be punished, regardless of age. Now he wasn't so sure.

He thought about Gary, the foster kid he had grown so attached to, the son of a junkie and a brainwashed Mormon. Before they had tracked down his sister, Foster had put him up. The kid was a one-man crimewave, feral and untamed, or he had been until Foster had taken him in for a few days. Now he was living with his sister, happily going to school, smart and streetwise. He was no model child but he had come a long way from the days when he racked up more than a hundred criminal offences. He had grown up, taking the second chance offered to him. Foster visited him every other weekend, when work allowed, took him to a football game, or the cinema. It was the highlight of Foster's month, if he was being honest. Gary was also a reminder that kids do bad things, but they may not be bad.

But what then of the victims? Their families who sought and required punishment and retribution in order to cope with their loss and the rest of their lives?

Foster snapped himself out of it; he wasn't here to debate the moral issues of the case. He continued to scour the transcripts, trying to find one comment which had stuck in his mind at the time, and not been dislodged in the years since. It was made during one of the last interviews before the case was passed on to the Crown Prosecution Service. He located it at last; Foster was conducting a final interview with Schofield, pushing him one last time on the events leading up to Chester's arrival at the Dean prior to the attack, a subject the boy was always vague and uncertain about. The narrative and detail had been supplied by Dibb, which they then recited back to Schofield, who murmured yes or no to indicate whether it fitted with his recollection. Often he gave a flat, monotonic 'Dunno,' said with such regularity that the officers who came into contact with him invariably ended up mimicking it in private, adopting his voice, which was unusually deep for a ten-year-old.

Q: Let me get this straight one last time, Craig. You went down to the Dean. You played a game of war.

A: Aye.

Q: For how long?

A: Dunno.

Q: Two minutes. Five minutes?

A: Aye.

Q: What was it, Craig?

A: Five minutes. Maybe more.

Q: That was inside the clearing?

A: Aye. And a bit outside. Hiding and that.

Q: OK. Then what?

A: We stopped playing that.

Q: What did you play next?

A: Dunno.

Q: You don't remember?

A: We just played, like.

Q: Both of you played? Did you stay in the
clearing?
A. Aye. Glen went off, said he wanted to find a
stick and left us there.
Q: By us you mean just you?
A: … I mean just me.

It was those ellipses, seemingly so prosaic, that he was
searching for. A world of meaning was contained in
those three dots. In Geordie dialect it was common
to use the plural 'us' when you meant just one person,
yourself. 'Are you going to give us one of those sweets?'
instead of 'Are you going to give me one of those
sweets?' Foster had grown used to it. The exchange he
read was unremarkable. Yet at the time, Schofield had
reacted strangely when he sought clarification for the
record. Rather than staring at the table in front, as
he did throughout, his eyes had flicked nervously side
to side. He then seized on Foster's explanation with
more alacrity than he had shown at almost any point
during the whole interrogation. Foster had moved on,
but it had stayed with him since. Had he really meant
'us' that time? Had there been someone else there?
Unable to shake it, he mentioned the idea to Jackie
Corrigan, but it was dismissed; the case was ready to
be presented and handed over. It was just a misunder-
standing; the flicking eyes were a manifestation of his
guilt and unease as the interview crept slowly towards
addressing the point when Chester showed up and
their frenzied attack began.

Reading it in bold print confirmed it wasn't a figment of his imagination, even if the text hinted at none of the boy's discomfort. Next he searched through the rest of the files for the letter that arrived only a week or so before the case reached court. There was no sign of it. No one had seen fit to hang on to it and it had probably been tossed into a drawer or a bin and forgotten. Details of the letter had come back to him the more he thought of it; it was from the boy's mother; she mentioned that she and the father had split recently, which might have explained her son's behaviour, but she thought there was more to it than that, that it all dated from the day of Kenny Chester's death and he had said a few things to her which troubled her, as well as overhearing a few things he had said to her nine-year-old daughter. He was at the same school as Dibb and Schofield, but the year above. Yet Foster was unable to conjure up any names.

Rather than rely on a reluctant detective to act as a sullen chauffeur, Foster chose a car from the pool, signed it out and headed for Mackington. Perhaps he could push this further on in the village where it all happened.

20

The light was bleeding from the day as he arrived in Mackington. Foster needed food. Given he had no idea who had sent the letter, he headed for a small cafe which he knew was still there, part of the paltry, half-closed parade of shops. It was closed, only open for breakfast and lunch. Next door was a grocer's. He wandered in and found a chiller selling unappetizing sandwiches, probably made and packaged days ago, but the best he was going to get. He chose the one with the least potential for food poisoning, cheese and pickle, and took it to the counter where a friendly old woman in a gingham overall and jam-jar glasses gave him a big smile in return for his money.

'Don't I know you?' she said, as she scrabbled for change for the note he'd given her.

'Not sure.' He had come in here several times back in the day for sustenance, hastily snatched pork pies or Scotch eggs, and there was every chance she'd worked here. In fact, he wasn't sure he didn't recognise her.

'The Kenny Chester case.'

He smiled. 'That's pretty impressive recall.'

She issued a small laugh. 'No one in this place is going to forget that summer in a hurry. You and all the other journalists in here every day, buying us out of all our stock. Business was never as good.'

A journalist. He couldn't stand for that. 'I wasn't a journalist.'.

She narrowed her eyes behind those immense round lenses. 'That's right. Police. You lot were in here slightly less. Those journalists. A bloody menace they were. For two weeks they were everywhere you looked, following people all over the place, sticking their cameras through hedges. Then the funeral and that was it, gone.'

'Yes, well, that's how they operate. The carnival moves on.' He was eager to eat his sandwich and quiet his grumbling belly, but he realised this affable, talkative woman might be helpful.

'It did that, love. And this place has never been the same since. Between that and the pit closing, the whole stuffing was knocked out of the village. People used to talk on the street, pop by each other's houses for a cup of tea, the pub and Institute were thriving, and this road was full of shops and that; not now. Everyone's more private, less trusting.' Foster could detect genuine sorrow and regret in her voice.

'Very sad,' was the only platitude he could muster in return.

He picked up his change and slipped it into his pocket.

'Aye,' she agreed. 'So what brings you back? Is it the death of them two bairns? Not that they're bairns any more. Nasty business. A lot around here are glad they're gone.'

'I can imagine. Not you, though?'

'I'm a Christian. I go to that church down the street every week and pray to our Lord. He tells us to forgive and forget. Way I seen it, them two paid their punishment, and they were given another chance. I say it's a shame they didn't get a chance to make amends in the eyes of the Lord. Maybe they did. Maybe they're with him now.' She leant forward conspiratorially, even though the shop was empty apart from them. 'Doesn't make me very popular. Even some of the congregation are glad they're gone, but they're a bit more Old Testament than me. Eye for an eye an' all that.'

'Well, it's pretty raw for people around here, isn't it? You bore the brunt of it. You all knew Kenny well.'

'I did. He was a good Christian too. I don't think he would've wanted them dead.' She paused. 'His family did, though.' Another pause. 'Are they suspects?'

Foster smiled uncomfortably, wary of setting the Mackington wires humming with gossip. 'No,' he said, mustering as much conviction as possible. 'You might be able to help me with something, though.'

She straightened herself. 'Certainly. How?'

'It's nothing to do with the Chester case but something else entirely. I'm trying to track down a family who used to live in Mackington. They may still be here, actually. I don't know.'

'What are the names?'

'That's the thing. I don't have the names. She was a single mum, split up from the dad about twenty-five years ago or so. She had a son and daughter at the primary school here. He must be thirty or so now; daughter would be mid-to late-twenties. Does that ring any bells?'

'It rings more than a few. Couples split up all the time now, what with the lack of work and that. Me and our Derek have been together thirty-seven years. Never even spent a night apart. But that was a different time.' She started to tap her fingers gently on the counter. 'Let me think. There's the Dawsons, they split a while back, but they had three lassies. He had an affair with the dental nurse in Cresswell. The McDonalds divorced around that time too, but they only had the one, a boy, a right spoilt little bugger too. He lives in London now, apparently. Doing well for himself, though heaven knows how.' She turned her head and looked out of the window, rifling through the Rolodex in her mind. 'It could be Cathy Underwood, maybe?'

The name chimed instantly with Foster. Underwood. That was it. 'Yes, I think that's her. Is she still in Mackington?'

'Aye. Keeps herself to herself, you know. The kids have long since gone. You never see them come back neither. She married again, Brian Dillard. He's fifteen years older than her. A widower. Ex-hewer. He's on incapacity. Wife died of breast cancer. Last I heard they lived up on Oakdene. One of the smaller terraces at the top of Halton Avenue. Can't remember which.'

'That's fine, thanks.' He finally picked his sandwich up from the counter. 'You've been more than helpful.'

'Thanks, love,' she called as he left the shop.

Inside his car, in between mouthfuls of stale bread and cheese, he put in a call and got an exact address for Cathy Dillard, née Underwood. He drove round and parked outside, relieved to see lights on inside.

The door was answered by a man, large and puffing slightly, with an unkempt beard, a blast of furnace heat from within hitting him full on. He asked if Cathy was in and he shuffled away to be replaced a few seconds later by a small, stick-thin woman with pale blonde hair in a T-shirt and sagging running bottoms. Time had taken its toll and her face was worn and pinched. The unmistakable smell of recently smoked cigarettes wafted from her. She eyed him suspiciously.

'Can I help you?' she asked, in a voice hesitant and withered.

He introduced himself. Her face did not move an inch. 'I was wondering if we could talk.'

'What about?'

He took a deep breath. 'A letter you wrote to the Northumbrian police twenty-five years ago.'

For a few long seconds she stood there, unmoving, eyes unblinking, and Foster felt certain he would feel a hot draught of wind as the door slammed in his face.

Eventually she shook her head. 'Is this some kind of wind-up?'

'It isn't,' he said. 'Look, I know this looks and sounds really strange, turning up so long after the letter was ignored. I'm sorry no one followed it up. Genuinely sorry. It's just that I've been going through the files and I really wanted to speak to you about it. It could be a great help.'

'Is this to do with the two lads that done it being killed?'

'Not directly. I worked on the original case. I saw the letter you wrote. I was very keen to come and speak to you about it but, let's just say, other things came up, which I regret. It's bugged me ever since. I'd genuinely like to rectify our mistake.'

She looked bewildered. Foster wondered if she was on some kind of medication, legal or not. Perhaps it might be better to leave it there, come back in the morning. Though he was keen to get as much done in Newcastle as quickly as possible and get back to London. His nostalgia had waned somewhat.

'Come in,' she said, pushing a lank lock of hair behind her ear.

Foster stepped into the house and the heat was almost overpowering. A bead of sweat slicked his forehead. He removed both his coat and jacket and held them in his arm. He followed Cathy through a doorway into a small sitting room thick with cigarette smoke. The man who'd answered the door stared at a late afternoon quiz show on TV. He wasn't introduced. Cathy lit a cigarette and stood at the man's side, one arm across her chest, the hand on the bicep of the other, which held the dangling cigarette. He wasn't sure what to do, so he sat on a sofa. The man muted the television.

'I'm Detective Chief Inspector Grant Foster.'

'Brian Dillard,' he replied in a flat voice.

'Warm in here,' he said, wiping his brow.

'Bri has got arthritis,' she explained.

'I need it warm,' he finished.

'I see.' The silence, like the lingering cigarette smoke, was oppressive. 'I was saying to Cathy that I worked on the Kenny Chester case. She sent us a letter just before the case went to court. We never followed it up. That's annoyed me ever since. I wanted to come and correct that mistake.'

'Oh,' Dillard said, reaching for his cigarettes. 'What letter was that, then?'

Foster thought he'd better let Cathy explain. But she said nothing, nervously and distractedly tip-tapping the stem of the cigarette, not caring or unaware of the particles of ash which fell to the floor.

'It was a letter she wrote about her son. Maybe she might be best able to explain it.' He looked at her hopefully. His hope was dashed. Her eyes were moist with tears and her shoulders had started to heave.

'Sorry.' She turned and scurried into the kitchen, closing the door behind her.

There followed a few seconds as they both watched the door. Then both men looked at each other. Dillard drew hard on his cigarette.

Foster felt sick from the heat and fags and sick with guilt. 'I'm sorry. It wasn't my intention to upset her. I suppose it was naive of me to think I could just barge in here and expect her to be happy to talk about something she needed our help with twenty-five years ago.'

Dillard didn't speak, just looked at him through a haze of smoke. 'The letter was about Ben?'

'Is that the name of her son?'

'Was.'

Shit, Foster thought. *Don't like the sound of that.* 'What happened to him?'

'The lad killed himself.'

That was the last thing he needed to hear. 'I'm sorry to hear that,' was all he said, and it sounded as pathetic and unsatisfactory as it hung in the air as it had on his lips.

He was about to get up and leave when the door reopened and Cathy shuffled back into the room, head bowed. 'Sorry,' she mumbled again.

Foster stood up. 'Don't even think of apologising. I'm the one who's sorry, barging in here like this. I didn't know. Brian just explained to me that your son took his own life. I should never have come round.'

'Wait,' she said, her voice firm.

He looked at her. Her eyes, so dead when he'd first called, were now alive. There was colour in her drawn cheeks. 'I want you to stay.'

Foster nodded and sat back down. He said nothing, wanting to allow her to approach it in her own way. She reached for another cigarette and lit it, this time taking short, aggressive inhalations.

'He didn't "take his own life",' she said, smoke billowing from her nostrils. 'His life was taken from him.'

'I'm sorry. Your husband said he committed suicide.'

'No. I said he killed himself.'

'I don't understand.'

'Drugs,' Cathy said. 'He got involved with drugs. Heroin, crack, you name it, really. He overdosed. He killed himself but he didn't mean to, is what Bri means.'

'When was that?'

'2000. He was twenty. He'd been using for years. When the pit closed, heroin became a big problem here, particularly in the 90s. There was nothing else for kids to do; no work, no future. Ben was already pretty troubled so it was no surprise he fell in with all that. We sent him away to live with Bri's sister in Morpeth for a bit but it was no use; he kept coming back. I threw him out and it didn't help.' Foster could see her eyes start to moisten once more. Sadness oozed from every pore of her body.

'You said he was already pretty troubled. Was that linked to the contents of the letter you sent to us?' She nodded, biting her lip. Foster went on. 'I tried to find the letter but I couldn't. It was a long time ago I read it, too. Can you remember what you wrote?'

'It *was* a long time ago. I can't remember to be honest.'

'I remember one piece, not exactly, but it said something about Ben not being the same since the day Kenny Chester was killed. Is that right?'

'Aye. He was nivver the same again. He was always a happy kid, easy as you like. Shortly after that day it was like someone flicked a switch. He got moody, had nightmares, started shouting. He got difficult.'

'What made you think it had anything to do with the Kenny Chester murder?'

She sucked on her cigarette, lost in thought. 'It was a few months after. He'd been a handful for a while. I took him to task about it, asked him why. I thought it might be something about Kenny Chester. He was at the same school as them boys and knew them. Lots of kids had been behaving strange. All the mums were talking about it. I thought I better have a word, you know? Well, he just went berserk. Said I didn't know anything. That there was more to it than just Kenny Chester being murdered. That if I knew what he did then I'd understand.'

'What did he mean by that?'

'I don't know. He wouldn't say. That's when I wrote to you lot. I tried again to ask him what it was all about and the same thing happened; he went apeshit. I just left it from then on. I wish I hadn't.' She wasn't sobbing but tears streamed down her cheeks. 'I should have helped him more but he just didn't want to speak to me. The only person he would speak to was Cheryl.'

'Cheryl?'

'My daughter. They were as tight as anything, those two. I spoke to her about it and she said he would get over it. He never did. Whatever "it" was.'

'Where is your daughter these days?'

'Excuse me,' Dillard said wearily, slowly extracting his bulk from the armchair. 'Going to get some air.' He shuffled away to the kitchen, blowing out heavily as he did, closing the door behind him. Foster watched him go.

'Is it something I said?'

She sighed deeply. 'Cheryl and Bri don't get on. They never did. It's been very hard.'

'I'm sure it has,' he replied, not knowing quite what to say.

'I met him not long before Ben died. Brian helped me through. He was my rock. I needed him. Cheryl couldn't understand that. But she was young and about to go out in the world. What does she know about what it's like being me? A failed marriage, a son who died because of drugs, I just needed someone. I didn't want to be alone. Bri's not perfect but he's a good man. Cheryl can be quite hot-tempered and Bri doesn't like the way she speaks to me. I say they're too alike but Cheryl won't have that.'

'Do you have any contact with Cheryl at all?'

'It's been four years,' she said, her voice a sad whisper. 'That was just a phone call. It's been longer since we actually saw her. Maybe six?'

'Do you know where she is now?'

'She went to London after she did her A-levels. She could've gone to uni but she said she wanted to earn some money. Friend of hers from school went to London, and she stopped with her. Did some waitressing and bar work. She was going to night school too for a bit. Then she got a job in a firm of solicitors. A good one too. As a paralegal. She wanted to become a lawyer.' She smiled almost absent-mindedly, and Foster gained another flash of the attractive woman that had been submerged under years of hardship and pain. 'Cheryl was always the bright one. She was doing well for herself. She probably still is.' The smile faded to be replaced by the worn and strained look.

'Would Ben have told her what was bothering him, what he knew, whatever it was?'

'She would have been the only one he told. They weren't like your usual brother and sister. They were very close, like friends. They barely had a fight, even.'

'Did you ever ask her?'

'Aye. Course I did. But she never told us. She just said Ben had his problems and he needed to sort them out.' There was a pause. 'He never did.'

Not for the first time, Foster wondered about the effects of crimes as grievous as the one committed on Kenny Chester. There were the obvious consequences on those directly affected; the grief, the loss, the questions, the anger and the desire to avenge or erase the past. But the echoes of these acts were felt wider.

'Would it be possible to get a last known address or contact number for Cheryl?' he asked.

'Why? What does it matter now? It's done, isn't it?'

It was a fair question. 'In some respects, yes. But there are still a lot of things we need to find the answer to. It would be good to put a lid on this once and for all.'

'Yes,' she replied. 'Yes, it would.'

With those words, she went to the drawer of a bureau, piled high with magazines and all kinds of junk mail.

'Do you want me to pass a message on to Cheryl if I do track her down?'

Cathy turned, a slip of paper in her hand, her eyes once more glazed, devoid of life or spirit.

'Just tell her I said hi.'

Foster left her at the door, glad to feel cool air once more. He didn't look back as he made his way to the car and sat in the driver's seat. By the time he did glance at the house, Cathy was gone. *Poor woman*, he thought. He looked at Cheryl's address, and then turned his mobile phone back on.

It buzzed. There were several messages.

The first told him that Barry Chester's youngest son had been taken in for questioning about the murder of Craig Schofield.

21

Foster drove the short distance to Barry Chester's house, just as he and Vince were loading a car with bags. Even in the twilight he could see the anger and impatience in Barry's movements. Foster got out and walked towards him. Vince saw him coming first and froze. It took a while for Barry to register.

'You've got a fucking nerve,' he spat out with a sneer.

Foster held his hands up. 'I've just heard, Barry. Nothing to do with me. The investigation into Schofield's death is in the hands of East Midlands.'

'Rob didn't do anything,' he hissed.

'I made a few calls. They brought him in because he wouldn't answer their questions about where he was last weekend. He'll need to loosen his lips about that, no matter how embarrassing.'

'He didn't do nothing,' he repeated, lifting another bag into the boot.

'I believe you, Barry. Schofield was last seen with a young woman, not a man. I suppose they think that woman might be linked to Rob in some way.'

For a second Barry smiled, a mirthless, humourless grin. 'That's a laugh. Rob's a spotty little git. No lass in her right mind would go near him, never mind kill for him.'

'He'll need to tell them where he was. Until he does, he'll be a suspect.'

'Aye, well, we're away to see him, knock some sense into him. He was probably sat around smoking drugs with his mates and thought he'd get into trouble for that, kept his mouth shut and landed himself with a murder charge.' He shook his head in disbelief. 'That's the kind of criminal mastermind we're dealing with here.'

Foster wondered if there wasn't something choreographed about the arrest, to show the watching world progress was being made while throwing the salivating press a bone to gorge on to buy time and space. God knows there had been precious little revealed about Dibb's death. Risky strategy, though. Barry and his family had been canonised in the press after the death of Kenny, held up as examples of the better angels of our nature, their close-knit family contrasted with the broken homes that had produced Dibb and Schofield. One of them being arrested on suspicion of murder would puncture that myth.

Dawn strode briskly down the garden path, holding the home phone, her hand over the receiver. Foster knew what she was about to say.

'It's the press, Barry. *Daily Herald*,' she said. 'They know about Rob.'

'Great. Tell them "No comment". Tell it to everyone who calls.' She nodded and walked back down the path. 'This is the last thing we need.' He put his hands on his hips and looked at Foster.

'We were just living our lives and all this blows up again. Do you know what it's like, having the press call you all the time? It's horrible. You can't move on. They won't let you. Every time there were any stories about those two, they called. Every time there was a similar case, kids killing or something like that, they called. It's like an open wound that never gets to heal. Just when it starts to scab over and you think it's OK, they call up and pick the scab right back off. We've tried everything: ex-directory, they find the number; getting rid of the landline, and they find out your mobile or they send someone round to knock on the door. It's not as if we've given them anything, either.'

He was right, Foster knew it. Compared to some victims' families, the Chesters had been models of dignity. When they did to speak to the press it was often with grace and consideration. He had always admired that. If it had been him, and the journalists were at the door, the temptation to ram a tape recorder where the sun didn't shine would be overwhelming.

'Now, with them being killed, and Rob being questioned, it's like it's happening all over again. There's no escape.'

'Does he have a decent lawyer?'

'Aye, we're meeting one there. Would have got him one sooner but they went round to speak to him at his digs. I don't believe he didn't tell us. Actually, I do,' he corrected himself. 'Daft little bastard.'

The last bag was in the car. Barry nodded at his mute brother. 'You ready, then?' Vince returned the nod. Barry fished the car keys from his pocket. 'We'd better be off, Detective Chief Inspector Foster. Try and clear up the shite your colleagues have landed my youngest in, eh.'

Foster smiled. 'I'll try.'

'Aye, well, I hope you divven't take this the wrong way, like, but I sincerely hope I never, ever see you again.'

Foster smiled once more. He hadn't told Barry that he was trying to track down information that could lead to the case being reopened. *Was it worth it?* he asked himself. *Just to scratch an itch after twenty-five years? To prove a point? If so, to whom?*

'I went to see Jackie Corrigan last night.'

'Did you? Was he pleased to see you?'

'Maybe,' he replied. 'I didn't know his wife had died.'

'Pauline? Lovely woman she was.' Barry checked his watch. 'We'd better head off.' He climbed into the driving seat, and Vince got in the passenger side. Dawn had returned and stood at the gate, arms wrapped around herself to protect against the cold. Together they watched the car pull away.

When the lights had disappeared, Foster smiled at Dawn and turned to walk to his car.

'Detective Foster,' she said in her high-pitched Geordie voice.

'Yes?'

She looked pensive. 'Would you like a cup of tea?'

He wouldn't; he wanted to get in the car, drop it off in Newcastle and try and get a train back to London that evening. There was little more he could do in the north-east and the place had lost all lustre for him. Yet something told him he should take her up on the offer. He said yes, mimicking enthusiasm, and followed her into the house.

While she brewed up – tea leaves, a pot, Nigel Barnes would be impressed – he plunged his hands into his pockets and looked at a few photos. Kenny Chester, a fine figure of a man for his age, took pride of place on the mantel. There were pictures of Barry and Dawn on their wedding day. Their daughter, Helen, at her graduation – beautiful, blonde, smiling. Rob in football gear, clutching a trophy. Dawn returned with the tea and placed the tray carefully on the coffee table. She caught sight of him looking at her son's picture.

'Does he still play football?' he asked.

'No,' she said, with some regret, handing him a mug of steaming tea. 'He doesn't play much sport now at all. It's a shame because he was good. He's more interested in going out and getting pissed.'

'Happens to all of us.'

'Aye, I suppose it does.'

'Is he doing well at uni?'

'Hard to tell, isn't it? He rarely phones, comes back for the holidays with a sack of washing that needs doing, asking for money. When you ask about his studies, he looks at you as if you're mad. I've to remind him it's the reason he's there. I'm sure he forgets.'

Foster smiled. He hadn't been to university. He sipped his tea, scalding his lips slightly. 'Lads of that age, they don't speak much to their parents. Unless they want something.'

'Not Rob. Rob tells me everything. He always has. He's the youngest. My baby. That's the reason I asked you in for a tea, to be honest.'

'Oh, really?'

She was sitting forward in the chair, cradling her cup between her hands in her lap. He had been in this position enough times to know when someone was about to open up.

'Last time he was up, a weekend a few weeks ago for one of his mate's birthdays, he told me something. I've never told Barry because I know he'd go postal and give him a hard time. And he has been stupid. I'm just a bit worried now that it'll count against him, once the police find out.'

He remained silent, leant against the fireplace, looking at her.

'You see, Rob was born five years after Kenny died.'

'Kenny was six. Helen was what, four?'

'Aye, there's a canny gap. Not for the want of trying. But the stress of it all, y'kna?'

Foster nodded.

'But it means Rob never knew his granddad. We held off the day we had to tell him the full details about what happened. He must have been about twelve or thirteen. Barry and I told him. Not all of it, obviously. But we did say his granddad was murdered by two boys. Over the years he asked more and more questions and we answered depending on what we thought was suitable for him to know.' She stopped to take a drink. Then she continued. 'Thing is, with the Internet and everything it was all out there for him to read. All kinds of stuff, even some that wasn't true. We didn't know but he read it all. It messed his mind up good and proper.'

'I can imagine it did.'

'Ah well, he's a good kid. We had a few problems with him for a bit at school, but it was hard to know what was normal teenage stuff and what was down to him finding out. The main thing was it didn't last. He knuckled down and did some graft and got his grades for university. We were all dead proud.' She smiled. 'As I told you, how he's doing there we don't know but he's having a rare old time, we know that.

'Anyway, he came home last month, was it? Six weeks or so ago. He was tired, been out and had a skinful on the Saturday and kipped over at one of his mates'. He came back the next morning looking

like shit turned backwards. I made him a fry-up.
The lad needs it because there's nowt to him. If he
took his shirt off he'd vanish. Barry was out playing golf; Vince was out terrorising small animals or
whatever he does when he goes out. We sat and had
a tea and we talked about things. I could see he was
champing at the bit to tell us something. I thought
it might be to do with a lass, because I been dread-
ing that sort of thing. He's one of the nice guys,
Rob, and at that age you don't want a nice guy. Most
lasses, anyway. I'm worried they'll run rings round
him. Turns out it wasn't a lassie – it was something
else. Where's me tabs?'

It took a few seconds for Foster to remember she
was referring to cigarettes. They were on the mantelpiece, close to where his right hand was leaning
against it. He threw them over. *Does everyone up here
still smoke?* he thought. He turned down her offer of
one and watched as she sparked up.

'I finally got him to open up. As I said, he'll tell
me anything. Anyway, it turns out he's been going
on the Internet, message boards and the like, where
people all talk and that kind of stuff. Not my kind of
thing but he likes it. He's been all over the place –
where all the crazy people hang out.'

The warp and weft of the Internet, he thought. 'Any
ideas where?' In Foster's experience, the places where
the complete nutters hung out were the ones you'd
least expect, on forums dedicated to caravanning or
driving vintage cars.

'He never told us. My first thought was, "Oh shit, he's gonna tell me Princess Di was killed by space aliens and expect me to take him seriously." But it was clear it was much more serious than that. He looked me in the eye and he said, "I been asking about Granddad's killers." I said, "What do you mean?" He said, "Who they are." I can be a bit slow on the uptake. "You know who they are," I said. He shook his head. "No, who they are *now*." '

She stopped to take a drag. 'Well, I went postal. I told him he was a fucking idiot, I told him he was going to get himself in all kinds of trouble, and I told him to stop messing about, that it was done and dusted and he should leave his Granddad's soul in peace.'

'You did the right thing,' Foster said. 'Did he say whether he found out the names?'

'No,' she replied quietly. 'That's the thing. I got so mad with him, I forgot to ask. I don't think he had but I don't know for sure. Vince came in a few seconds later and that was it. Barry drove him to the station after tea and he was away. Only thing I had the chance to say before he left, and I've repeated it on the phone, is "Keep your head down." Look at him now. In police custody?'

Foster sighed. 'He'll need to tell them all this. They'll find out eventually and if he's been hiding it, it won't look good.'

'He didn't do it, you know. He was the sort of lad who didn't even crush an ant when he was a kid. I know that for a fact.'

'I'm sure he didn't, but he needs to tell them that. At the very least, it could be that those names were circulating the web. We scour all those sites and are doing so now, but it'd be good to know which one.'

'How, though? How do I tell him to tell the cops? Barry will go berserk.'

Foster thought about it. Barry should know what his son had been up to, but he could see that Dawn did not want her little darling being the subject of both a police interrogation and the rage of his father. There was no way he was going to keep quiet about it. Perhaps Rob was not the timid little darling his mother imagined to be.

'Look, if you want, I'll call the person who's heading up the Midlands inquiry, let them know what you told me. They can ask Rob about it in his father's absence.' He paused. 'You'll just have to hope he's savvy enough to tell them the truth.'

'He will,' she said with utmost certainty. 'Barry jokes about him being daft, but Rob's no dummy, just like I'm certain he's no killer.'

'What about Helen?'

Dawn raised her eyebrows. 'She's no killer either, though she's got more balls than he has.'

Something about the way she blew the smoke out of the side of her mouth, disdainfully, told Foster all was not right between mother and daughter.

'You and her all right?'

'Not as such.'

What was it about mothers and daughters? he thought.

'It's not just me and her. It's her and all of us. She thinks we're obsessed with the past. She can't be doing with it all. Us living in the house and that. Apparently, we haven't "moved on".'

The last two words were said with withering sarcasm.

'I think you've done all right myself,' he said.

'Well, tell Mother Superior that.'

This clearly wasn't a subject worth pursuing. He also saw this was not a mother and daughter thing, just like Cathy Dillard and her daughter's problems weren't. He remembered something Nigel Barnes had told him. That seismic events, like the Chester murder, created a series of aftershocks, rippling down the years. Sometimes the damage was reparable. He suspected Helen and the Chesters would make up eventually. Other times, like the shocks that spread beneath the feet of Cathy Dillard and her family, it brought the whole structure of their lives crashing down.

22

The digitised electoral registers he owned gave Nigel the previous occupants of Lara Harrison's house going back more than half a century. Cross-referencing these names with online birth, death and marriage indexes allowed him to see how many of those were living. The next step was to trace the handful of names that remained and where they lived now. By the end of his search he was left with the names of two families, one who had lived there for seven years before Lara Harrison, the other who had been their predecessors but one, residing there between 1996 and 2003. Given that they had lived longest at the address, he felt they might be the best place to start.

The family were named the Keiths, and had moved out to St Albans. The records told him they had four children, the youngest of whom was now fourteen, the eldest twenty-five. Their house, spacious and detached, was on a quiet, tree-lined avenue on the outskirts of the town. Nigel had called in advance and left a message, but rather than sit around waiting for a phone call that might never arrive he decided to be proactive and took the short rain ride from King's Cross.

His luck was in. The door was answered by an avuncular man in good shape for his age. He smiled in friendly yet quizzical fashion when Nigel introduced himself and explained that he had been hired to compile a history of their former house by its current occupant. This induced another curious look from Mr Keith, who had the calm, patrician air befitting his profession as a general practitioner. Still, he invited Nigel in and led him through to the kitchen, explaining that his wife was at a conference, and he was in charge of the house for a few days.

He made tea, asking why someone would want a history of their house. Nigel shied away from the truth and said that some people were interested to know who had passed through their home and contributed to its story.

'I suppose that makes sense,' he said. 'One doesn't usually think of houses having stories as such, but when you think about it it's pretty obvious that much happens within the walls of a home.'

'Exactly,' Nigel said. 'Few people think of their homes as witnesses to history, but they are. Not the sort that is taught in schools, but the history that we all experience.'

They sat at a large pine table. A teenage boy sauntered in, grunted an indecipherable greeting and buried his head in the fridge.

'We moved when Liam was born,' he explained, gesturing to Liam. Then he sighed, almost knowingly. 'Though, of course, had we stayed for a few more years then we could have sold when it was worth a terrific amount of money. But we weren't to know the property market was about to rocket.'

'Why did you move?'

'Space, mainly. Outside space in particular. There being no garden to speak of, which is a drawback when you have boisterous children. Plus I'm rather fond of gardening, or I am now at least; back then all we could do was grow a few herbs. Though neither was there as much space as you'd think inside. Have you visited the property?'

'Once,' Nigel said. 'Though I didn't get a tour. Just the downstairs, mainly.'

'Oh, the ground floor was fine. We were the ones who knocked through from the sitting room to the kitchen and opened it out. Made a world of difference in terms of space and light. It became a very pleasant space indeed. No, it was upstairs where we felt a bit short-changed.'

Nigel sensed a note of hesitancy. 'Why was that?'

Keith laughed. 'The whole configuration was out of whack. Someone had taken a perfectly good bedroom and made it smaller.'

'What for?'

'I've no idea. There's an entirely unnecessary wall there, which seems to have been in situ for heaven knows how long. We did consider reconfiguring the upstairs, but all our funds were swallowed up converting the ground floor and we never got round to it. You learn to live with most things after a while.'

Nigel scribbled in his notebook. 'When you were there did you ever notice anything strange? An atmosphere of any kind?'

He furrowed his brow. 'Are you asking me if it was haunted?'

'I suppose I am, after a fashion.'

'Nothing whatsoever. I mean, it's a fairly old house and it has its quirks, but certainly nothing that went bump in the night.'

The next question felt even more embarrassing, and Nigel prefaced it with an apology. 'Sorry if this sounds weird, but did all your children sleep well in the house? In particular, when they were young?'

Dr Keith grinned once more. 'That does sound weird.'

To avoid further embarrassment, Nigel decided to break cover and explain the full story: first about Lara Harrison's daughter's sleep problems, then the strange death of Esther Bathurst and the case of Yvette Franklin.

'Wow, now I know why you're asking about ghosts. What a tragic story. I've seen a few cases of cot death in my career and from what you say, there's every chance it was an accident rather than murder. Goodness.'

'So you can see why I'm asking if any of your children experienced sleep problems.'

'It's difficult. Some children just aren't good sleepers. Our first two boys were fine, as far as I can remember. Claire wasn't so good. Awful, in fact.'

'Was that when you lived in Chiswick?'

'It was. But I'm not prepared to accept there were other reasons for it. She was just a poor sleeper.'

'Did she have nightmares?'

'Yes. But children do.'

'About anything in particular?'

He fell silent for a few seconds. 'I really don't remember anything specific. You would have to ask my wife, though. Her memory for these things is slightly better preserved than mine. 'Claire was quite unsettled for some time.

'Has she remained a bad sleeper?'

Dr Keith snorted with amused derision. 'You're kidding, aren't you? We can't get her out of bed these days.'

Nigel smiled. That was all he needed to know.

'You've been very helpful,' he told Dr Keith as he left.

'I don't feel like I have,' he said. But Nigel assured him he had been.

On his way back to London, he rang Lara Harrison and asked to meet her the next day.

23

Foster rode the train back to London that morning, the table around him strewn with newspapers. Usually he made a point of avoiding the news, and if he did read the paper it was to scour the sports pages, but he wanted to see what had been said about the arrest of Rob Chester.

The press didn't disappoint. The morning newspapers were certain of two things: Rob Chester was in some way responsible for the deaths of Dibb and Schofield; secondly, his actions, while wrong, were driven by an understandable need to right a grievous wrong. The tabloids pointed an accusing finger at those they believed to be ultimately responsible for the whole mess: the 'liberal' judges, 'do-good' parole boards and 'out of touch' politicians who didn't lock the boys up and throw away the key all those years ago. 'Had the catastrophic decision not been taken to release the boys, Rob Chester would not be in custody and the two young men themselves might still be alive,' one editorial leader thundered.

The night before, he had called Heather to get an update about the investigation into Dibb's death. There was little new of any note; they had failed to trace the person he was speaking to animatedly on his phone in the seconds before he became a fireball.

The rush hour was beginning to ebb when his train pulled into King's Cross. Foster took a Circle line train to Paddington, before catching the Bakerloo line to Queen's Park. From there it was a short walk towards Kilburn High Road along a wide street lined with newly pollarded trees, whose shorn, knuckled branches cast a bleak shape against the grey, featureless sky. He took a left onto a dead-end street and searched out the address handed to him by Cathy Dillard.

It was a flat halfway down the street. He had asked someone at the office to go through almost every legal firm in the city looking for an employee named Cheryl Underwood. So far, with no luck. The address was worth trying. But when he pressed the doorbell, there was no reply. He checked his watch. Most people would have left for work.

He tried the flat downstairs. A woman's voice answered and when he introduced himself, she appeared at the door a few seconds later, a young child in her arms. She was a young black woman, tall and striking, the child pudgy-faced and cute.

'I'm looking for Cheryl Underwood,' he explained.

'Cheryl? she replied. 'She don't live here any more. She fell out with Justine.'

'Justine is her flatmate?'

'That's right. She's still here. Lives with her boyfriend. They'll be out at work. I heard them leave.'

'Do you know where Cheryl went?'

'I have no idea,' she said emphatically. 'I don't know what happened between her and Justine but I tell you what, it weren't pretty because she never speaks about her any more. It's like she died. One minute she was there and the next she was gone. I asked but she wouldn't talk about it.'

Great, a feud. Perhaps Cheryl had left London. And when he tracked down Justine, it seemed unlikely she would know where she had gone.

His mobile rang. It was Heather. He thanked the young mother and walked away before answering.

'Yes?' he asked.

'You back in London?' she asked without greeting.

'I am.'

'Come and meet me quick. You're never gonna believe this.'

Foster hailed a cab and took it north-east to the border of Hackney and Islington, near the sprawling De Beauvoir estate and a small row of custom-built terraced houses, nestled in the lee of some larger, grander Victorian townhouses. It was so hidden the cabbie had no idea where it was and would never have found it had it not been for the phalanx of cop cars, ambulances and cordoned-off onlookers. He paid the cab, sprang out, went through the tape and along the lane to where Heather stood, tight-lipped and anxious, at the gate.

'Follow me,' she said brusquely, leading him inside the house.

He followed. The house smelt of furniture polish. The forensics team were gathering in the hall, preparing to fan out across the house. She took him into the sitting room. There was a woman's body in the middle of the floor, her spread-eagled corpse framed by a crimson slick of blood. There was a single bullet hole in the front of her forehead. She was young and blonde.

'Do you recognise her?' Heather asked.

He studied the face, leeched of all colour and life. He was about to say no when a memory came into focus. Then he knew.

'Jesus Christ.'

'No. Kelly Thurston.'

Kelly Thurston had been just fifteen when she was asked to babysit for Matthew Craven, the baby of her neighbours, Max and Tina Craven. They had gone out and the baby woke up. The child had screamed continuously. Thurston lost control and shook the child. He died as a result of his injuries. While she had known she had hurt the baby, when the parents returned she had accepted her money and lift home without mentioning a word. The couple didn't discover until the next morning that Matthew was dead.

Thurston pleaded guilty and was sentenced to ten years for manslaughter, commuted to six. The family of the murdered child were horrified. They had threatened to track her down and exact their own justice. For her protection, Kelly had been given a new identity and a chance to live a normal life free of the stigma of her teenage crime.

He stood over the body.

'Come upstairs,' Heather said.

'Another body?'

She shook her head. He followed her up. At the top, three uniformed officers stood sentry at a door. Heather brushed past and opened the door. On a bed sat a man, his head in his hands. He looked up as they went in. Foster recognised him immediately.

Max Craven.

24

Max Craven was whippet-thin. He was completely bald, and his face wore the pallid look of the long-term boozer. He looked like he'd aged forty years in the twenty since his son had been killed. Foster had read about how his marriage had disintegrated, the pain he had endured, his attempts at suicide. He remembered Barry Chester's words about how the press had picked at the family's sores like a scab. Craven and his wife had suffered a similar fate. They believed that Thurston had killed their baby in cold blood. They had not known at the time, but she had been dumped by Craven's nephew only a few days before and was said to be extremely bitter. Killing the baby was her revenge. The defence interpretation – that this was a young girl, unable to cope, who had panicked – held sway, and there was no evidence to prove that she meant to do it.

Craven sat across the interview room from Foster and Heather with a smile so contented it was almost beatific. His lawyer was sitting beside him. Heather had been forced to use all her skills of persuasion to get him to hire one. He kept repeating that he wanted to confess and do his time. Eventually he relented.

Once the lawyer was summoned and briefed, Foster pressed the tape and went through the usual niceties. Finally, he asked the pressing question, and this time it wasn't motive; that was blindingly clear.

'How did you find her, Max?'

The smile on Craven's face faded and he knitted his brow in concentration. When he spoke, his voice was quiet and measured.

'I set up an Internet alert.'

'For what?'

'For Kelly Thurston.'

'OK. Then what?'

'There used to be tons of them. At least a dozen every day. Even I was surprised how often her name was mentioned, on news sites, message boards, blogs, that kind of thing.'

'What did you do with them?

'I followed every link.'

'Every single one?'

Craven nodded.

It wasn't the press scratching an open wound. He was doing it himself.

'So what happened?'

'Well, as I said it usually led to a report or something written about her murder of Matty. I've had one set up for well over a decade. I must have read thousands and thousands of words about her.'

'Is that why you set up the alert? To read about what people were saying?'

For the first time a trace of impatience flashed across his face. 'No! Why would I do that?'

'I don't know, Max. I'm just trying to work out why you'd put yourself through that.'

'I was waiting for what happened a few weeks ago.'

'What happened?'

'An alert led me to a message board. It was Austrian.'

'What was the website?'

His eyes narrowed. 'I don't remember.'

'No problem. We'll come back to that,' Foster said. 'What did you find on this website?'

'Someone was saying they'd seen a list with the new identities of killers on it. People who'd been given new names and stuff. They said it was an English list but that some of the names were of famous killers. The name they gave was Kelly Thurston.'

Foster felt his heart beat harder against the inside of his chest.

'Who was this someone?'

Again, Craven put on his game face. 'I don't remember.'

'OK. We can come back to that too. What did you do?'

'I asked him if he knew what Kelly Thurston's new identity was.'

'Did he know?'

Craven nodded. 'I paid him for it.'

'How much?'

'A thousand pounds.'

Bloody hell, Foster thought. *All the money that was lavished on protecting Kelly Thurston, all the work, the man-hours involved, sold down the river on an Internet idiotboard for a grand.*

'How did you pay?'

'Paypal.'

'I don't suppose you remember the name of the account you paid?'

Craven shook his head.

'I thought not. So, once you paid, what happened?'

'He emailed me her name.'

'What was that, then?'

'Phoebe Trant.'

Foster nodded. That was her new identity. 'Any more info?'

'No. Just a name.'

'What did you do then?'

'I went back on the Internet and started searching.'

'What did you find?'

'I went through a lot of social networking sites. Facebook, mainly.'

'Surely she didn't sign up for any those?'

Craven shook his head. 'No, she wasn't that stupid. But I found her.'

'How?'

'Have you heard of reverse imaging software?'

Foster hadn't. 'Enlighten me,' he said.

A small, slightly smug grin appeared across Craven's face, like a kid who's just been told he's clever. Foster had to remind himself he'd shot someone in cold blood a few hours before.

'It's a search engine for images. It uses face recognition technology so you upload a picture rather than words. I got a picture of her from when she was arrested. I put it into the search engine. It's capable of not only looking for a match, but also modified versions of it. Which means it'll find someone who looks like that.'

'But that picture was taken about twenty years ago.'

'Well, she's just a modified version of that girl. So any pictures of her will be a modified one of that image.'

'And you found her?'

He nodded eagerly. 'Not without a lot of effort. But I scoured every single social network site. I got lots of hits. But some of them were just lookalikes. Nearly all of them. But I found her.'

'Where?'

'A work colleague of hers had taken some pictures at a Christmas party. Obviously they didn't know she was a killer in hiding so they named her in the photo.' Craven was warming up now. 'So not only did I have a likeness to the image, but the name Phoebe Trant was attached to it. Confirmation, in other words.'

Foster was almost stunned into silence. It was everyone's nightmare about the death of privacy made real. 'So then what?'

'I found out what I could about the friend who posted the pictures. Mainly who she worked for.'

He discovered Thurston/Trant had been working at a call centre in central London. Ironically, not far from the offices of Glen Dibb. He wondered if they'd ever passed in the street. Two child-killers blithely unaware of each other's chilling secret.

Craven went on. 'I came down to London yesterday. Got a room at a B & B in Kings Cross. I went to the office where she worked. I spent a day staking it out, watching people come and go. When it came to the end of the day, I saw her leave. It was definitely her.' He let out a little laugh. 'It's funny. I'd been dreaming of this moment for nearly twenty years and how I'd feel. Part of me was worried that when I saw her my nerve would go, or I would have some kind of … feeling for her, a sympathy, and I wouldn't be able to go through with it.' He stopped talking, shaking his head in disbelief.

'But that wasn't the case?'

'Not at all,' he replied. 'Not in the slightest. It was all I could do to stop myself from running up to the bitch and blowing her brains out in the street. But that would have been traumatic for those who witnessed it, and if it went wrong people might have been hurt. I didn't want anyone to get hurt. Just for her to die.'

'So what did you do?'

'She was with some friends so I followed them. They went to a bar off Oxford Street. She had one drink and left. I followed her.'

'Then what?'

'I waited until I was ready. This morning I went round, nice and early, before she went to work. I rang the doorbell. I expected her to answer it on a chain and have to kick the door down. But she, no, she just opened it up, like that.'

Again the smile, as if he couldn't believe his luck. The lawyer was scribbling away. Probably working out a plea of diminished responsibility. Not that it would work. What he had just been told confirmed the mind of someone who knew exactly what he was doing, carried out with a cold precision.

'We found her in the hall. Did you shoot her there and then?' Heather asked.

'She looked at me. She recognised me straight away. Again, I had thought for years about what I might say, or how I might do it. But the fact is she was too shocked to speak. She was about to turn and her face was contorting into a scream. There was no time for words. I just stepped forward, lifted the gun and shot her. She went down instantly. It was dead easy.'

The smile returned. 'I went in, closed the door. Made myself a cup of tea. Then I called Tina and told her.'

'What did she say?' Foster asked.

'Not much. She was a bit taken aback. We've barely spoken in years. I just said, "She's dead. Thurston's dead. I just shot her." She was like, "Oh." I told her I had to go and call the police and I was sorry for all the shite we had been through and that it should be at an end now. Then I put the phone down and called you lot. That's it, really.'

It was. 'We'll need the name of that website where you found out about her new identity. You can either tell me now and save everyone a lot of trouble, or we can ransack your house and seize your computer.'

'You'll have a job,' he replied. 'I got rid of it.'

'We'll find it.'

'Good luck.'

Foster stood up. He needed a team on it straight away and any further questions could wait. In the meantime he needed to speak to his boss, Detective Superintendent Harris.

Then he needed to speak to the Home Office.

They sat in a wide, spacious office in Whitehall, Foster glancing at his watch, wondering what was keeping the junior minister, Adrian Gorton. Foster had read that he was beleaguered because there had been a few breaches of confidential data on his watch, and it was believed he might walk to save the Home Secretary's skin. She was being tipped as next party leader, a future prime minister; others were more expendable.

He looked across at Harris, in full uniform, cap under his arm like a general at ease, smoothing down a few imaginary creases. Foster had called him, expressed his concerns over the latest murder and what it meant. Harris immediately convened this meeting and ordered him to attend.

The door opened and Gorton walked in. His face was tight and troubled as he acknowledged them. From the way they greeted each other, Harris excelling himself with an emollient 'Good morning, Minister,' Foster guessed his boss was no stranger to Gorton's office. He'd probably spent more time scratching backs in the corridors of power than he ever had at a murder scene.

Harris, permanently tanned and healthy, introduced Foster, who felt shabby and worn, to Gorton. The handshake was wet and limp. He went behind his desk and sat, pushing a pad of paper out of his way, and asking a PPS to be good enough to get some coffee. Eventually he remembered to ask if they wanted one and when they said they did, the long-suffering assistant was told to be quick. While they waited, Harris made small talk, asking if he was busy. 'The usual chaos,' Gorton said, and Harris laughed obsequiously.

'I know exactly what you mean, Minister,' he replied.

Spare me, thought Foster.

The aide returned with a tray of coffees. Foster dimly remembered reading that Gorton had briefly been an officer in the army before he left to practise law. He could see the progression: public school, Oxford, a year at Sandhurst, seven years as an officer, then into the law and sacks of cash, before becoming a politician and a minister by his forty-fifth birthday without ever having to spend any time in the real world.

'So, what's so urgent?' the junior minister asked.

'I'll let my colleague DCI Foster tell you,' Harris replied.

Gorton switched his gaze to Foster. 'I hope it's not too serious,' he added, mock nervously.

'You've got a leak.'

Gorton's face fell immediately. 'Fuck,' he said simply, almost matter-of-factly. 'Fuck and double fuck. What makes you think that?'

'The death of the Kenny Chester murderers. Then this morning we found Kelly Thurston, the killer babysitter.'

He pulled a face. 'I don't see the link.'

'They were all given new identities, which have been compromised, unless we're looking at some gargantuan coincidence. What we need to know is if there's a Home Office list where Dibb, Schofield and Thurston might appear.'

'I wouldn't know,' he said. 'Give me a second.'

He left. Harris asked if he couldn't be slightly more 'subservient' to the minister in his tone, before Gorton returned with a couple of civil servants in tow, both men, both middle-aged, both looking irritated.

'Tell them what you told me,' Gorton asked.

Foster explained again about Thurston and Dibb and Schofield. Their bored expressions grew more concerned as he spoke. He repeated the question about the list. Both men looked at each other and Foster could see their worry.

One of them, a taller man as grey as his suit, spoke eventually. 'We have a list of people who have been awarded new identities by the state for their own protection.'

'All criminals?' Foster asked.

'No,' the grey suit said, shaking his head. 'The only criterion is that they were at risk. In some cases that was because they perpetrated a crime; in others it might be because they were related to someone who committed a notorious crime, or it is linked with a matter of national security – the only qualification is that they have been given a new life and their life would be in danger should their true identity be revealed.'

'Who has access to it?'

'Very few people, as you may imagine. I can think of only a handful of people who might be aware it exists and only three or four who have access to it. And you're looking at two of them.'

Foster nodded. 'Well, you'll need to conduct a thorough investigation and see if the details have been removed, or copied, or hacked or whatever. Then you'll need to report back to me as swiftly as humanly possible. Like today.'

'Speed is paramount,' Gorton added, unnecessarily.

'And I'll need a copy of the list,' Foster said.

At last the civil servants recognised Gorton's presence. It was clearly his decision. 'I'll need to check with the Home Secretary,' he said.

'It's actually something you could authorise your-self, minister,' the grey man said, with more than a hint of condescension.

'It is? Oh.' Gorton went silent, weighing up the political implications.

'I am sure Scotland Yard will respect the confidential nature of the list, minister,' creeped Harris.

'I'm certain you will. My concern is that once you look at it, presumably to assess the safety of those on it, we will have to arrange some kind of security for those you feel are in danger. There is a financial aspect to that; but also, a political one. Some pretty notorious people are on there, I should imagine, and it will cost a lot of money and manpower to make them secure, or even relocate them and provide a new identity, with all that entails. The public tends to resent its money being spent on making people safe who perhaps they feel should not be on the streets. I'm not sure how this plays out vis a vis the public relations scenario.'

'With the greatest respect,' Foster said, 'banging people up in prison for life doesn't come cheap. I can assure you the only people who will see the list are those who need to. I guess it's been leaked somehow so it's worth nothing anyway. You'll need to speak to your boss, and anyone else, to discuss how to go forward. But the best way to protect those on it, and keep all this under wraps, is for us to catch whoever leaked it, and who is responsible for these deaths, and we can do that quicker if we know who they're after.'

Gorton had leant forward. The colour was draining from his face, as his brain struggled to compute all the implications. Foster felt a twinge of sympathy for a second; there would have to be a hell of a clear-up, and Gorton was toast if it became public. But there were more important people to consider. As the civil servants had confirmed, some innocent, vulnerable people were on that list, entirely unaware their lives were in danger.

'OK,' Gorton said weakly, nodding. 'Get the list.' His face darkened with anger. 'Then I want to you to find out if this is leaked, how, and if the person responsible is in this building.'

The head civil servant nodded. 'May I suggest you find someone from another department to conduct the inquiry, Minister? After all, we have access to the information ourselves; it might not be in our best interests to be as thorough as necessary.'

'Yes, of course,' he said. 'Leave it to me.'

They left the room. While they were gone, Gorton also left, saying he needed to make some calls in private.

'Poor guy,' Harris said.

'He's still alive. I prefer to think of those less fortunate.'

Harris shook his head, probably more concerned about whether his invites to dinners and charity balls would be affected if Gorton was bounced out of office.

Gorton was still out when one of the civil servants returned with the list. He brought it to Foster and handed it over. 'It's probably best if we deal only in hard copies. This is a summary,' he said. 'For obvious reasons the originals and other documentation is kept elsewhere.'

Foster took it from him. It covered two sheets of A4. There must have been fifty or so names in total. On the left-hand side were their old identities. On the right, their new ones. The only other detail was their date of birth. No mention of what they had done to warrant being placed there. 'Thanks,' he said.

The civil servant left. Foster started to read down the list, recognising several names. It was alphabetical. He saw Dibb's name and new identity. Then Schofield's, then Thurston's.

He was almost at the end when the penultimate name caused him to stop.

'Jesus,' he mumbled.

'What now?' Harris said.

He didn't reply. It wasn't the first column which had alerted him. The name Christopher Wilkinson meant nothing to him.

But the new identity given to that name did.

Nigel Barnes.

25

Nigel was about to leave for Lara Harrison's house when Heather walked through the door with Grant Foster. The clock on the wall said it was mid-afternoon. They were in the middle of a high-profile murder investigation. What were they doing back here?

'I was just leaving,' he said.

Heather and Foster exchanged a nervous look. She managed a forced smile.

'Is something the matter?' Nigel asked. *Oh no,* he thought, heart sinking to his brogues. 'It's Lara Harrison, isn't it? What's happened?'

Foster looked puzzled. Heather spoke. 'It's nothing to do with Lara Harrison, love.'

Love? he thought. She never called him that. 'Babe' quite often. 'Sweetheart' a couple of times. The occasional half-ironic 'darling'. But never 'love'. This must be serious.

'Take a seat,' Foster said, nodding at the sofa.

Nigel sat down, in his head doing an inventory of all the people he knew who might warrant a double-handed visit from these two. He came up empty.

'I'll put the kettle on,' Foster said.

'Right, now you're just scaring me.'

Foster disappeared from view. Nigel used tea leaves, a strainer and a pot. Foster was definitely a tea bag man. *This could get messy,* he thought.

'What is it, Heather?' he asked.

She gently pulled his shoulder down so they were sitting side by side on the sofa, she turning to face him, one hand on his lap. 'We found something out today.'

'OK,' he said nodding. Health. This was a health scare. Him or her? But why was Foster here?

'About you.'

'Am I a suspect?' he joked weakly.

Heather smiled, but it was still forced. 'No, you're not a suspect.' Foster had re-entered the room and was standing at the back with his hands plunged deep into his pockets, looking everywhere but at Nigel.

'It's about your past.'

If she was going to collar him about an ex-girlfriend he doubted she would have brought Foster along. 'What about it?'

'Grant saw a list today. It was made up of people who had been given new identities by the state for their own protection.' She moved her hand from his knee and grasped his hand with it. 'We think you were on it.'

Nigel had heard and read about people in a state of shock being aware that other people were speaking but that their words didn't make sense. He had thought it was a myth. Now he was beginning to know how they felt.

'Run that by me again.'

Heather nodded earnestly. 'It's a headspinner, I know. As part of our current investigation, Grant was shown a list by the Home Office today of people they had granted a new identity to in order to protect them from harm. Your name was on it.'

'It was definitely me?'

'It has the same birth date. There's a chance it refers to another Nigel Barnes. But we think it's you.'

A million questions ran through his mind. 'My name was on it? Nigel Barnes?'

'Yes.' She took a deep breath. 'Another name too.'

'What do you mean?'

'There was your name ... and your real name.'

'My real name?' Nigel was beginning to feel light-headed. 'You mean my birth name?' Heather nodded. He still couldn't shake the idea that this was some kind of joke. 'This isn't a wind-up?'

'No,' Heather said with utter certainty. 'I would never joke about something like this. I know how you feel about your past.'

What past? he thought. He was a foster child. He'd always known that. There had been no details of his real parents, and no paper trail to follow; as if they had vanished into the ether or he'd been delivered by stork. 'What is my real name?' he said.

'Christopher Wilkinson,' Foster said.

'Christopher?' he spat out.

'It could be worse,' Foster said, shrugging. 'I was at school with someone called Greville.'

'Christopher? Are you sure?'

'Foster's right, Nigel. It's not a bad name. Quite nice if—'

'No, no,' he interrupted. 'There's nothing wrong with it. It's just, I was always told my birth name was Nigel. Bloody hell.' He paused. 'Jesus, this is surreal.'

'I can imagine,' Heather said. 'Actually, I can't. But Foster told me straight away and I knew you would want to know. It'll take a bit of time to sink in, I'm sure.'

'So I'm in danger?'

Heather once again deferred to Foster. 'Possibly,' he said.

Then, through the shock, it clicked: Dibb and Schofield and their new identities; the woman this morning who had murdered an infant, her own violent death now all over the TV news. Nigel felt queasy, as if he would be sick.

'You OK?' Heather said. 'You've gone pale.'

'What did they do?'

'Who?'

'Who do you think? My bloody parents! This is a list of people who have killed, isn't it? I think I deserve to know who my parents were and what they did!'

Heather looked lost. Nigel felt guilty for biting her head off. Yet this news was so bewildering, all sense of perspective was spinning away from him.

For years, since he was a child and discovered he was fostered, he had wondered who his real parents were and what had happened to them, his imagination veering between the wild and the fantastic to the prosaic and mundane. Never in his craziest fantasies had he considered they were criminals.

'The simple truth is we don't know,' Foster said.

'But my existence on this list means they did something bad, right?'

'Not necessarily. I asked them if they could tell me what it was. They went away and came back and said it was a matter of national security. There's any number of explanations. If it'd been a case of murder, or of some other crime, I'm pretty sure they'd have told me.'

'Can I find out?'

'Again, I don't know. I asked but the decision would be taken at a level much higher than the people I was speaking to. Maybe even a different agency or body. I'd be speculating if I tried to guess what it was they were involved in.'

'Are they alive?'

Foster spread his arms. 'That's another question I can't answer yet. Sorry. I did ask. I even asked for their names, but it's all classified information.' He paused. 'You knew your name was Wilkinson, though?'

'Yes, as I said, my foster parents told me. But that's all they told me. They didn't know anything else. Or so they said, and I had no reason not to believe them.'

Nigel ran his hand through his hair. That was only part of the story. In his foster mother's drawer one day, searching for clues to his past when no one was at home, he came across a small bundle of correspondence. In one of the letters a woman had exhorted his mum to 'look after Nigel'. He copied the name – it was a common name, Smith or Jones, he couldn't remember which – and the address from the back of the envelope. At the same time, he wrote to the adoption agency asking for contact details for his natural parents. The address he was given matched the one on the letter. A few days later he rode a bus to the woman's address. She was dead and had been for some time. She lived alone and no one knew of any family. Nigel traced her ancestry and found no evidence of any children, or any immediate family. It was a dead end, and he was unable to summon the courage to ask his foster mother about it because he didn't want her to know he had been rifling through her private correspondence. They had been good to him and it felt like a betrayal of their trust. There the matter had rested. Until now.

His initial shock gave way to a curiously flat feeling. The mystery of his origins had been solved for a few tantalising seconds. Even if the explanation was unedifying, it was an explanation nonetheless. But the truth still remained out of his reach. There was enough information to make a start.

'You probably need some time on your own to digest all this,' Heather said.

'Yes, I do.'

'There's a small problem,' Foster interjected.

'What?'

'Well, three names on that list have turned up dead. Technically you're in danger. The secrecy of that list has been compromised. Who knows who has it. Including, and it's a long shot, whoever the authorities had in mind when they changed your identity.'

'We can't take any chances,' Heather said.

'Don't I get a say in this? How likely is it that I'm in danger?'

Foster shrugged. 'There's lots of other people on the list, so there's some safety in numbers. But until we either catch the person responsible or trace where and how the list was compromised, we have to assume you are in moderate danger.'

'I'll take my chances,' he said. 'After all, I live with a policewoman.'

'I'm not trained in security detail, Nigel,' Heather said.

'I don't want a bodyguard. That would just be weird.'

'I don't think it would be a good idea for you to go anywhere alone in the near future.'

'Well, then we have a problem. Because I have an appointment in half an hour.'

'Who with?' Heather asked.

'Lara Harrison.'

Heather paused.

'Heather, she has paid me. I am helping her. And I'm *going* to help her. Right now.'

Foster opened his mouth as if to speak but Heather beat him to it. 'OK. Cab there, cab straight back? Deal.'

'Deal.'

'Then later tonight we talk about the best way forward,' she added.

'Like what?'

'There's one possibility you need to prepare for,' Foster said.

'What?'

'Until we know why your identity was changed, it's hard to be certain, but if someone saw fit to protect you with a new identity back then, there's a chance they may decide to protect you now that identity has been breached.' He paused. 'You might have to be given a new name. Even set up somewhere else.'

This was getting even more surreal. Heather's eyes were moist with tears. The prospect of changing his name, moving away from London, asking the people he loved to move with him or leave them behind? It was hideous to contemplate. 'No,' he said, shaking his head. 'No way. I'm Nigel fucking Barnes and I'm staying that way.'

'Let's just hope we don't have to reach that stage,' Foster muttered.

'I don't care. I don't shed skins. I stay in this one. Come what may.'

He meant every word. He would rather die if it meant not being with Heather and not being Nigel Barnes. It was the only identity he'd ever had. Take that away from him and what was left?

'I better get going.' He just wanted to get out of there and think.

Heather glanced at Foster. He shrugged. Ignoring them, Nigel walked over to a small utility cupboard by the entrance.

'And don't worry,' he said as he disappeared inside. He pulled out a sledgehammer. 'I'm going armed.'

26

Lara Harrison was understandably surprised when Nigel turned up at her front door with a sledgehammer on his shoulder. The events of that afternoon had not left him in the mood for small talk, however.

'Let me in and I'll explain,' he said, as she hesitated on the front door step.

In the kitchen he put down the sledgehammer, opened his bag and pulled out a rolled-up piece of A2 paper. He unfurled it on the table and used a salt and a pepper mill at each end to stop it curling back into a tube.

Lara stood at his shoulder, arms folded.

'These are the floor plans of the house. I got them from the 1910 Valuation Office Survey. Surveys are good. We need more surveys.' His finger pointed to an area between the front bedroom, currently India's, and the bathroom.

Lara leaned forward for a closer look.

'Notice anything?' Nigel asked.

'My God,' she said. 'There's a room there.'

'There still is,' Nigel said. 'Both doors to it have been sealed up.'

Lara continued to stare at the plans. 'That's a room? I always thought it housed pipes or something.'

He glanced at the sledgehammer. 'I suggest we find out.'

Lara bit her lip. It was clear that she wasn't too enamoured with a genealogist smashing down the wall of her house.

'There are bookshelves on the bedroom wall. I'd rather they weren't damaged.'

'Of course. But the entrance from the landing isn't obstructed.'

Lara nodded. 'OK, but let me lay down a few sheets first.'

A few minutes later the landing floor was covered. Nigel knocked on the wall where the plans showed the door to be. It was solid. He cursed. He'd hoped for some plasterboard or the Edwardian equivalent. No such luck.

He and Lara stepped back and looked at each other. She shrugged. 'Go for it,' she said softly.

He picked up the sledgehammer and eyed up the middle of the wall where it might be weakest. He felt a force of anger wash through him, which he transferred to the swing of the sledgehammer. It struck the wall with a mighty thud and a small dent appeared. Another swing and a large spidery crack appeared. One more and the outer surface gave way, exposing wood. Two more hits and there was a tiny hole. Something overtook him and soon he was swinging away for his life, a mass of dust and noise erupting in front of them. Finally, he stopped, the acrid smell of dust in his nostrils, coating his face and hair. In front of him was a gaping hole twice the size of his head.

'Bloody hell,' Lara murmured. 'There seemed to be a bit of feeling going into that.'

He turned. She was smiling. He tried to smile back.

'Tough day.'

'I'll get a torch,' she said and a few seconds later she returned with one. She switched it on and both of them made their way cautiously to the hole in the wall. She aimed its beam through the gap and they both leaned in as close as they could. Nigel smelt a familiar smell of the old. The musty odour of things hidden or ignored.

They looked in silence as the torchlight crept across the far wall.

'Oh my God,' Lara said.

Nigel said nothing, but he knew why she exclaimed.

'It's that little girl's nursery, isn't it?' Lara said.

She moved the torchlight to the far corner of the little room. Then she dropped it on the floor and gasped. She stepped back. She looked at Nigel, hand over her mouth, her eyes wide with shock. Nigel bent down and picked up the torch and shone it back towards the corner.

A small white wooden cot. The same one Esther Bathurst had slept in. And, Nigel suspected, the same one she had died in.

Someone had put a wall around the past. Hoping to hide it for ever. But he knew that wasn't the way it worked, and he knew, then, why India had been haunted by those dreams.

The hidden past had found a way to escape.

It was still light when Nigel arrived home. No one was there. *Good*, he thought. He needed a drink. The past few hours had been more than a headspinner, as Heather had put it. It was a mindfuck. The whole of his life, his sense of self, had been thrown into flux. The whisky brought calm and a sense of perspective.

He threw his mind back to Lara Harrison's house. She and India had gone to stay at her mother's, unable to face being in the house with that tragic little room exposed. They had agreed a date to meet, with a builder, to knock the down the wall completely and expose the nursery to the light. Then she would convert it into one room.

Expose to the light.

As he sipped his drink, this thought held extra resonance for him. The time had come to find out who he really was and where he had come from. To knock down the walls built around his own past. He knew what he must do.

The birth, marriage and death indexes were his start. Years ago he had checked for Nigel Wilkinsons.

There were many, but none born on the same day as him. Now, armed with his real identity, or what he was told was his real identity, it might be different. Christopher Wilkinson, his birth date, which meant the second quarter of 1976. He started the search.

It was fruitless. He tried every sound-a-like and alternative spelling of both names, with no success. But while there were many Christopher Wilkinsons, when he phoned through to his contact at the General Register Office to get the results, there were none sharing his birth date. He even checked the years after and preceding 1976.

Just my luck, he thought, *if I also discover I'm older than I always thought.* One Christopher Wilkinson was born two days before his birthday and he asked for that copy to be sent. He sighed and took another slug of his Scotch. If his parents' activities had been so precarious that he warranted a new identity, it was probably too much to expect them to have registered his birth with the state. Maybe there was a secret index, populated by the children of people in peril. Not having eaten much, and with the shock of all this discovery and the Scotch, he was feeling slightly drunk. It felt good, distracting. He poured another measure and tried to think around why his name was not in the birth indexes.

There were several options, some more convincing than others. First and most believable was that he wasn't registered. If so, this was a dead end. Maybe he had been born overseas and brought back. There was also the chance that Christopher Wilkinson was not, in fact, his real name, though as it had been entered on an official Home Office list then he would have to accept they had got it right.

Then he remembered the woman who had corresponded with his foster mother; there was one avenue he could explore. It would involve going back into his past. Knocking down the last existing wall.

And exposing to the light a place he had once called home.

27

The bus slowed, and shuddered through the centre of the town, passing the monstrous 1960s carbuncles which Nigel knew only too well, and the breezeblock shopping precinct. A small commuter town with no history, just a mundane present.

He shouldn't be so cynical, he thought. It was just that he'd been making this journey every single week for almost eight years. No matter what was happening in his life, whether he was assisting the Metropolitan Police with a murder case, falling in love with a female detective or working so hard that he could barely walk through exhaustion, the only debate was whether he got the train from Waterloo on a Saturday or a Sunday. He'd made this journey in every type of mood, every type of weather.

Perhaps that was why this felt so different. Because it was midweek. The world was working. Or it may have been the news that Heather had given him. The whole of his past, the whole of his life, seemed different now. Out of the murk, a narrative of his early life was emerging, to throw illumination on those dank early years he had spent in this place. Where there once had been a blank sheet of paper, someone had drawn a huge question mark.

On his normal pilgrimage, he was buried in a book, or some research, or thinking about a problem that needed solving. Not this time. Everything he saw was cast in new light. Behind a thicket of trees – there were precious few patches of green – he saw the old church, the only place that was more than fifty or sixty years old, rather than ones that looked like they were, such as the pubs with mock Tudor frontages.

They passed over two mini-roundabouts and a busy crossroads. At the next mini-roundabout the bus turned right, onto a long winding street. Here he usually glanced up. Approaching on the right, Nigel could see his old secondary school, set back from the road. Once so big and sprawling to him, it now looked small. A few lights shone in the windows. The kids would be in class. Rather than just looking absent-mindedly looking through a window, he wanted to get off, go in, have a look, walk the halls, get that old school smell in his nostrils. His childhood now seemed very fragile.

The school was soon receding into the distance behind him; he counted down the roads. Elm Tree Road; Beech Avenue; Oak Crescent and then ...

He turned, as he always did, to look down Sycamore Grove, towards the bungalow at number six, the house in which he had grown up. It was gone quickly as the bus continued its journey. Eight years ago he had moved his father out of the house for the last time, just a few months after his mum died. Sold to a family with an only child, just like he was. He wondered if they were still there. Again there was a sudden urge to get off and knock on the door, have a look around the old place, the first time he'd experienced that in all the many times he'd taken this journey in the past seven years. The only part of the whole town he missed was that three-bedroom, one-storey, pebble-dashed house. He smiled at the recollection of his father, ever practical, doing the pebble-dashing himself. Nigel must have been four, or was it five? Whatever, his father had let him fling the first few stones at the soft concrete covering himself. Right until the day the place was sold he was able to identify those bits of gravel.

A further half a mile up the road and the bus reached his stop. From there it was a good ten-minute brisk walk to the nursing home. It was rare that he wished he could drive, but there were times visiting his father when the thought of a warm car made sense. He soon shook off the idea. This journey, the effort, was his penance – his duty. If it were too easy it wouldn't be worth it.

The wind bit deep as he walked, hands buried in his pockets. Ten years ago his father had had a stroke, which left him with most of his faculties but affected his movement. Always an immensely capable and practical man, who loved to build and mend, and play with gadgets and machines, his disabilities had pitched him into a deep depression. Nigel's homely, devoted mother had done all she could to pull him out of it, but it had proved beyond even her ample powers. There had been signs of a recovery, but his state of mind lagged well behind his physical improvement.

Then, no doubt exhausted by having to care for him, his mother's already enfeebled heart gave way during a bout of gardening one glorious summer's day. Nigel had been at Middlesex University during his ill-fated spell there. His father called. Mum was dead, he said. Nigel had gone home immediately. He and his father sat around drinking tea, neither knowing what to say or do. His mother had always compensated for his father's dark moods with a selfless effervescence, summoned from God knows where. The forced jollity and bonhomie had, he suspected, eventually, killed her. As he and his dad sipped cold tea and watched the sun blaze down on the spot where his mother had dropped dead, it was all he could do not to blame him for it. But to issue blame was futile.

His father sank fast. Since his wife's death he had remained almost catatonic with depression and grief, and Nigel, unwilling to and unable to sacrifice his life in the way his mother had, found him a place in a nursing home at the end of the road and made his weekly visits. A few friends dropped by, though some of them had now also died; his mother's sister, Auntie Wendy, went as often as she could, but his father was hard work for whoever visited. He rarely spoke, choosing instead to stare out of the window onto a small garden, or watch TV with avid interest, the one gadget he had deplored before his stroke. He never used to watch it. Now he did little else.

Every time the phone rang late at night, Nigel imagined it to be the nursing home with bad news. When it turned out not be, he felt a mixture of relief and regret. His dad got no joy from life any more. It was a hollow charade. Recently, his weekly visits had become twice monthly; he found excuses not to go. It was tough to admit it, but when he was first hired to work on the killings in Kensington, and heard how Foster had helped his father kill himself to spare the pain of the last agonising stages of his terminal cancer, he had felt a combination of respect and envy.

Yet here he was, turning onto the gravel drive of the nursing home, a large, almost Gothic Victorian house which had once belonged to a rich landowner, on an unscheduled visit, hoping the hollow human shell that had once contained the soul of a vigorous and active man might shed some further light on the mystery surrounding his past. He had not told Heather what he was doing; she would have insisted on coming, or sending someone along to protect him. That was too much fuss. A Tube, a train, a bus and a long walk – even the hardiest of killers might have baulked at following him all that way.

The door was opened by a male nurse, a personable young man in his twenties, ears pierced, hair spiked and gelled, called Michael.

'How do,' he said, letting him in. 'Special visit?'

'You could say that,' he answered, happy to be warm again. 'How is he?' Nigel asked every time. The usual response was 'OK' or 'You know, the usual.'

'Pretty spritely, actually.'

'Really?' Nigel said, surprised. That was rare.

'Remember the new meds he was starting?'

'Yes,' Nigel lied. They had tried so many pills on his father his mind fogged over when they started to describe them to him. Sometimes, there was a short-term boost, but it was always brief, and he soon lapsed back into his usual monosyllabic despair. Maybe his timing was good. This was a sign.

Nigel signed in at the book on the counter. 'Bit too cold to wheel him outside, eh?' When the weather allowed, he took his dad into the garden he stared at so longingly from his window.

'Think so, I'm afraid,' Michael said. 'He's in the main lounge, by the way.'

'Really?' Nigel repeated. This was turning into a red-letter day. The main lounge was where the sociable residents congregated to watch TV, play cards, read or chat. His dad usually went in there only under sufferance.

'How's the research going?' he asked, putting down the pen. For the past few months, Michael had been tracing his family tree, and Nigel had been helping with a few tips and discussing the results of his labours.

'Very well. Discovered one of my ancestors got sent down.'

'Brilliant! Something juicy, I hope.'

'Demanding money with menaces.'

'Interesting. Know any more? Might be worth checking out the local paper to see if there was a report of the case, if you have dates?'

'I was going to do that. I think he was living rough. I thought it might be begging.'

'Could be. Have you worked out how he came to be on the streets?'

'Not yet.'

'When was it?'

'1880s.'

'Well worth checking at the local record office, see if there was ever any application for poor relief. Often they divulged a fair bit of detail in there.'

'Thanks,' he said.

'No problem.'

Nigel wandered down the lushly carpeted corridor, smiling at a few other nurses that passed. A bead of sweat broke out on his brow. The place was too warm; given the soporific hum that pervaded the whole place, it was no surprise half the inhabitants spent most of the time asleep.

He took a right and the corridor opened up, glass doors leading to the inner garden on one side – there was a larger though less interesting garden at the back, behind the house – and double doors that lead through to the main lounge. He walked in and cast his eyes around the room. There was a smattering of people, several fast asleep, heads lolling on shoulders; a group in the corner playing cards; in front of the TV a few rows watched an afternoon quiz show. At the back, his dad had his arms folded, staring at the screen, brow furrowed; his usual TV pose, as if daring the set to entertain him.

Nigel walked over quietly, trying to not to wake or interrupt anyone. An old lady gazing into space gave him a warm smile, which he returned. He didn't know half the people; his dad barely socialized with anyone, so there were few opportunities for introductions.

Reaching his father, he tapped him gently on the shoulder. He got a strong smell of shaving foam. Another good sign; often his father let his personal hygiene slip.

'Oh,' his father said. 'Hello.' His face flickered briefly with confusion. 'It's not Saturday.'

'No, Father,' he said. 'It's Friday.' He leaned forward and gently kissed the old man's forehead. The hair, or what was left it beyond the crown, smelled clean too. 'You're looking well.'

The old man ignored the compliment, turning back to face the screen.

'Sorry, do you want to carry on watching this?' Well groomed, out from his room, *compos mentis*, Nigel was reluctant to break the spell.

He pulled a sneer. 'No. It's all a load of rubbish anyway, isn't it?' That sounded more like his father of old. 'I only came in to watch the news bulletin. Fancied a change of scene.'

'Good,' Nigel said. 'How about we move to the back, so we don't disturb those watching?'

'OK,' he said, getting up. Yet another good sign; on his bad days, in fact most days, he refused to move unless being wheeled by chair. Here he managed to get up and with his rolling gait – it was his left side the stroke affected – half walked and half limped beside Nigel to a table at the back of the room, enough distance away from the card school not to interrupt their game.

Nigel helped him get in his seat. 'Can I get you a tea or a coffee?'

'Are you getting one?'

'Yes, I think I'll have a coffee.'

'No, I'm all right.'

Nigel shook his head, trying not to laugh. He might be more chipper but the cantankerous, slightly odd man he had become was still very much there.

There was a machine in the far corner that dispensed free coffee, not much more than hot coloured water, but it still contained caffeine and he could do with a fix. From a small adjoining table he swiped a mini-pack of shortbread biscuits. A sweet tooth was the one thing his father had retained from his life prior to the stroke.

'Biscuit?' he offered, sitting down.

His dad's eyes lit up briefly and he tore open the wrapper and popped one in his mouth. He chewed for a few seconds, pulled a face. 'It's a bit dry without a tea,' he said, crumbs spilling out of his mouth.

Nigel got up and got his dad a tea, reminded, not for the first time, of why his mother's weak heart had given way after waiting on her husband hand and foot. He brought it back and pulled across an occasional table to sit it on. For a few minutes or so they sat there in silence, munching on biscuits, interrupted by a slurp of their hot drinks.

'How's life?' Nigel asked eventually.

His father shrugged one shoulder. 'Same as usual.'

'Good, good,' he said, then cleared his throat. 'Not much to report from me either.' Nigel was used to having to volunteer information rather than being asked. His dad was simply uninterested in anything other than himself or things that affected him. Which is why Nigel knew his next comment would provoke a reaction.

'Though I learned something new about my real identity,' he said matter-of-factly.

The words seem to hang in the air for a few seconds.

'I don't understand. What "real identity"?' his father responded.

Nigel took another drink of his coffee. 'My birth name,' he explained. 'I knew I was called Wilkinson, but I always thought I was called Nigel by my birth parents. It turned out they named me Christopher.'

His father said nothing, but remained, half-turned, looking at him. 'I didn't know that.' He turned away, clasping his limp left hand in his right. 'Are you sure?' he added, swivelling back.

'That was my reaction too. And yes, I'm pretty sure.'

A few more seconds of silence passed. 'I always thought you came to us as Nigel. I don't remember changing it.' The last sentence was said with a rise of intonation, as if he wasn't sure. He shook his head. 'Your mother would know.'

'Maybe,' he replied. More silence followed. 'How much do you remember of all that, Dad?'

Nigel had often broached the subject of his adoption with his mother, though increasingly less when it became clear she knew didn't know much. She had always told him a bare bones version: of them not being able to have kids, of falling foul of the adoption authorities, of being offered him, aged fourteen months, through an intermediary and falling in love with him on first sight. She said she knew nothing about his real parents.

His father's response took some time in coming, and was preceded by a sigh. 'It was a long time ago. We couldn't have kids. Broke your mother's heart, that. We looked into adoption. There was an issue about your mother's heart. It was a bit dicky back then. We were offered the chance of you, a private adoption. But we did it above board as far as we knew.' He paused. 'And we loved you as if you were ours.'

It was as much as he'd ever heard his father say for the past few years, bar the time Nigel had bought him some wireless headphones which he could use to watch the TV. Then, on first use, he had marvelled at the sound quality at length and in detail. But talking about the past, this was as loquacious as he'd been. It was still totally devoid of the detail he craved, however.

'Who arranged it, Dad? There must have been someone you dealt with.'

'A woman.'

'Can you remember a name?'

More silence. 'Why do you want to know this now?'

'I told you, I found out my real name. It's on a list. It's set me thinking about who my birth parents were and what happened to them.'

'I think they died, son. That's the impression we got.'

'I know that. I'd like to know how they died, who they were.'

'Can't help you with all that, I'm afraid. Your mum just wanted an assurance they would never come back for you. That would've broken her heart. We were told they never would. We took that to mean they were dead, and you were an orphan. For your sake, I wished we could've found out more. But we didn't. I'm sorry about that.'

'There's no need to be sorry,' he said emphatically. 'You never, ever have to say sorry about anything. You gave me a home, a good upbringing; I'll only ever be very thankful to you and Mum.'

He nodded. 'She'd be glad to hear that. She doted on you, you know.'

'I do.'

He wanted to get back to the reason he was there. There would be no certainty his father would be anywhere near as expressive and open the next time he visited. The shutters might come down and it would be grunts and unintelligible mumbles.

'The woman. The one who fixed the adoption. Do you remember her name?'

Time slowed to a crawl as he willed his father to recall it.

'It was double-barrelled.'

Nigel thought back to the woman he had traced. He was certain it was something common, Smith or Jones, so unremarkable the passing time had erased it.

'Yes. I'm sure of it. I used to take the mickey a bit. There was a Tory MP from the sixties who had the same name.'

His father was and always had been a staunch Labour man. 'Douglas-Home?'

'No, not him.' He paused. 'What a fucking dickhead he was.' That was another consequence of his condition. Until recently, the strongest curse he'd ever heard him mutter was 'heavens to Betsy'. Even when he smashed his finger with a hammer. But the past few years he'd started using the salty language of a docker. Nigel quite enjoyed it.

His father was deep in thought, his brow creasing. 'What was it?'

Nigel went through every double-barrelled politician he could think of, and they were few, each one meeting with a shake of the head from his father. He gave up.

'That's it,' his father said.

'What is?'

'Navin-Jones. Susan Navin-Jones.' He smiled triumphantly, like a child proud of completing a task.

Nigel had never heard of a Tory politician with that name, but he didn't care. Here was a start. 'Well done, Dad. But I'm puzzled: what was her role?

Nigel could see his father tiring. He usually spent most of the afternoon asleep. He yawned, then frowned. The window for discovering anything new was closing. 'Truth be told, we were just glad to have you. It had been a difficult ordeal, all the rejection and the doubt. We didn't ask too many questions. This woman called us and said they had a child and were we interested. We went to see you. Said yes immediately. It was all done and a day or so later, maybe more, we had you home. Your mother was so happy. We both were.' He smiled, eyes misting over, lost in a reverie.

'So you never met Navin-Jones?'

'Never laid eyes on her. I spoke to her on the phone twice. Once when she called to tell us about you. The second time when we called to confirm we wanted you.'

'Didn't Navin-Jones say who she worked for, and how she had heard of you, or got your details? I mean, I could have been stolen for all you knew.'

'It wasn't anything like that,' he said, with a hint of anger. 'She said she worked for a private adoption agency. There were a lot of them back then, and we had signed on with most, as well as the public ones. It was difficult to keep track of them all. She said they had a child who needed a home. They thought we sounded a perfect match. I know it sounds slipshod, but at the time it seemed OK – and you have to remember we were desperate for a child. We'd had a lot of knock backs because of your mum's heart.' He yawned again. 'I should take a nap.'

Nigel had a hundred more questions; most of them could wait. He knew enough about adoption from his work to know that while there was an official adoption register that dated back to the 1920s, there were other organisations that arranged adoption, as well as a burgeoning unofficial 'scene' operated by various churches and faith organisations. 'You don't remember the name of the agency she represented?'

'Sorry,' he said, yawning yet again. 'It was a different world then from now. You took people at their word. There wasn't the Internet where you could go and check people out. If we'd asked more questions, then we might never have got you. I'm certainly not going to apologize for that.'

Nigel smiled. He couldn't argue with that either. His upbringing had not been perfect, and he had been desperate to escape, but he had been given love and stability and comfort, which, in the final reckoning, is all a child needs. 'Why don't you go and have a lie-down?'

'I need it,' his father said. 'Thanks for coming. Does this mean you won't be here this weekend?'

'Probably not tomorrow. But I'll be here a week on Saturday.'

His father laid a hand on his shoulder. 'Good. I'll look forward to it. Safe journey back.'

He shuffled wearily towards the door. Nigel watched him go, hoping this meant a permanent upturn in his dad's mood. He felt a tinge of guilt. To question the process that had brought him two loving parents was churlish.

But there were so many questions he still needed answers to.

28

The young, suited man sitting in the same room in Kensington where Foster had interviewed Max Craven could not have been more different. Where Craven's benign, accepting face was emotionless and calm, this one wore the look of the hunted. The internal Home Office inquiry had not taken long to reach a verdict. There were very few who knew about the list, and even fewer with access to it. Just a couple of shakes of the tree and the culprit fell out: Martin Clements, a young civil servant, in his late twenties, who had been assigned to the Home Office only a few months before.

This wasn't his first interrogation; an internal team had already questioned him. Neither would it be his last; another police team were eager to question him about potential breaches of the Official Secrets Act, which brought a lengthy prison sentence. Compared to that prospect, being given the once-over by Foster would be a breeze. There was no charge in this case, just information that might lead to the killers of Dibb, Schofield and how Max Craven had obtained the initial information he needed to track and gun down Kelly Thurston.

Foster was in no mood to be charitable. The killer was out there, people were in danger. All because of this young fool.

The statement Clements had given to the internal inquiry was concise to the point of being useless. He had put the information on a memory stick, taken it from the office and lost it.

'Let me get this straight,' Foster said. 'How did the list come to be put on a memory stick?'

'My client answers that in his statement,' the lawyer said.

'He didn't give the statement to me, and he's not being charged with anything. This is a murder inquiry, which I'm heading up, and I need to get things straight. So, if you can advise your client when it comes to the law, rather than advising me of my job, then we'll be OK. There is no real reason for you to be here, after all.'

The lawyer pursed his lips, folded his arms. 'My client asked me to attend. As did his employers.'

'So which one are you representing? The Home Office or Martin?'

Clements sat perspiring, eyes glancing everywhere but at Foster. He wore his hair mussed and untidy, though sculpted to look that way. His jaw was square and he was blue-eyed. A good-looking lad. Must have been bright to have got the job in the first place. He was about to be ejected from the civil service with some force, but if he steered clear of jail, and they would find some way to keep him out if only to avoid the publicity, Foster guessed he would do all right for himself in the end.

The lawyer looked distinctly uneasy. 'Both.'

'Look, this is how we'll do it. You leave right now. You tell your employers I demanded to see Martin on his own, and he voluntarily agreed to that. Because I think you're here to make sure he doesn't say anything to embarrass them and I don't want to interview him with you looming over his shoulder. So get yourself off.' Foster gestured to the door. 'Tell your employers that if they have any complaints, and I'm sure they will, then they should address them to my boss, Detective Superintendent Harris.'

The lawyer, fixing Foster with a disdainful glare, gathered his papers. 'I'll accede to DCI Foster's wishes,' he said to Clements, 'But don't feel you need to answer all of his questions and do terminate the interview at any point you want to.'

Clements looked torn, both relieved yet terrified to lose his minder. Foster guessed the statement in front of him was a confection, drawn up to save as many arses as possible. The lawyer left. Foster sat back, arms behind his head. Clements licked his dry lips anxiously and continued to look everywhere but at him.

'Don't think they will protect you, Martin. Right now they will, because they don't want this to go public. But you're eminently expendable. Your best option is to tell the truth and face the consequences, because if you lie, or cover up, no matter what they tell you, the truth will get out. That list is out there in the world, and when the shitstorm breaks, as it inevitably will, there will be reporters crawling all over it, and they will want a patsy and a fall guy, and that person will be you, and you'll be fucked every which way. Don't be blinded by any misguided loyalty.'

The press weren't yet linking Dibb's and Schofield's deaths with that of Kelly Thurston. But it was only a matter of time until news of the leaked list was out, given that the people who knew about it were policemen and Home Office mandarins, two of the most porous professional groups that existed.

He thumped the table with his hand. 'Lecture over. Where were we? Yes, I remember. You were going to tell me how the list ended up on the memory stick when it is categorically prohibited from being copied or taken out of the office in any way, shape or form.'

Clements had been nodding, fringe matted to his sweating forehead. He was in a grade A funk. 'There had been requests for a look at documents pertaining to the witness protection program. There's a review pending on its operation ...'

'Cut the bureaucrat speak, Martin. I'm not a junior minister or a mandarin. You've got quite a broad London accent – I doubt this is the way you speak about work with your friends. As a US congressman once said of the Bible, "If the Queen's

English was good enough for Jesus Christ, then it's good enough for me." '

Clements was in no mood for humour. 'OK. They're reviewing the way the witness protection program functions. There've been a few incidents recently of people going into the program and delivering little. The idea is that there should be some criteria a person must fulfil before they are allowed into the program.'

'You want them to sing like a canary before they get a new identity?'

He paused. 'In a nutshell, yes.'

'Good luck with that,' he said. 'Carry on.'

'I was asked to produce a report for the evaluating team. I copied a host of files. The new identity register is in the same part of the system. By accident, when copying those files, I copied some others that weren't relevant, including the new identities.'

'Copied them onto what?'

'A memory stick.'

What was it with civil servants and sensitive data? he wondered. In the old days it had been briefcases or files being left in cars. Then it was floppy disks and CD-ROMs. Now it was memory sticks. The technology was getting smaller and easier to lose.

If it really was lost. Foster thought it was too convenient when some of these documents were 'lost' and wound up in the news. Yet this latest act of misplacement was another level of seriousness entirely. As had been proved, people would kill for this information. He wanted to believe it was a complete accident.

'You were allowed to take files about people in the witness protection program from the office?'

Clements shifted nervously in his seat. 'I didn't take information about people on the program, any other lists or that sort of thing. It was files relating to the procedures surrounding the witness protection program.'

'So, you were careful enough not to copy any files that would compromise people in witness protection, but you were careless enough to inadvertently copy over this file with the new identities on it?

More squirming.

'I can only say it was because I was being so careful not to copy the information about witnesses, that I managed to overlook the fact I had copied the new identities register.'

'Hmmm,' Foster said. 'Let's move on. When was this again?'

He cleared his throat. 'Three months ago.'

'Three months. Jesus, Martin. And you didn't come forward about it until the inquiry?'

'I didn't realise I had lost the memory stick until it became known that the list was leaked.'

'Yeah, let's have a look at how that works, shall we? You take the memory stick home with you. Did it reach home?'

'Yes, I spent the weekend working on the report. I delivered it on the Monday morning.'

'Then what happened to the memory stick?'

'I can't with all honesty say.'

'You can't honestly say,' he repeated. 'It just slipped your mind.'

'I suppose. I fully intended to erase the contents and reuse the stick. I never got round to doing that.'

'Do you remember taking the stick out of your place?'

'No, I don't.'

'Been burgled?'

'Not that I'm aware of.'

Foster got hold of a pad and a pen from the table in front, and pushed it across towards Clements. 'Then I want you to write down a list of everyone who has been in or near your house in the past three months, with addresses and numbers if possible.'

Clements looked at him, open-mouthed.

'What's the problem? You told me you didn't remove it, so the obvious conclusion is that someone else took it from your flat. Therefore we'll need to speak to everyone who's been anywhere near your place since the date you took the memory stick. Your cleaner, your mates, every girl who comes in for coffee. I'm assuming you live alone?'

He shook his head. 'I share with a friend.'

'Well, there you go. We'll need to bring him in.'

'She's a she,' he muttered quietly. His skin had turned pallid, and he was perspiring even more than before.

'Well, she's prime suspect number one.'

He took the pen. His movements had become slow, almost as if he was drugged. He was about to start writing but stopped.

Foster kicked on. There was a file in front of him. In it were pictures of Dibb's charred corpse. He took the least gruesome one – though it was relative – and tossed it on the table in front of Clements. 'Maybe she was behind this?'

He stared at the photograph, nonplussed. Then his eyes connected with his brain. He vomited. Foster went to the door and called for assistance before opening a window to get rid of the stench. Clements continued to cough up his guts. Foster poured him a glass of water. A PC turned up with some paper roll. He ripped off some sheets and handed them to Clements to wipe his face, while he put another batch on a small stain on the floor and stood on it to help soak up the moisture. Then he put away the picture.

Foster gave it a few seconds. Then he spoke. 'You see, Martin, we think that whoever has got that list is doing some pretty terrible things. They might well continue to do some terrible things unless we catch them. Right now, you're the only lead we have which is any use. Now, we can carry on playing the game, following the story you concocted with or without the help of your colleagues, and turn your life inside out, and cast suspicion on everyone you know. That will cause a lot of upset and we'll still get to the truth in the end, but in the meantime your life will have been made a misery and you'll be no better off for it. Or, we can cut the crap and bullshit and you can tell me exactly what happened to the list and we can stop more people being murdered.'

He sat back down in his seat.

Clements was leaning forward, arms on his knees, gazing at the floor. He said nothing.

'I can guarantee you'll feel better for it. I don't just say that. In my job, I've seen hundreds of people come in here, trying to cover themselves, concocting all kinds of cock and bull stories. It *destroys* them. We nearly always find the truth and in the meantime all they've done is damage themselves and the case.'

Still Clements continued to look down. Foster was about to reach for the picture of Kelly Thurston's body when he finally spoke.

'OK,' he muttered. He lifted his head and took a deep breath. He looked utterly defeated and broken. Foster said nothing.

Clements ran his hand through his mane of hair. 'Maybe I need a lawyer here,' he said.

'Your call. But we can talk about it first. Off the record. Nothing taped. We can come to the formal interview later if necessary. Someone else will do that. I just want a start here so I can go and catch a killer.'

More pause while he thought. 'I met her in a pub.'

'Who?'

'She said her name was Lydia.'

'A surname?'

'No. I don't think her real name was Lydia either.'

'Carry on.'

'She came on to me. We shared a few drinks. I'd had a few. Usual thing happened, the people I was with left, we carried on, went on somewhere else, then back to mine.' He paused. 'She left the next morning.'

'Taking the memory stick?'

'No. Not then. There was no memory stick then. She scribbled an email address. I was really keen to see her again. We'd had a great time. I was going to give it a few days, like you do, you know? Not to look too keen. I lasted a day. Suggested we meet up again. She replied and said she'd like that.'

'You still have that email?'

'Yes. I think. I'll need to check.'

'Where did you meet?'

'Same pub we met in. Lamb and Flag near Covent Garden. Upstairs.'

'Did you have any other contact details, a phone number?'

'No, we met that night. Similar thing, a lot of drinks, we went on to a few places, then back to mine.'

'Was there anything more to it than drinking and sex?'

'There was for me. We talked a lot. She is gorgeous, good fun too. She was interested in what I did. Very interested.' He looked apologetically at Foster. 'I shot my mouth off a bit, like you do.'

'What was she interested in?'

'The Kenny Chester killers. Their real identities. She said she was a journalist.' He started to shake his head. 'God, was I ever fucking dumb?'

Foster said nothing. 'What did you do?'

'Well, we had another great night. I was pretty into her.'

'You got her the info?'

He nodded. 'I copied the list onto a memory stick. We met again a few nights later. I was just going to give her the Chester killers' identities. The fact is, I didn't. Or at least I thought I hadn't. I told her I had the info, back at the house. I wasn't stupid enough to bring it out with me.'

No, thought Foster dryly. *Very wise.*

'We went back, had sex. She left early the next morning. Woke up, she was gone. She left a note. I didn't notice the stick had gone for a while. I thought I hadn't given her the information because we never spoke about it.'

'What did the note say?'

Clements looked a little abashed once more. 'Thanks for the bed, the sex and everything.' He let out a mirthless little laugh.

'You didn't notice the stick was gone?'

'No. I've lots of them, and they're all together in a pile. It was only when she kept ignoring the emails that I got suspicious and checked. It wasn't there. Still, I wasn't sure she had actually taken it. Then I read about the Chester killers being found dead. I thought it might be coincidence. Or rather, I prayed it was. But then there was the inquiry…' His voice tailed away.

'She disappeared after that second date?'

'It was our third night together.'

'Have you had any contact since?'

He shook his head. 'The emails just disappeared into the ether. Then they began to bounce back, no such address. She'd obviously cancelled the account.' A bitter laugh. 'I was completely played.'

Totally, Foster thought. 'Obviously, we're going to need a detailed description. But is there anything else you found out about her, other than her name, her profession and this email address?'

'She said she lived in Manor Park.'

'Anything else?'

He scratched his head absent-mindedly, palpably embarrassed. 'Not really…'

'Any biographical details? Family, where she came from, previous jobs, that kind of thing?'

Again it drew a blank. 'I know it all sounds pretty cheap and sordid,' he said.

'I never said that.'

'But it does. I just want to say it wasn't like that. It wasn't cold and mechanical. We got on great. That's the thing; she was funny and we had a laugh. I really, really wanted to keep seeing her. I genuinely thought we had something, and not just a physical connection. I can't believe she could fake that much interest.'

A dark, troubled look swept across his face, a canvas that showed every emotion. There was very little guile to him. 'But then I'd never believe for a second she would kill anyone. If she can do that, I'm sure she can run rings round like a sap like me.'

In one, Foster thought. 'We're going to need to come to your place and do some forensic tests. When was the last time you changed your bedsheets? Tell me it was ages ago.'

'I change them every two weeks.'

Trust me to get the only fastidious heterosexual twenty-something male in London, Foster thought. 'Do you still have the note she wrote?'

'I don't know. I can have a look.'

'Please do. Look, I'm going to send in a sketch artist to do a detailed ID. I want you to give as good a description as you can. It may be all we have. Then I'll come back when you're done and you can go.'

'Really?'

'Being made a fool of by a woman isn't a crime, Martin. If it was, we'd all have done time.' He paused. 'There will certainly be some comeback for taking the information from work but that's not for me to sort out.'

Foster went and grabbed a coffee while the sketch was done, and handed 'Lydia's' email address to the computer forensic team to see if they could pick up a trail. After an hour or so, he went back to the room and looked at the sketch. In his hand was one that had been scanned and sent down from the East Midlands, drawn on the recollections of the pub bar man. They showed blue eyes, beautiful bone structure, full lips and blonde hair. All pretty generic. The eyes in both, however, were closer together than usual and the forehead slightly high. They were the same woman.

The sketch artist left. Foster began to gather his papers.

'There's one thing,' Clements said.

'Yeah?'

'I took her photo.'

Foster almost dropped his papers in surprise. 'You what?'

'With my mobile phone.' His face had turned crimson. 'It was that third night. Or rather the morning. She was in my shower. It's an en suite. She came out and I was there and I had the phone and took a picture. I thought it was a bit of fun. She was quite, er, playful.'

'You still have it?'

'God, no. She went bananas. Took the phone off me. Deleted it immediately and told me not to be so fucking stupid. I took it to mean she was a bit more prudish and less liberated than she had appeared. Now it's pretty obvious why she wanted to delete it.'

'I need your phone.'

'Is it recoverable?'

'We'll try.'

29

Susan Navin-Jones. The name was pinned above Nigel's computer terminal. The woman who had approached his parents and offered him for adoption. The person who had been entirely responsible for the shape of his life, more than any other. Why had she chosen his adoptive mum and dad? Had she known his birth parents? Was she one of them? So many questions. Yet he knew absolutely nothing about her. No biographical detail beyond her name.

He started with some logical guesswork. He had been adopted in 1975. He guessed she would have been no younger than twenty and no older than sixty, which meant he was looking for someone born with that name between 1915 and 1955. Searching through the indexes, he found only two candidates considering the possibility that Navin-Jones could be her married name, and the result of her joining surnames in marriage.

In his spread of years, he estimated that she might have married between 1933 and 1973. He went through the marriage indexes, noting down the union between any man bearing the Navin-Jones name. There were more than seventy. From each he obtained the maiden name of their spouse. Then he cross-referenced these entries to discover the Christian names of the woman who married. By the time he finished, his shoulders were arched and aching, his eyeballs weary from scouring through reams of entries, but he had three potential hits. After taking a break and dosing up on caffeine, he traced the two women born Susan Navin-Jones down the years to see if they married. One had, the other remained single. There was no way of knowing if the married one had taken her husband's name so he could not strike her from the list.

Five possible matches. Was she among them?

The next step was to glean as much autobiographical detail as possible from death and marriage certificates. He phoned his contact at the General Register Office and endured a painful wait as they found time in the schedule to fulfil his request. Thankfully, it was a quiet day and a series of scanned documents arrived in his email inbox a couple of hours later.

He opened the attachment eagerly, hoping the crucial give-away detail would leap from the copies in front of him. No such luck. The results were interesting but unrevealing. Two were housewives. Could he rule them out? Foster had mentioned that his case was an issue of national security. It seemed fair to assume that the Susan Navin-Jones he was searching for was in some way connected to the security service.

Would a housewife be attached? If it was a cover, it was certainly deep. He demoted those two to a lower priority with another, a Navin-Jones who had lived and died, only a few years before, in Edinburgh. His dad had mentioned nothing about a Scottish accent. Nigel knew that affluent Edinburghians often had soft accents, so it might have gone undetected. Still, that went to one side.

Which left him with two Susan Navin-Joneses. One was the unmarried Susan, born 1924, died 2005. The death certificate gave her occupation as 'secretary'. She had lived at an address in north London at the time of her death. The other candidate was a Susan Reardon, born 1942, who married Guy Navin-Jones in 1969, and was still alive. Her marriage certificate gave her occupation as 'solicitor', the same as her husband. *Thank God for the professions*, he thought. It would not take too long to track down the legal career of both husband and wife. Perhaps she was his birth parents' solicitor, and had been appointed by them, by either their will or their word, to find him a home to go with his change of identity? She lived in Bristol.

The Internet told him that their practice, bearing their name and those of two other partners, was still going. Their website indicated they had retired, but their son was still a partner. That was good news; there was a place he could visit, someone who could answer his questions.

Not so for the unwed Susan. She had died in the Royal Free Hospital at Hampstead, the cause entered as 'metastatic lung cancer'. No family member was there to witness the certificate's signing. Yet Nigel knew that sometimes the dead could speak, often clearer and with more brevity than the living. If she had died a spinster, or even had a partner she had not married by law, then there would be every need for her to make a will; elderly women in Hampstead rarely died penniless, particularly if there were no children to bleed them of all their cash. Her will and its contents would still be protected. Before setting his sights on Bristol, Nigel decided to deal with Hampstead first.

Time was short, so he took a cab to the British Library. Armed with her date of death, he requested back issues of the *Hampstead & Highgate Gazette* for the weeks following. He scanned through, finding no news story. However, there was a notice. It mentioned her death, and that she was to be buried in Highgate Cemetery that Friday. Unusually, there was no reference to a family member, or her being a beloved aunt, sister or relation to anyone. She had died alone.

A picture was building in Nigel's mind. Often these were inaccurate, yet more often they proved to have some connection with the truth. In this case he saw an elderly, bookish spinster, who had been a secretary, perhaps even personal assistant to someone of importance, who paid well enough to support her and a small cottage in an expensive part of London, perhaps supplemented by some family wealth. Her father had been an officer in the army, and maybe picked up a well-paid job once he resigned his commission, it being the time when the right regimental tie could go a long way. Susan had not married, though maybe there had been the right man – she would have been fifteen or sixteen when the Second World War began, in her twenties when it ended. Perhaps he was a casualty of the conflict and there had been no one else since, and as the years passed she became gradually accustomed to and fond of her own company, unwilling to compromise on the pleasant if slightly cold and unfulfilling life she had created.

It was based partly on facts and hunches – London being more plugged into the network of national security than Bristol – as well as intuition, but he felt as if he was getting close. As if he *knew* this woman, even though the idea was impractical and preposterous. Yet as he stumbled out from the library into the chilly night air, he was unable to shake a feeling of anticipation. He took another cab to Hampstead.

The small cottage that had once belonged to Susan Navin-Jones, on a quiet mews, looked empty. Nigel rang the doorbell next door, but the tenants had only been there a year so had no recollection of her. The other properties were deserted. He stood for a few minutes, unsure if he should wait until people started to come home from work. She had died more than four years ago, an age in a transient London neighbourhood like this. Yet there must be one person who knew her, who had lived here then, and might be able to tell him where she went and how she lived.

There were footsteps behind. He turned to see who they belonged to. It was a man, in his sixties Nigel guessed, though remarkably well preserved, lean and fit, with a mane of grey hair and a pair of expensive glasses. He was wearing a dark woollen overcoat and leather gloves.

'Hello, Nigel,' he said, unbidden. The voice was firm, friendly and well-spoken.

Nigel didn't know what to say. He felt a sudden lurch of terror. Heather had warned him not to leave the house. Suddenly his bravado about not wanting protection, determined to find out about his past whatever the cost, seemed foolish and empty.

'Don't be worried. You have nothing to fear from me,' the man said, his voice soft.

Nigel glanced left. No more than fifty yards away was a busy road; he could see buses, their decks lit and filled with passengers, passing by regularly, while pedestrians streamed past on their way home from work. Yet the mews was empty save for him and this stranger.

'Who are you?' he asked, a crack in his voice.

'My name is Henry Mann. We've never met.'

'How do you know my name?'

The man looked around. Nigel felt another undulation in the pit of his gut.

'Look, there's a pub around the corner. Busy enough to make you feel reassured, not so busy that we can't hear ourselves speak. Let me get you a drink.'

Nigel paused. *Never go anywhere with strangers.* Prescient advice at the best of times, but particularly pertinent when your name has just wound up on a list of protected persons whose cover has been blown, and other people on it have started turning up dead. 'You haven't told me how you know my name.'

Henry sighed. 'We've been following you since we discovered the list with your name on it was leaked.' Nigel's face must have shown surprise. 'You don't think we'd leave you dangling in the wind, exposed like that, do you? You could be in danger. We knew you would try to find out why you were on that list when you were told. We've kept an eye on you ever since.'

A discreet one, Nigel thought. 'You followed me to the nursing home?' He remembered checking the car park and road behind him as he arrived at his dad's home and seeing no one.

'To the nursing home? Yes, we did.' There was a pause. A young woman walked up the mews, looking anxiously at the two of them standing in the middle of the road. Henry Mann smiled warmly, which put her at ease. Nigel toyed with asking her to get help. Yet the strange thing was that he suddenly felt reassured. They watched her go into one of the cottages.

'Let me buy you that drink. We can talk.'

Nigel's curiosity was triumphing over his caution. The pub was on the main street. Henry ordered two pints of bitter at the bar, Nigel watching his interaction with his drink carefully in case he happened to slip something into it, before they found a table in an empty corner.

The two of them sat opposite each other, neither saying a word. Henry took a sip of his pint and wiped the foam off his top lip. 'Decent pint.'

Nigel drank. It was good. Better than he'd expected. 'If you're keeping an eye on me then why have you broken cover? Am I really in that much danger?'

'We don't know. There's a chance you might be and it's not a chance we're willing to take. That's not why I came to talk to you, however.'

'Oh, why did you?'

'Because we can see what you're doing. And we want to tell you it's not worth it.' Henry had a calm, patrician air and a soothing voice. Nigel had to force himself to listen and analyse his words, because it would be easy to let the tone and the gentle way it was delivered wash over him.

'What isn't?'

'Chasing your past like this.'

'And what gives you the right to tell me that?'

'That doesn't matter.'

'It does to me.'

'OK,' Henry said, taking another drink, as if composing himself. 'The house you were outside belonged to Susan Navin-Jones. I know you're aware of that. She and I used to work for the same company.'

'What company was that?'

'MI5.'

It was no surprise; he'd suspected this was connected to the security services. 'You knew her?'

'Knew of her. It's a big place. I know she was involved in setting up your adoption. That is all I know.'

Nigel had too many questions to take that as hint to not to probe further. 'Why are you here, then? I don't know my past, you don't know it, Susan is dead. I don't see the point.'

'That's rather what I'm trying to say: there is no way you can find out about your past. It is out of bounds, hidden from view, classified. What you are doing here is wasting your energy. I can understand why you would want to find out. Who wouldn't? Especially you, Nigel, with your skills. But there is no way you can find out what you want. There will always be a dead end.'

'I can apply via freedom of information …'

'And you will be told the information is classified.'

'And you think I'll stop?' Nigel's voice had risen an octave. He'd had enough of being lectured to. 'You're right, it is easy for you to say. You don't have all these questions. This gaping hole. You showing up like this just compounds it. There's always a paper trail. I'm going to follow it.'

Henry nodded, as if agreeing. 'As I said, I understand. More than you might think. One thing I do know: nothing good will come of you pursuing this.

Just a great deal of frustration. What I can give you here is an assurance that you will be protected and looked after. There will be no need for you to go into any sort of hiding, or to change your identity and give up the successful life you have forged. You can carry on living that life. You *should* carry on living that life. I know this is anathema to you, but the past in this case is a closed book; it is gone. It cannot be dug up. For once, think about the future.'

Nigel felt his mind reel. All his life had been spent wondering about the past, both in private and in work. Switching that off wasn't easy. 'What if I can't? Are you saying you won't protect me? Is this some kind of threat?'

Henry held up his hands in a calming gesture. 'It's nothing of the sort. We'll always keep an eye on you. We will keep you safe. But, if you keep digging, and keep chasing, then that job becomes more difficult. Which is my polite way of saying you'll put yourself at risk. It's not worth it—'

Nigel struck the table with his fist, stopping Henry dead, shocking him and a few others in the pub. 'But I have nothing! I'm finally on the verge of finding out who my parents are, or at least some hint at who they might be, and therefore who I really am, and you're asking me to stop? Here's a deal. You tell your friends at MI5 to let me know who my parents were and what happened to them. I don't have to have full names. I just want the story. The truth.'

Henry started to shake his head as Nigel finished his rant. 'I can't do that, Nigel. I wish I could but it's out—'

'Then you and all your secret service spook friends can go and fuck yourselves,' Nigel said, and got up to leave, grabbing his coat and scarf, and heading out into the London night.

30

The forensic team ran a software program on Martin Clements' phone which extracted and restored all his deleted images. Among them the picture of the enigmatic Lydia, ambushed emerging from a shower. Her surprise was impossible to gauge as the image was blurred. It was just about possible to make out she was blonde, that she was topless, but she must have moved as the picture was taken. Any other details were impossible to make out. As a tool for identification, it was useless. But Foster made sure the image was sent to a lab to see if it could be made sharper and salvaged as a potential lead.

A trail of events began to weave together in his mind. Foster knew what needed to be done, starting with Cheryl Underwood, last seen storming out of her flat in north-west London after a row with her flatmate. An electoral roll search suggested she had moved to an address in Bermondsey, but a call revealed she had left there more than a year before. A few more enquiries turned up a law firm in Colliers Wood, where she was working as a conveyancing solicitor. Foster drove there as quickly as the teeming London traffic would allow him. Gridlocked amid the grime of Elephant and Castle, Foster was reminded of why he rarely ventured to the wilderness south of the river.

The solicitors' office was on the main artery that took people south out of London, the sort of place where lawyers were dedicated to helping the dispossessed and downtrodden rather than seeking to enrich themselves. No one came to Colliers Wood to enrich themselves. The office was across the road from a rundown apartment block which looked as though it was made from soggy cardboard, up a set of stairs decorated by a threadbare carpet, peeling wallpaper and the not unpleasant yet pungent smell of the neighbouring Indian restaurant.

A receptionist or secretary sat behind a small desk. She smiled and closed her eyes behind a pair of thick-rimmed glasses. Foster made his introductions, asking if Cheryl Underwood was free, apologising for not having an appointment. The woman betrayed no surprise; Foster guessed the police were no strangers here. It turned out she was with a client and they took a seat and waited. Ten minutes later an Asian man emerged, behind him a tall, slim young woman. Cheryl Underwood. She turned to smile at him.

He followed her through to a meeting room to one side of an open plan office. There was one other person sitting there, a young man, going through a pile of files and papers. Cheryl explained the two partners were out at court, while she held the fort. He voice still bore a trace of the musical lilt of her Geordie upbringing.

They went to an airless and stuffy meeting room which smelled of stale sweat. Cheryl went to the only window and tugged it open, while Foster sat at a long table. She sat opposite and smiled.

'How can I help? Is this about Jamal?' She was wearing little make-up and her hair was tied back, her manner brisk and officious, as if she was trying to suppress her natural good looks.

'No,' Foster said, wondering who Jamal was and what he had done. 'It's about you, actually.'

She pulled a face. 'How do you mean?'

'I'm investigating the deaths of Glen Dibb and Craig Schofield.'

She said nothing at first. There wasn't even a hint of recognition on her face. 'Which has exactly what to do with me?'

Foster sat forward. 'I really don't know.'

The noise of the traffic through the open window filled the silence. In the distance he could hear the blare and whirl of an ambulance siren.

'So why have you come to see me, then?'

'I was in Mackington last week.' He paused. 'I saw your mother.'

Did he notice a slight wince? He wasn't sure. Her fingers had started to pick at each other. She glanced towards the window. 'Detective, I really can't see what...'

'She told me about Ben.'

Her eyes came back to meet his. The stare was granite hard. Again, she said nothing.

'I worked on the original case,' he continued. 'You may not know this, but your mum sent us a letter. It was towards the back end of the investigation. She was worried about him, about his behaviour, ever since the day Kenny Chester was killed.'

She carried on giving him the same unyielding gaze. 'And what did you do about that letter?' she asked, her voice flat and without emotion.

'We did nothing. To my shame.' More silence, more traffic noise. He realised she wasn't going to offer any information voluntarily. 'I'm sorry about that.'

'Yes, well, you've made your apology, now if you don't mind…'

'Was he there, Cheryl?'

'Who?'

'Ben. Was he at the scene? Was he with them?'

She looked down at her hands, picking some more. The draught blowing through the open window had brought a chill to the room.

'No,' she said simply. There was the answer to his first question, he thought. As if sensing his thoughts, she stood up, and without speaking closed the window, before smoothing down her skirt and sitting down.

'Then why was he so affected by it all?'

She sighed. 'We were all affected by it.'

'We?'

'The whole village.'

Foster didn't believe a word of it, but wanted to tread carefully.

'I know that. I was affected by it. But as far as I know, your mum was the only person to write a letter because she was so worried. No other mothers did. And to the police, too. Not social services, or the school, or anyone else who might have helped and offered some counselling. The police.'

He looked at her. Her face held firm, giving away nothing. 'Talking to your mum was something I should have done ages ago. She told me about Ben and how he changed. I can only think that he was in some way involved.'

Her nostrils flared, and for a second her eyes blazed anger. 'Never!'

'How do you know that, Cheryl? He may have kept it secret.'

'We had no secrets!'

'Again, how do you know that? He may have been so ashamed ...'

'I was there!' she hissed.

'You were there?' he repeated. 'At the scene?'

She nodded, eyes moistening. The hands had stopped picking and started to tremble.

'With the boys?'

She shook her head, wiped a tear from her cheek. 'No,' she said in a hoarse whisper.

'You were passing by?'

'No,' she replied, more firmly, as if angered by his slowness. 'I was with him.'

The last word was said with venom and disdain.

'Kenny Chester?'

'Yes,' she said. '*Him.*'

In his mind he rifled through a list of circumstances where Cheryl Underwood would be in the care of Kenny Chester. He couldn't think of any.

'Why?'

She wiped her eyes, hatred and defiance now burning from them. The phone on the table started to ring. She picked it up. 'Give me five more minutes, Eunice,' she said calmly.

Five minutes? It would take him longer than that to unpick this.

'I was off school that day. I was sick.'

'I don't understand why you were with Kenny Chester.'

'He was a friend of my granddad's. They worked down the pit together. My mam worked, so I spent a lot of time with my granddad. We both did, Ben and I. He suffered quite badly from angina. That was the coal dust. Kenny Chester was fitter. He'd go for a walk every day and pop round to see my granddad. We were there after school sometimes when he came round. Or I was, because Ben would be out playing.' She started to blink back a few more tears, her hands shaking once again. 'Kenny would offer to take me for a walk. My granddad got out of puff climbing the stairs. He used to take me down the Dean Bank.' She shook her slowly. 'My granddad said he was the fin-est man he ever knew. Saved his life. I believed him. Who would believe he wasn't? Who would believe a six-year-old girl?'

It was only then, with the tears streaming down her face, that Foster realised the meaning of what she was saying. 'You mean ... he used to abuse you?'

She bit her lip, then nodded slowly.

'How many times?'

'More times than I could name.'

'Down at the Dean?'

'Always. He'd never do it near my granddad. Always took us for a walk. I'd always go, too. I dared not.'

'That day, the day he was ...' His voice trailed away.

'I was off sick. I was at my granddad's because our mam couldn't get the time away from work. He came round. Said I could do with the air because it was a belting day. I said I felt sick. He said it would do me good. I didn't know how to get out of it. We went, him holding my hand. He had hot sweaty hands. I would be so scared my throat would dry up and con-strict and I'd never say a word. He'd talk about the weather, all kinds of stuff, and I would just trudge along like I was going to the gallows. We got to the entrance to the Dean and we were heading for the clearing, which is where he'd usually do it.' She took in a deep breath. 'Something in me clicked. I just ran. He was old so I got ahead pretty quickly. I heard him say something but I just kept running. I was so scared … God, I wish I'd just kept running and never stopped.'

'What made you stop?'

I saw the two of them playing. I thought they could help. I looked back and I still couldn't see him coming. For a second I thought he'd gone home. I went up to them. I was gabbling, crying. One of them, Dibb, he said, "You're Ben's sister, aren't you?" I said I was. I told him, or I tried to. I can't remember what I said. I don't think they understood but they saw how terrified I was. I turned around and Kenny was coming. Dibb went off to get a stick and the other one just stood there with me, watching him come.'

The moment Schofield was alluding to in his interview, Foster thought.

'Kenny was fuming. Dibb came back. Kenny lost it with them, saying he was going to tell the headmaster, for them to bugger off. They were giving him lip back. He went at them with his walking stick and they were laughing and carrying on.'

'I just couldn't stop meself. I said, "He's a dirty man. He's going to fiddle with us." He stopped, looked at me like he was going to kill us. Them two started laughing and chanting, "Dirty man, dirty man." He turned bright purple. I thought he was gonna keel over. But he got his stick and started whacking me. Really really hard. They just turned on him. Started beating the living daylights out of him. He went at them with his stick but then he fell over. They'd lost it. They were kicking him and kicking him. I asked them to stop. They didn't. I was crying. I was scared. I just turned and I ran. I ran all the way back to my granddad's. He was asleep on the sofa.'

The silence was profound when she stopped. Even the traffic beyond the window had ceased its incessant roar, as if in awed shock. Foster let her carry on.

'So, as you'll see, I have no reason to kill these boys. I have every reason to thank them. What they did to him was wrong, but they protected me. They stopped him doing what he had done to me countless times.'

'But – your brother, the letter your mum wrote …'

'Ben was the only person I ever told. I wish every second of every single day I hadn't. But I told him: about the abuse, about Glen and Craig. I swore him to secrecy. I think it must have been guilt and anger at what had happened to me, his failure to protect me.' She spread her arms wide. 'Who knows? He was always troubled. Maybe he would have ended up that way regardless.'

'No one spoke to you? No one saw you with him?'

She shook her head. 'I sat and I waited. All through the days afterwards I expected someone to come and see me, that the boys would say something. But they didn't. It was torture. Everyone mourning Kenny Chester and me knowing he was a monster. That's why I told Ben. I had to tell someone.'

'Why didn't you tell your mother? Or your granddad?'

'I was six years old. I was terrified. Kenny Chester was a hero.'

'A lot of us fell for that story,' he murmured. He'd always had the inkling that someone else was at the scene, a witness, but never imagined anything like this.

'I felt culpable,' she added in a small voice. 'Guilty. If it hadn't been for me being there, saying what I said, then it might never have happened.'

Though the abuse would have continued, he thought.

'There's been times when I thought I should come forward, during the trial and the publicity. But I was just too scared. It ate Ben up inside, the whole thing. I just learned to carry it around with me.'

'You never told anyone apart from Ben?'

'I've had therapy. I've talked about and dealt with the abuse, or tried to, though not the circumstances surrounding it. I've never told anyone that.'

There was another long silence.

'One thing I never understood,' she added, looking straight at him for the first time in a while. 'The two boys, why did they never say anything? I've seen the reports. It never came out. Not a hint.'

'I don't think it was allowed to.' Foster knew why, and he also knew who was responsible.

'The damage that was done,' she said, shaking her head.

Foster nodded slowly.

The phone on the table rang once more. 'I must get back to work,' she said. 'Clients…'

'I understand. Thanks for your time. And I know it means little now, but sorry.'

She shrugged. 'There's little we can do to make it right now, though, is there?'

'Maybe.' He felt his phone in his pocket vibrate. 'Mind if I take this here?'

'Take your time.'

He smiled as she left, then looked at the screen of his phone.

It was Harry Stokes.

31

The rain drilled against the windscreen as Foster drove north, his mind replaying Cheryl Underwood's words, and the images it evoked of that balmy summer day two decades before. Exhaustion hit him as he left the M1 and joined the Great North Road but he ploughed on, determined to reach his destination by late afternoon and not waste a second more. So much had been wasted in twenty-five years; so many lives damaged beyond repair.

His first stop was the county archives office in Ashington. Nigel Barnes had told him where to look. He got the employment records for Mackington colliery. It confirmed what he already knew. Then he headed towards the coast.

The gates to Jackie Corrigan's house were closed. That much he expected. He buzzed the intercom and there was no answer. There were lights on in the house but they could be switched on by a timer. He buzzed once more. Once again, nothing.

He ran his hand over his head, then pinched the bridge of his nose, trying to clear his head, fogged by nearly five hours of peering through rain-streaked glass. The cold wind helped, but in a few minutes it would be enervating rather than invigorating.

Foster reached into his pocket and found the piece of paper. A photocopy of a news report written four years after Dibb and Schofield were sentenced. It had vaguely caught his attention at the time, but he had moved on, trying to put the case and the city behind him.

The uncle of child murderer Craig Schofield was yesterday found dead just a few hundred yards from where his nephew brutally slayed an elderly miner.

Warren Schofield's body was found on a side street in Mackington. Police refused to state the cause of death, though a police source said it was believed he might have fallen after a night of heavy drinking.

Mr Schofield, 32, had chosen to remain in the village despite his link to the notorious killer, Craig Schofield, who, along with school pal Glen Dibb, kicked 73-year-old Kenny Chester to death in July 1992 in a crime that shocked Britain.

Friends said Mr Schofield had denounced his nephew and no one had a vendetta against him. They also confirmed that he had been drinking heavily in the hours leading up to his death...

Just then two glowing lamps appeared over the crest of the headland. Foster stood and watched as they swept closer. He saw them dip, believing the car would sweep past, but he could hear the hum of its engine – expensive, powerful – start to decelerate.

As it slowed to turn in, he could see it was Corrigan's Bentley, a silhouetted figure at the wheel.

Foster stepped back. As the car turned, some mechanism causing the gates to open, its light illuminated him, and he could see Corrigan at the wheel, leaning to the side to catch a better look at the stranger at his gate. Foster thought he wasn't going to stop, but a few yards on, as the car was about to pass the point where the gates would swing shut, it came to a halt. There was a whirr as the passenger window rolled down automatically.

'Get in,' came the familiar Geordie voice, sounding irritable.

Foster glanced back at his car left on a grass verge at the side of the road. Not the best place to leave it, but it would have to do. He strode forward, opened the door and climbed in. The interior was warm and smelled of leather and musk. Corrigan gave him a cursory look, said nothing, put the car back into gear and crunched slowly up the gravel drive.

He parked in front of the house. 'Been somewhere nice?' Foster asked.

Corrigan did not reply. He climbed out and Foster followed, all the way to the door of the house. He hadn't noticed it when he was here the week before, but four CCTV cameras were mounted at various points around the exterior. Turning the key tripped the alarm and, after opening the door, Corrigan went straight inside to a small panel to punch in a code. He was wearing a long blue woollen overcoat, which he unbuttoned. Underneath he was wearing a suit. 'I just need to go and disable the back-door alarm.'

'You've got this place locked tight,' Foster said.

'We don't make many friends wearing this uniform. You know that.' He disappeared along a small corridor. 'Follow me,' he said.

Foster went through to a huge kitchen diner, with tiled floors and a gigantic oak dining table. A pair of sliding doors looked out onto impenetrable darkness. Corrigan opened a small corner cupboard at the far end of the kitchen units and Foster heard him enter another code.

He then went to another cupboard, this time pulling out a bottle. 'Drink?'

'No thanks.'

'Suit yourself. He grabbed a small tumbler and put it on the counter, filling it halfway with whisky. 'Took the car to a civic reception. Never had a drink.' He picked up the glass and took a large sip. 'So, what's brought you back again? Not a word for nigh on twenty-five years, then I get two visits in little more than a week.'

Foster walked forward, put his hands on the back of a high-backed wooden chair that was set around the table. He could sense Corrigan's unease. He let him stew in it. The wall to his right was filled with pictures and paintings of pitmen and collieries, poignant images of men and a way of life long gone. Foster walked over, plunging his hands deep in his pockets, sensing Corrigan watching him closely. He scoured the pictures; grimy-faced men, with proud sculpted faces beneath the dirt, some hollow-eyed and exhausted from a day's work so tiring they could barely stand. *We have it easy; this was dirty, dangerous work, about the most difficult there could possibly be. These men risked their lives and broke their backs down in gloomy, claustrophobic caves, the weight of the North Sea pressing down on them, danger and death ever present colleagues.*

'Your dad worked down the pit, didn't he?' he asked Corrigan.

'Aye.' Foster heard him make his way over. He could smell the aftershave and the booze. 'That's him there.'

He pointed to a group of men, faces so black their eyes and teeth looked fluorescent, like some grim parody of a minstrel act. They were smiling all. The face he was pointing to belonged to a tall man, bearing the same aquiline nose and granite jaw.

'It was his job to bring down the shaft. When they finished hewing a seam, my old man and his mates came in to collapse it.'

'Dangerous work.'

'Probably the most dangerous there was. And that's saying something. It was proper work, though. He gave all he did down that mine to provide for us, in that hot, dark, stinking place, and he never moaned once. Because he was a working man. He sacrificed it all to give us a better life and we all had much better lives than him. It took it all out of him; his back was fucked, his ears were knackered, his lungs filled with dust and crap, but he never whinged a bit. It was what he had to do. I am eternally grateful for every backbreaking second he put in down there.'

Foster turned from the wall to face him. 'He was in the cave-in, wasn't he?' Corrigan said nothing. 'Your dad was one of the guys Chester dug out.'

Corrigan sighed. 'Kenny saved his life. Saved all of their lives.' He took a large sip of his Scotch, seeming to savour the taste of it on his tongue. 'There were five of them down there. They were collapsing the seam. They heard cracking, a terrible rumbling noise too. They knew what it meant only too well. The whole tunnel was coming down. They tried to run. Kenny was at the end. He could have got clear easy. But when he heard the noise of it coming down, he went back to try and get them and got swallowed up in it all.'

Foster said nothing. Just the thought of it, of being so far underground and to be buried alive, made a cold sweat slick his palms.

Jackie's eyes had narrowed, a film of moisture across the slits. 'Kenny had a broken arm, it was pitch black, and there was pile of rubble and rock and timber. But he worked himself free and then started digging for the others. Only the light on his helmet to guide him – that ran out after a few hours. It took him all day and night but he got all of them free. Then he kept them going for nearly seventy-two hours, talking to them, singing, reminiscing, doing all he could until the rescuers came. Some of them were in a bad way. My dad had concussion, his lung

DAN WADDELL

was punctured and he could barely breathe. Another of the fellers had a broken back.' He paused. 'Kenny Chester never bought another pint in his life. There were men queuing up to stand him one.'

'I bet they were,' Foster said. 'I bet people were willing to do all sorts of favours. You never told me all that at the time.'

'Was it relevant?'

'I don't know. Was it?'

Corrigan looked across at him coolly. He took a slow mouthful of his drink, let it roll around his tongue and mouth before swallowing. His shoulders were back, his chest out and his jaw jutting out defiantly.

'What's this about, Grant? Do you have something you want to tell me?'

'I know there was a girl at the scene, Jack.'

Foster let the words hang in the air. Corrigan continued to look at him in the same unflinching way. If anything, his defiance seemed to turn to disdain. He shook his head slowly. 'You wouldn't let it lie, would you?'

'The truth has a funny way of coming to the surface.'

'What truth would that be, then?'

'That Kenny Chester sexually abused a little girl. That he was about to do that again when he was interrupted by Dibb and Schofield. That if those facts had been known by a judge and jury, the case might have turned out very differently.'

'That's your opinion. There was no evidence he was sexually abusing anyone. They were going for a walk. All the evidence pointed to a violent and unprovoked attack on a defenceless old man. Or is it all right for two lads to set about an old fella like that, whatever the provocation?'

'No evidence? We never tried to get any. As for the two lads, you took both their first interviews. They said nothing about seeing any girl. Did they tell you, Jackie? Did they tell you and you told them to, or made them, shut their mouths? Or is it all right for a senior policeman to intimidate two terrified young lads like that?'

'They were fucking animals!' he shouted, cheeks turning puce. 'They didn't give a shit for that little girl. If there were any allegations to be made about Kenny Chester then they should have gone through the proper channels.'

'They were ten years old, for God's sake. And he set about her and them with a stick. Defenceless, my arse. What do you expect them to do?'

'Run away. If he were half the bogeyman they made out, they would've done. They buried him. You can't dress this up as something it wasn't, Grant.'

'And you can?! Make out this was some frail old man who got in the wrong place at the wrong time and was killed by two sadistic little ruffians? When the truth was he was an old pervert who was tormenting and abusing a bewildered little girl on a regular basis, and would have done again had these two not stepped in. They went too far, but we don't know what he said and did. But we know they were denied a chance of a decent defence, all because you wanted to step in and save the reputation of your dad's mate.'

Corrigan banged the table with his fist. 'He saved his life! I was six years old, man. Do you know what it was like, knowing your dad was out at work, and he might never come home? That siren went off to signal there had been an accident and you could hear the pit machinery come to a stop. The silence was awful. Your stomach lurched. It made you sick. And each time I thought it was my dad. One day it was. He didn't come out. We thought he was dead. Me mam cried her eyes out. My little sister walking around in a daze, asking where her daddy was. The agony of waiting, all gathered at the pithead. The looks of pity. Then the relief when they said they were alive. Learning that Kenny Chester had been responsible for saving him. You don't have any idea what that means.'

'It never gave him the freedom to do what he did to Cheryl Underwood. And it never gave you the right to decide how the law should be applied. Those lads never got a fair trial.'

'Well, they're dead now,' he said dryly, draining his glass. 'Case closed.'

'Yes, convenient that, isn't it?'

'What goes around …' he said with another shrug, then wandered back to the sideboard where he had left his whisky and poured another glass. 'You can show yourself out,' he added, not even looking up.

Foster didn't move.

'I have a panic alarm here, you know. One press and there'll be a squad of cars here.'

'Have a lot of enemies do you, Jackie.'

'A good copper can't help but make a few.'

'And a bad one can make a lot. Do you remember Harry Stokes?'

'The journalist?'

'The same. He called me earlier today, as I was setting off.'

'Friend of yours, is he? That's nice.'

Foster smiled. 'He told me that Dibb had been in touch with a newspaper before he died.'

'Good for him.'

'Apparently he was keen to talk about the murder of Kenny Chester.'

'Like I said, bully for him.' There was a look in his eye, hazy and unfocused, and his cheeks had a glow; perhaps the first sign of drunkenness.

'He said he wanted to tell the full truth about it.'

Corrigan laughed mirthlessly. 'I bet they loved that. A convicted killer wanting to sell his story.'

'He didn't want any money, Jackie. He was clear about that. He also said he was willing to come out into the open, to be photographed, to tell people about his new identity and take whatever conse-quences came his way. You see, his little girl had been picked up from school by someone and taken home.

She'd not walked there herself. She'd been taken. He'd got a phone call from someone telling him that. He was terrified.'

'Always prone to exaggeration, that lad.'

'The person who phoned had a lot of control over him. Had the ability to scare him shitless. So scared that he was willing to top himself in the most hideous way to protect his family. You see, his uncle had been killed within hours of his arrest. No one found the killer. Could have an effect on a ten-year-old, that. See what happens if you don't toe the line. Same with Schofield a few years later, an uncle of his was found beaten to death. No one found the killer. It was blamed on him being pissed and falling, even though he was riddled with injuries.'

'No idea what you're talking about.'

'I think you do. Around the same time as the uncle died, they were both moved to new prisons. Better conditions. I remember the outcry. Did you fix that too? Show them your power? Or remind them of it, more like?' He paused. Corrigan's face was growing steadily redder. His mentor; their tormentor. 'You made them think you were some kind of god. Or the devil, more like. They were terrified of you. You made them do what they could to keep you happy. And whenever you felt the lead was getting slack you gave it a pull. You heard Dibb was thinking of grassing you up, and you gave him a scare. Put the fear of the devil in him by threatening the person he loved most, his daughter. Then you decided to go all the way and use the hold you had over him to force him into setting himself alight. What were you going to do if he didn't, Jackie? Kill a little girl?'

'The paper didn't use the story, did they? It's all fantasy, Grant.' There was a slur to his voice now.

'It's not, Jackie. To save the reputation of a dirty old man, you controlled, ruined and destroyed the lives of those two lads. Then to save your own reputation you had them killed.'

Corrigan's glassy eyes stared at him, though it was difficult to tell. 'What you gonna do, Grant? Take me in? You'll need more than your theories.'

He shook his head slowly. 'Just tell me who you got to kill Schofield. Who was the girl?'

Corrigan remained silent.

'Is it this housekeeper of yours? How old is she?'

'Jealous, Grant?'

'How well do you know her?'

'Well enough. I knew her dad. Her granddad too.' There was a leer on his face. 'Helen has turned out to be immensely helpful.'

Helen Chester? For a few seconds Foster was speechless. Her father had said she had nothing to do with them because they were lost in the past. 'Grateful enough to kill?'

'I'm not letting you get her, Grant. I look after her.'

'The same way you looked after Dibb and Schofield?'

'Aye. I would have done if they'd kept their mouths shut.'

He could see what had happened. Jackie went around each year. He saw her grow up. He didn't want to think when he had first approached her. 'She got their new identities, didn't she? You didn't want your prints on the trail. But you knew where she should go. Willing to let her sleep with someone else in order to get it.'

'I'm an old man, Grant. You need to give these young lasses their head. I'm not so proud that I don't know she needs to have a bit of fun every now and then.'

Foster shook his head at the whole sordid saga. 'Where's she now?'

'Out. I don't own her.'

'No. I think that's clear.'

His eyes narrowed. 'Why d'you say that?'

'Because she either still has it or has sold or given away the list their names were on. Not just Dibb and Schofield, but all the others. Innocent people, many of them. But now their new identities are compromised, their lives in danger, all because your young girlfriend decided to make a few bob. It's all over the Internet.'

The colour had started to drain from his cheeks. 'What do you mean?' Foster could see him trying to evaluate this revelation, see where it would leave him and his precious reputation. 'I don't know…'

'I need to find her and I need to find her now. Tell me where she is?'

'I don't know.' His voice was flat, diminished.

'Where is she?'

'She has a place of her own too.'

'Where?'

Jackie didn't speak, just took another slug of his Scotch. His hand was shaking.

'Will she be coming back here?' Foster

'Not tonight, no.' His voice had become small, almost withered. 'We had a row...'

Foster turned to leave mid-sentence, unable to be bear breathing the same air as him. He hustled out of the door and away from that tawdry, corrupt old man as fast he could manage.

He didn't look back.

32

Foster couldn't believe the news about Helen Chester and Jackie. How had this seedy, murderous union come into being? Jackie Corrigan was many things – corrupt, arrogant – but he'd never had him down as a dirty old bastard. Maybe it was not as sordid as he imagined; wealthy, well-connected Jackie made a good sugar daddy. *Scratch that thought*, he told himself. It made his stomach turn to think of any man dating a woman old enough be her father, never mind grandfather.

He put in a call to the office in London and got an address, on the outskirts of Morpeth. Her dad had told him she lived in the city. It was the basement of a Victorian house sectioned into four flats. Foster pressed the doorbell repeatedly, with no luck. All the lights inside were off. He would have to wait.

As he turned to go back, a car pulled up on the road above, the engine running: a taxi. He heard a woman's voice and the slam of a car door; then the outline of a figure appeared in the gloom at the top of the stone steps. It stopped dead when it saw him looming at the door.

'Who are you?' The voice was soft, wary, with a subtle accent.

'Detective Inspector Grant Foster,' he said.

'Hello, Mr Detective.'

Foster had to fight to suppress a smile. It was how Helen had referred to him as a girl during the investigation. She had been four at the time.

'You remember me.'

She breezed past him to the front door, trailing a scent of perfume and cigarette smoke.

'Well, it was a pretty pivotal moment in a young girl's life,' she said as she put her key in the door.

A security light came on above the door, casting a harsh light on them both. Foster suffered most in its glare. Helen was revealed to be the same blue-eyed blonde she had been as a child, though she looked different enough not to be recognisable as the slightly chubby little thing with a bewildered look on her face who had padded quietly around the house while her parents cried and shouted, and detectives and neighbours spoke in hushed, enigmatic whispers. There was no way Schofield or Dibb might have recognized her, even if they'd known her by sight back in Mackington before the murder. Not that ten-year-old boys paid much attention to six-year-old girls.

Now she was slim and elegant and beautiful: he wondered instantly how a woman of her looks and youth could bring herself to sleep with an old man like Corrigan.

'You'd better come in, then,' she said as she opened the door. He followed her into a narrow hall. She dropped the bag to the floor and carried on down the passageway which opened into a large open-plan kitchen. He saw her clothes, her jewellery, and wondered how much of his ample pension Jackie lavished on her.

'Tea?' she asked, holding up the kettle. Inside, illuminated by the lights, she looked even better.

'No thanks,' he said.

She shrugged. 'I've got something stronger if you'd like.'

'I'm fine.'

He sensed she was pretty well-refreshed. 'Suit yourself, I'm going to have a glass of wine.' She went the fridge, found a bottle of white wine and poured liberally into a bulb-shaped glass.

There was silence as her hand ran up and down the stem. 'How can I help you, Detective?' she asked, looking over the top of her wine glass as she raised it to her mouth.

'Do you know why I might be here?' he asked.

'I love your voice. Has anyone told you it's very sensual?'

'Not recently, no,' he replied. The last time anyone had mentioned his voice, it was the woman at the scene of a crime who said he sounded like he had swallowed Orson Welles. He preferred sensual.

She was drunk. Foster had not been out of the game for so long that he didn't realise when he was being flirted with.

'But in answer to your question, yes I do,' she said.

'Really? Do you want to tell me?'

'I suppose you're here to arrest me for murder?'

'Which murder would that be?'

She smiled and nodded, then unclasped her earrings and laid them on the counter. 'I see. We're playing that game, are we? Have you been to see Jackie?'

'Maybe. Why did you do it, Helen?'

'Do what?'

'Enough of the cryptic shit. This isn't a game. Craig Schofield. You poisoned him.' Looking at her, he could see a withdrawn loser like Schofield never stood a chance.

She said nothing, just stared into her glass. 'Oh, let me see, ' she said. The softness, any attempt to disarm him, had gone. 'Perhaps because, you know, he murdered my grandfather in a hideously brutal manner.'

'I paid a visit to your mum and dad.'

The faintest curl of her lip appeared when he mentioned her parents.

'They said you have little to do with them any more,' he added.

She shrugged. 'People outgrow their backgrounds.'

'They told me you couldn't bear to be around them because you think they're obsessed with Kenny's killing, can't get over it, living in the past.'

She looked at him, eyes burning. 'Well they fucking well are,' she said. 'They live in that house, the same one Granddad lived in, as if it was some kind of shrine to his memory, in the same village, with the same reminders of what happened there. It's pathetic.'

'And you've moved on?'

The anger returned. 'There's a big difference between living in the past, frozen in time, and actually doing something about it, so people and generations to come can live their lives. That killing has hung over my family like a cloud, a horrible miasma that refuses to lift. None of them were going to do anything about it.'

'So you did?'

She shrugged once more. 'As I said, it was a pretty pivotal moment in my life. I've had to endure it for so long and I was fed up of being yet another victim of those two little bastards.'

'And Jackie? Where did he come in?'

There was a gleam of amusement in her eye. 'You think I've been shagging him, don't you?

Foster was momentarily taken aback. Helen shook her head. 'Men are all the same.'

'It was purely platonic?'

She scrunched up her face. 'Purely necessary. He could help me. He was willing to help. Yeuch,' she added, sticking out her tongue. 'I'd do many things but I wouldn't do that. Jackie wanted them dead; so did I. Call it a meeting of minds, a collaboration. He knew my granddad; his father worked with him in the pit.' She flicked a strand of hair casually from her brow. 'Granddad saved his dad's life after a cave-in.'

'I know.'

'Then you'll understand why he was as keen as I was to see those two rot in hell.'

'You're willing to go to prison for this?'

Once again, the shrug. 'If necessary. But Jackie will protect me. I know he will.'

'I wouldn't bank on that,' Foster said.

'You really don't know him, do you?'

'Oh, I do. Crooked, corrupt, duplicitous, criminal...I could go on?'

Her eyes narrowed. 'You and him had a falling out, didn't you? Was it tough in his shadow?'

Foster said nothing.

Any hint of flirtation had now gone. She picked her phone up off the counter in front of her, and without taking her eyes off Foster started dialling a number.

As the phone rang and rang without answer, her expression changed from defiance to something less certain. 'Maybe asleep,' she said, and dialled once more. When it rang out again she looked uncertain. 'Must be a deep sleep,' she muttered, glancing across at a digital clock on top of the cooker. It read 10.15.

'Very deep,' he agreed.

'I'm not saying any more until I speak to Jackie or a lawyer,' she said, folding her arms across her chest.

'That won't be necessary,' he explained.

'I don't understand. You're accusing me of murder?'

'Not yet I'm not. You're the only one that's talking about murder. That can wait. For now.'

'Then what are you here for?'

'The memory stick, Helen. The one you screwed that poor sap at the Home Office to obtain.'

The smirk appeared on her face. 'You know about that!' She shook her head. 'God, he was dumb. Beautiful, granted, and very, very eager to please, but very dumb.'

'What did you do with the stick, Helen?'

'I passed it on to Jackie, or at least the information we needed about Dibb and Schofield. We didn't want there being a trail back to him, or to implicate any of his former colleagues or friends.' She paused. 'He cared about the people he worked with. The ones he thought anything of.'

He ignored the slight. 'Then what? When you had what you needed?'

'I sold it.'

'You sold it?'

'I worked hard to get hold of it. There was a market there for the information. It seemed a question of basic capitalism. It was rude not to. The people on it were all murderers. Why should they be protected?'

'They weren't all murderers, Helen.'

Her face didn't change, save a flicker of doubt. 'What do you mean?'

'Exactly what I said. They weren't all murderers. Some are completely innocent people who had to have their identities changed for their own protection. But they didn't do anything wrong.'

The colour was bleeding from her face, and with it her fortitude. Her eyes cast about anxiously as she tried to comprehend what she had done.

'But Jackie said . . .'

'Tell me who you sold it to, Helen.'

'There was more than one,' she stuttered. 'It was online . . . I really need to speak to Jackie.'

'In a minute. Who did you sell it to?'

'I don't have names.'

'What do you have?'

'Online identities, avatars, that sort of thing.'

'I'll need them.' She looked unsure. 'Helen, if you don't get me that information there is a very real chance that innocent people will die and all this will begin to look even worse.'

Her eyes had glazed over. 'Give me a second.' She went down the hall to a room, flicked on the light. Foster paced back and forth across the kitchen, occasionally glancing down the hall. The sound of fingers on keyboard offered reassurance. A few minutes later she returned with a scrap of paper. She tossed it on to the table in front of him. There were three names. It was a start.

'We'll need to take the computer,' he said. 'These will mean nothing without it.'

'I'd better call Jackie,' she said flatly, walking to the telephone. 'He'll know what to do.'

'He won't, Helen.'

She turned around quickly. 'Why?'

'He knew the real truth about that day, Helen. It doesn't surprise me in the least that he didn't tell you.'

He felt sorry for her. She thought she had found common cause with Jackie. But he had used her.

'Tell me what?'

'Do you know Cheryl Underwood?'

'Aye. Her granddad was friends with mine.'

He took a deep breath. 'Your granddad used to sexually abuse her.'

She said nothing, but he could see the anger welling in her. He ploughed on. 'On that day, he was taking Cheryl to the Dean to do what he had done many times before. Dibb and Schofield came across them. Cheryl blurted out what he was doing. He went after her with his stick. They came to her defence. So he went after them with his stick. So they turned on him.'

Her eyes misted with tears. Her head shaking in disbelief. He continued.

'Jackie put the frighteners on them straight away to protect Kenny's reputation, paying back the favour he'd had done for him. He screwed the living shit out of those two boys, made them believe he was God. There was no escape. I didn't see it then. But I see it clearly now. Their trial and their convictions were abominations. Their murders, too; Jackie duped you,

Helen. You should've been able to deal with all this years ago.'

How she was supposed to have dealt with it, he didn't say, because he didn't know. What he did know was that if the truth of her grandfather had been revealed at the time, the two boys given a fair hearing, and due process followed, then the open wound of the past two decades might have healed.

Helen looked shattered, as if she had been dropped from a height and her body broken. Her head was slumped forwards, her shoulders sunken.

'I don't believe you,' she said in a withered voice. 'He never touched us. Jackie would never...'

'Jackie lied, Helen.' He let the words sink in. Her shoulders slumped further and her head was almost on the counter.

He sat and he waited. Seconds ticked by, perhaps minutes. If she had any questions he wanted to be able to answer them. She deserved that much. Helen Chester was as much the victim of this tragic episode as anyone else. The murder in her heart was born of a lie. Too many people had been tainted by the events of that summer's day.

She lifted her head. Instead of desolation, there was anger. He could tell from the way her eyes burned it was directed at him. He saw a glint of steel. A knife. She rushed towards him.

There was time for him to push his hands forward to meet the force of her charge. He felt something brush his arm, but he was able to grab her arms.

She was shaking her head, screaming, demented. He managed to grip tighter, pull her arms together in front of them both. Then she screamed in pain under the pressure and the knife fell to the floor. She fell forward to her knees and he picked the weapon up, only then seeing his sleeve was torn and blood was beginning to pour out.

'Thanks for that,' he said. Another scar to add to the collection.

On the floor, she had dissolved into tears, her shoulders heaving. He grabbed his phone and called for assistance, or whatever he could get from the local cops. He couldn't bet against another attack.

'But he never touched me,' she sobbed.

He sat down beside her on the floor and put the arm that wasn't cut around her shoulder.

33

Since his aborted drink with Henry Mann, Nigel had been contemplating what he had been told. He detested secrecy of any kind. Even the concept of protecting and archiving official documents for fifty years offended him, even when there was good reason for it. He believed the truth should be out there and the public had a right to know. If politicians and civil servants knew their decisions and motives would come under immediate scrutiny, they might be inclined to act with more honesty.

But here he was being forced to live with the idea of his own past being concealed. He thought of the ongoing puzzle of Susan Navin-Jones and why his parents' identity was a state secret. He had managed to dig out back copies of the civil service list, the imperial calendar, and Navin-Jones was there, her department given as National Security. This only increased his curiosity. Were his parents spies of some kind? That was as far as the official paper trail would take him. There was no mention of Navin-Jones in files in the National Archives, and while he had submitted a request for any relevant documents under the Freedom of Information Act he knew it would take months and even then was unlikely to be granted.

He kept trying to think of new ideas to pursue the elusive Miss Navin-Jones and came up empty, knowing that the harder he tried to find inspiration, the less likely it was to strike. Eventually, as the day gave way to dusk, he gave up and fixed himself something to eat for the first time since breakfast.

The buzzer to his door went as he grated some cheese for his toast.

'Yes,' he said, picking up the receiver.

'Delivery for flat seven.' The voice was accented, European.

'I'm on my way down,' Nigel said. 'Leave it at the door.'

Nigel wandered down the stairs and tried to remember what he might have ordered recently. Probably a book.

Halfway down the second flight of stairs he heard the door open and close. Nigel peered over the edge of the stairwell. He could hear footsteps coming up the concrete steps.

'The door was open,' he heard the accented voice say. 'It's heavy so I'll carry it up for you.'

'OK,' he said. 'Need a hand?'

'No. Should be OK,' the voice came back. Definitely Germanic.

Nigel went and propped the door of the flat open, as the delivery man rounded the final flight of stairs leading to his door. He was thin, wiry and tall, and older than Nigel had expected. Mid-fifties, he guessed. Yet the box, which the man cradled in both arms, did not appear that big.

'Evening,' Nigel said. 'Let me...' He moved towards him with his arms outstretched.

'No,' the man replied. 'It's OK. It's my job.'

Nigel wondered briefly whether a middle-aged man should be lugging boxes up and down stairs for a living.

'Just pop it on the floor through there,' he said with a smile as the delivery man crossed his threshold, rustling in his trouser pocket for some change to offer as a tip. He wouldn't normally, but this was service above and beyond the call of duty. London flat-dwellers were used to having delivery men turn and run screaming at the sight of stairs, while this chap had put his vertebrae at risk without complaint.

The man bent down and slowly laid the box on the floor, then stood and wiped his brow. He had thick grey hair but his eyebrows were still dark, which gave him a look of intensity. The face was pale and his skin stretched taut across it, yet the eyes crackled with life.

'Do I need to sign?'

'Give me a second,' the man said. He was wearing a set of blue overalls. Nigel wondered which mail services used that as a uniform. None he recognised. The delivery man reached into a deep pocket to find a pen.

Instead he produced a gun.

Nigel spent a few witless seconds wondering what that had to do with the delivery. Then his heart froze.

'I think you'd better sit down,' the gunman said, cracking a thin smile, though his eyes danced with relish.

34

Without even taking his coat off, Foster headed for the cellar and a good bottle of red. He brought it up to the kitchen, took the cork out and poured a glass without even letting it breathe. Then he took a seat at his kitchen table and took a long deep slug of the wine.

After Helen Chester had been taken away, Foster had had his wounded arm stitched and then given a statement to Derek Whelan as a yellow-tinged dawn rose over the city. The detective said nothing as Foster recounted all that he knew, about Helen, about Kenny Chester, Cheryl Underwood and Jackie. When Foster had finished, Whelan rose from his chair.

'No questions?' Foster asked

Whelan sighed. 'Thousands,' he said wearily. 'But none for you.'

Foster nodded. 'I idolised him too. Once.'

Whelan grimaced. 'I've got somewhere to go.' He turned to leave, just as another detective burst into the room.

The detective looked anxious, agitated. He glanced warily at Foster.

'It's OK, whatever it is, you can say it,' Whelan told him.

'Jackie Corrigan has killed himself, sir. Got a call from someone saying they heard a gunshot this morning. Officer attending found him dead.'

Whelan dropped his head and put his hands on his hips.

Figures, thought Foster. That coward was never going to face the consequences.

'I'm off back to London,' he said. 'You know where I am if you need me.'

He walked to the door.

'Wait a minute,' Whelan said.

What now? Foster thought.

'Safe journey,' Whelan said.

Foster nodded.

'And good work.'

There was a pause. 'Good luck with it all,' he told Whelan.

Then he got in his car, and drove back to London, stopping only to load up on coffee.

Now he was seeking a different form of fuel. It had been a five-hour drive; he was exhausted. He was going to sink this bottle and then sleep for as long as he could.

His phone rang before he took his second sip. He was tempted to ignore it, but it was Heather.

'Are you still up North?' She sounded panicked.

'No, I'm back in London. What's wrong?'

'I need you here now,' she gasped.

35

The man stalked around the flat, as if on the hunt, while Nigel sat in the chair, his hands and feet bound. His mouth was dry and he felt sick to the pit of his gut. The nausea he attributed to excitement as well as fear. At least now the riddle of his past might be solved.

'Who are you?' he asked the man, who was peering from the lounge window across the rooftops. Since he'd tied Nigel to the chair he'd not uttered a single word.

Nigel asked again who he was.

'Shut up,' the man replied finally. 'Unless you want me to gag you also?'

Nigel gave a cursory struggle to test the tightness of his bonds. Enough to realise it would take a great effort to free himself. How had it come to this? It was six in the evening; depending on what had developed at work, Heather might be back in an hour or five hours. He pictured her walking in and shuddered. What would this lunatic do? What did he want?

He stayed silent while his captor continued to patrol the flat. Once he was satisfied that there were no hidden mysteries in the cupboards, or behind the curtains, he sat on the sofa, next to where the box he had brought in had been placed. Nigel had assumed it was a dummy, but the careful way he handled it suggested otherwise. He slid a finger between the folds to release the loose binds, and delicately pulled back either side of the lid. From where he sat, Nigel could see some kind of packaging that looked like bubble wrap. The man reached in with utmost care, as if the wrong move might give him a shock. Then he pulled out a long black container, the same size as a violin case but thinner. He put it on his lap and flipped open two metal catches.

It was some kind of sniper rifle, with a telescopic sight. Had he been checking the windows for vantage points? Was he going to start taking potshots at the outside world? Nigel's flat was at the rear of the building, facing away from the crowds of Shepherd's Bush where he would be able to cause mayhem. All you could see from Nigel's windows were a few side streets and the backs of endless terraced houses. Hardly rich pickings.

Once assembled, the man got up and laid the gun down on the sofa as gently as if it was a newborn. Then he returned to the box, knelt down and pulled out some more wrapping and padding. He leant in and played with something. Other than a glimpse of another black case, Nigel couldn't see what he was fiddling with. Some sort of radio or communications system. He could see what he thought was the top of some kind of clock. Before he could glean any more clues, the man stood up and closed the lid with extreme circumspection.

He seemed reassured. After wiping his palms on the front of his overalls, he looked over at Nigel.

'I don't live alone,' Nigel said, almost reflexively.

'I can see that.'

'You can?'

'For sure. There is a woman's hand on this flat, that much is clear. Your wife?'

'Girlfriend.'

'The policewoman?'

'You know her?'

'I know you have a policewoman as a girlfriend. I know she is at work.' His voice was bloodless, mechanical, almost entirely stripped of colour and emotion.

'How?'

'For a few days, I have watched.' He went over to the phone and picked it up.

'What is her number?'

'I don't know.'

The man sighed. 'What is her number? Please, it is advisable you do as you are told if you want to live.'

Even though this confirmed that Nigel's life was in danger, he was surprised how calm he felt. As if he was detached in some way, a spectator watching events unfold rather than experiencing them directly.

'I don't know. I don't know anyone's number. They're either in my address book or the contacts of my mobile phone.'

Another sigh, more exasperated this time. 'Where is your mobile phone?'

'Good question,' Nigel said. He thought. 'The holdall that's by the front door, it might be in the side pocket. I think.'

He left the room. Nigel could hear the zip being released, the sound of rustling, then another zip being pulled. He returned with the phone.

'It's under "Heather",' Nigel said.

The man poked at the phone suspiciously, as if unfamiliar with its technology. Eventually he located the number and then picked up the home phone.

Before he dialled, he looked at Nigel. 'You're going to tell her you're being held here. That the person who is holding you wants to see your father. That the person holding you is well armed. That if your father does not present himself here by seven a.m. next morning, you will be shot. That if they do anything to storm the building or any such act of rescue, there is a bomb of sufficient power to raze this building to the ground, killing everyone in it.'

He started to dial the number. *A bomb? Fucking hell*, Nigel thought. But the phone was ringing in his ear, and there wasn't much chance to cogitate over what he had just been told.

A few rings and there was Heather's breezy voice. A few seconds of ignorant bliss for her before life as they knew it changed, possibly irrevocably.

'Yes, babe,' she said.

'Er, hello,' he stuttered.

She sensed a problem immediately. 'What's wrong?'

'Nothing,' he said. 'Actually, that's a lie.'

'Don't be cryptic, Nigel.'

'I'm being held hostage.'

A silence. 'Is this a joke?'

'No. It certainly isn't.'

'OK.' Heather's voice, her whole attitude changed in those two syllables. 'Does the person holding you know you've called me?'

'Yes. He's holding the phone.'

She didn't pause a beat. 'Where are you being held?'

'At my flat.'

'What does he want?'

'My father.'

'Your father? Your adopted father?'

'No. He wants my real father, I think.' He glanced up at the man holding the phone. He nodded confirmation.

'Do you know who your real father is?'

'No, I don't know who my real father is,' he repeated, for his captor's benefit.

'OK. Is he issuing any other demands, any other threats or conditions?'

'Yes. He has a gun. Two guns, actually. He says that if my father isn't here by seven a.m. tomorrow morning... then I will be shot.'

'OK,' she said simply.

'He also says he has a bomb. That if you try and do anything to free me, like storm the building, then he will blow it all up.'

This time she remained silent. 'Have you seen a bomb?'

'There's a box...'

'That's OK. Is he asking for anything else?'

The man took away the phone. 'That is all you need to know. By seven tomorrow morning or he dies. You will keep everyone in the building. If I see them being evacuated, I will detonate the bomb.'

He ended the call and for a second Nigel felt as helpless and bewildered as he ever had done in his life. Then anger kicked in. 'I don't know who my fucking real father is. How is he supposed to make it here for seven o' fucking clock in the morning if I don't know who the fuck he is!?'

The man ignored his anger. 'Someone knows. They are the police. They will be able to find out. We have given them enough time. Don't worry yourself so much. This will be a long night. It's advisable to save some energy.'

He turned away and went to the window. Nigel glanced at the clock. He had perhaps twelve hours to live. Then he tried to picture what Heather would do, who she would call. Foster. How would they track down his father? He wanted to call back and pass on Henry Mann's name. He might know more. But would they be willing to give the information up? He wasn't sure who this guy was. Was it the policy of the security services to negotiate with kidnappers? Maybe his death would pale into insignificance when compared to the consequences of giving up his father. Whoever he might be. For God's sake, he didn't even know if he was alive.

'Is it true that you don't know who your father is?' the man said, still looking from the window.

'Cast-iron truth,' he said. 'Do you know him?'

He laughed and shook his head. 'I will ask the questions. Do you mean to tell me he has not been to see you or meet you since you were young?' He closed the curtains and turned to face Nigel.

'Never.'

Again, the shake of the head and mirthless laugh. 'Typical,' he muttered. Then he muttered a word in another language Nigel didn't understand, but which confirmed his Germanic roots.

'So you can see, asking my father to be here by the morning is slightly complicated because I don't know who he is.'

'He will be here. There is enough time.'

'Why are you so confident? I don't even know whether he's alive or dead.'

'He is alive, I feel sure.'

There was a lengthy pause.

'I am going to turn off the lights in here now,' he said. 'I will leave the hall light on and I have a torch, so we will not be in total darkness.'

He flicked the switch and light dimmed to almost blackness.

'Who are you?' Nigel asked once more. 'Seeing as you're threatening to kill me, I feel I deserve some kind of explanation.'

He held his breath in the silence that followed. Eventually the man's robotic voice spoke. 'OK. This much you do need to know. Are you sitting comfortably?'

'Actually, I need the loo.'

The man laughed. 'I will need to accompany you and keep your hands tied. I hope you are not shy. Then we will talk.'

36

Foster flashed his badge and made his way across Shepherd's Bush Green – now deserted because the area had been evacuated. He headed towards the side street that led to Barnes' building. Armed coppers stood idly by. Then he saw Heather cast in the amber glow of a street light. *Poor kid*, he thought.

She saw him coming and instinctively flung her arms around him. This probably wasn't the best place for her, he thought. Decisions would have to be made in the best interest of the many and not the few. Ones she might not agree with, which could cause her great distress. But he didn't have the heart to tell her to go.

She ended her bear hug. 'Sorry,' she said.

'What for?' He placed a hand on her shoulder. 'How you holding up?'

'Not great. We're not getting anywhere, Grant. Nigel doesn't know who his father is and trying to find someone who does is impossible.'

Brian Harris had come across to join them, nodding at Foster. 'The place is surrounded?'

'Yes,' Harris said. 'As discreetly as possible. Most people evacuated from the houses nearby, apart from a couple of old dears who are reluctant to go.'

'And Barnes' building?'

'We're working on it. We've managed to stop people going in.'

'Any chance of getting a shot off through the window?'

'We've got shooters at pretty much every vantage point. We can see his window. The curtains are closed. Lights are off. It's too tricky.'

'Do we know what sort of detonator he has?'

A slow shake of the head. 'We're not even sure there is a detonator. It could all be colossal scaremongering. A hoax, just to get what he wants. But, of course, a risk we can't take. Bomb squad are here. They're discussing using an EMP style device that might be able to jam the detonator remotely. We don't know how sophisticated this one is. It might not be possible to jam it.'

'Have you spoken to Adrian Gorton?' Foster asked.

'He's on the case.' He paused. 'German security forces have positively identified the guy as Thomas Dreher.'

Somewhere in the back of Foster's mind was a flicker of recognition at the name. 'Who's he?'

'A former terrorist. Or at least, not so former. Do you remember the League of Liberation?'

'German communists from the 1970s?'

'Radicals, communists, call them what you like. Dreher was their leader.'

'Jesus,' Foster whispered. One thing was certain – he'd know how to build a bomb. Neither would he be scared to use it.

'I've never heard of them,' Heather said.

Foster filled her in. 'This was the 1970s, the height of European terrorism, when every Tom, Seamus and Tarquin was taking up arms against the state. The Liberation League were brash and flash, wore sharp haircuts and black, and there were women involved, good-looking ones too. So they got a better press than scowling Irish men in platform shoes and big sideburns. The LL carried out a few spectaculars in the 70s, usually banks. Said they were reclaiming the finances of the nation for the people. Steal from the rich and give to the poor. Rudolph Hood. Except they missed out the giving it to the poor bit. Gained a lot of notoriety. Then they all got caught. Presumably Dreher was released.'

'Two weeks ago. He'd spent thirty years inside,' Harris confirmed. 'But what the hell does it have to do with Barnes' father?'

'What's the plan?'

'We keep trying to find the father. In the meantime, we get as many people out of that building as possible.'

'And if we don't find the father?'

Foster didn't need an answer to that. He could tell from Harris' face that it wasn't something Heather needed to hear.

37

The man had lit a cigarette. Nigel could see the tip glow and swell in the dark with each deep drag.

'There's an ashtray in the kitchen ...'

'My name is Thomas Dreher,' the man replied, ignoring him.

'German?'

'Yes. Though the German state is not one I recognise. I pay no heed to the propaganda of nationhood. It's all just a method of control by those in power, who wish to keep power.'

'How did you know my father?'

'I met him for the first time in 1974, in Berlin. He was a good socialist. Or so he seemed.'

'He was German too?'

He could see the cigarette tip shake in the dark. Laughter? 'No. He was English. Very English. He told me he couldn't bear this place any more. What was the word he used now? Yes, he said it was "drab". It was old, it was tired, and he wanted to leave. West Germany was a vibrant place. There were ideas and passion. It was on the border of east and west. This was the height of the Cold War and it was felt things could go either way. We wanted it to go the way of the east. His mother was also German, so he could speak the language. He said it was home.'

My grandmother was German, Nigel thought. The blank page was starting to fill.

Another drag; this time Dreher's face, creased and wrinkled from years of smoking, lit up briefly.

'What is his name?'

'Roland. Roland Wilkinson. That was his real name. I knew him as Kris Bargeld'

Nigel repeated the words 'Roland Wilkinson' time after time in his mind, rolling them around, seeing how they felt. His father's identity.

'You knew him well?'

'We were like brothers. More so, because we fought side by side, unlike most brothers.'

'You fought?'

'Yes. We were in a war. A war with the German state, its economic and political institutions.'

'I don't understand.' Nigel thought he knew his history, but he couldn't recall any German civil wars or insurrections.

'We were called the Befreien Klasse. The Liberation League as the English called us.' He stopped to take another drag. Nigel recalled a few newspaper articles and news reports about the group he mentioned. Beyond a fleeting recognition of their name, he couldn't remember any other details. 'In 1974 we took up arms against the state. Your father was one of us.'

He inhaled again. He sucked in cigarette smoke like a choking man grabbed oxygen. 'As was your mother.'

'My mother?'

'Christa Andregen. We met as students. I introduced her to your father. She was impossibly beautiful. They were very much in love.'

So many revelations that Nigel felt his brain might burst. 'She was in the same gang?'

'The BK, yes. There were ten of us. We robbed seven banks.' His flat voice rose slightly as if swelled by pride. 'We were the most wanted people in Germany. Perhaps even Europe. Yet they couldn't find us or catch us. For two years we twisted and tied them in knots. Until...'

'Until what?'

'Until the day your father betrayed us.'

'How...?'

'A bank job. In Magdeburg. We planned it like all the others. Nothing left to chance. But they were waiting for us. We were trapped, fish in a barrel. I saw your father walk away to the other side while we came under a hail of bullets. He walked away from your mother, from me, from the group. Your mother was shot and killed. So were seven others, including my partner, Elsa. Your mother was lucky. One bullet through the brain and instant death. Elsa, not so. I saw her writhe in agony, shot in the gut. Her blood spilling on the floor, her life bleeding out of her drop by drop, in the most excruciating pain. I found out later the pathologist said she was ten weeks pregnant.

I was shot four times but I was the unlucky one. I survived. How I wished I had died. Thirty years in jail. There was not a day when I haven't thought of the revenge I will get if I ever see your father again.'

'Where was I? During the robbery.'

'With friends. We had a commune of sorts. Not everyone took part in the actions. You were six months old.'

'You said my father walked away.'

Dreher nodded. 'Uh huh. Just like that. He had told the police where we would be and what time, the amount of guns we would have. Once we were in place and were about to carry out the job, he walked away.'

Nigel had learned that his father was an anarchist double agent, his mother a radical who had left him behind to rob a bank and was shot and killed because of his father's betrayal.

This was going to take a therapist some time to unpick.

'How did you find me?'

'As I said, I know he came back here. I was also sure that you would be given new identities.'

'You got hold of the list.'

'I did. An old comrade said some information was for sale on the Internet. I needed help. Thirty-five years in jail and much has changed. I knew about the Internet but I didn't know it would be quite so useful. With his help I enquired. It turned out the information I wanted was there. So I came here. It took me a while to work out who was the right one, but as soon as I saw you I knew you were the one. I have to say, you look a great deal like he used to.'

'What will you do to my father if he comes here?'

'There is no "if". He will come.'

'You seem so sure. You've just told me he was willing to see his wife killed.'

'This is different. He will come.'

'Why is it different? He's shown no interest in me all my life. Why would that change?'

'Because you are innocent. Have no fear, he will come.'

'And when he does?'

'I will kill him.'

A tangle of different emotions clashed in Nigel's mind. He did not want to die. Yet he did not want his father, a man he had never met, to come through that door and be killed because of him. There would be no guarantee that Dreher wouldn't turn the gun on Nigel too after that.

'Can I make a phone call?' he asked Dreher.

'No,' came the reply. 'Please don't get any thoughts of noble self-sacrifice. If your father doesn't come, then I will kill you. If he does come, only he dies.'

'And the bomb?'

'That is to ensure the police don't act rashly. If your father comes, no one will be blown up.'

'But you will be killed too, then.'

'So be it. I've spent thirty-five years thinking of revenge. Your father's death is the last thing I desire. Then I am done. I am prepared to die.'

38

An incident room of sorts had been set up in a coffee shop on one side of the Green. It was almost three in the morning. Usually there would be a steady flow of traffic – Foster had once had a flat near the Bush and used to think the distant drone of the traffic leading out to the Westway sounded like a river – but because of the cordon, it had all been diverted. Outside, the air was unseasonally balmy, not a cough of wind.

Harris had gone to take a phone call. The Home Secretary had finally been tracked down and briefed. They hoped now she had her teeth into it the rest would come away in chunks. Yet there was still no news on whether this bloke had even been located. Foster glanced at his watch. He was doing it every few minutes. Soon, as time cascaded away, that would become a few seconds. In a corner, Heather sat nursing a coffee, staring into space. There was little he could think to say to her that didn't sound trite and hollow.

In front of him were files and clippings about Thomas Dreher. He was no back-garden anarchist but a fully fledged terrorist. He'd masterminded seven successful bank robberies. He had killed a security guard in cold blood who'd had the temerity to try and resist. The LL had burned down various safe houses to destroy evidence once they felt their cover had been blown, not caring whether nearby buildings were damaged or people injured. An eleven-year-old girl had suffered serious burns in one of the blazes. They were experienced in using explosives in their missions. Once, they had attached a bomb to the car of a right-wing politician, which exploded before he could get in. There had been enough power in the blast to blow the car forty feet down the road. It might have been wired badly, but it was one hell of a homemade device. Did he have a bomb? Who knew for certain, but his record guaranteed no one was going to take any risks.

He had been sentenced to life, the only one of the gang captured alive. Another member was reported to have got away before the robbery was busted. He was never found. Foster knew he held the key to why Dreher was now here.

The escapee was called Kris Bargeld. Very little had been known about him. Some reports said he had committed suicide, but there had been a lacklustre effort to find him. Once Dreher was sent down the case was closed, the Liberation League banished to a small footnote in history. Foster would bet any money that the guy who escaped was a double agent, and that he was Barnes' father. It would explain why Nigel's identity had been changed, in case any followers out there slipped through the net and came looking for him to try and get to his father. Just like Dreher had.

Dreher did not turn up to his first parole meeting after release and a feeble manhunt was launched. They must have believed an ageing ex-commie was the least of their worries. So far, they had not been able to piece together any of Dreher's movement since he arrived in London, or when that might have been, only some grainy CCTV footage of him arriving at Barnes' block of flats.

Harris returned. He looked energised.

'He's coming.'

'Barnes' dad?'

He could sense Heather's concentration click back into the here and now.

'When?' she asked.

'Soon.'

There was an awkward silence. Harris looked at Foster, then glanced from the corner of his eye at Heather. He got the message.

'Heather, we need to chat in private.'

'Of course,' she said softly. 'I need some air anyway.'

'I'll fill you in.' They watched her depart. 'She has a right to be kept in the loop,' he said to Harris.

'Fine.'

'Do you want to tell me what's happening?'

'The head of MI5 is on her way here with Barnes' father. She has the plan. She can explain. It has my support. First we have to make a phone call.'

39

The ringing phone broke the silence, waking Nigel from a light slumber, his head slumped to one side. When had he drifted off? At about 2.30, Dreher had fallen silent, rousing every now and then to peer behind a flap of curtain, or to go to the front door to look through the spyhole and listen, before returning to the sofa and his two guns.

'Hello,' he heard him say into the phone. From a clock on the DVD player beneath the TV he could see it was almost 3.30 a.m. He shook the sleep from his head and remembered his predicament.

Dreher remained silent for what felt like an eternity, but may only have been a few seconds. Then he spoke. 'He comes alone on the stroke of seven a.m.,' he said with utter calm, as if relaying a bus timetable. 'If I see or even sense there is someone with him, then I will detonate the bomb. He comes unarmed to the front entrance. He rings the buzzer. I will let him in. He walks up the stairs, hands held up. If they go below the waist I detonate the bomb.'

More silence.

'No, I release Mr Barnes when his father sets foot in the flat and not a second sooner. Goodbye.' He replaced the handset. Nigel's eyes were by now accustomed to the dark, and he could make out Dreher's features. He appeared to be smiling.

'Looks like you're going to meet daddy.'

Dawn came slowly at about 6.35, imperceptibly at first, but by 6.45 there was enough light for Nigel to make out everything in the flat. Dreher turned on the light, causing both him and Nigel to blink like owls facing sunlight. The last few hours had crawled by. Each man said little. Each movement of the clock caused Nigel's chest to tighten, his breath to become shallower. His mouth was so dry he could hardly speak. He managed a cracked whisper asking for water, and Dreher held a cup to his mouth for a few seconds – a mug of Heather's, studded with polka dots – before draining the rest himself. It seemed he shared Nigel's apprehension. While Nigel might live, whatever happened, the likelihood was that Dreher had experienced his last sunrise.

'Are you going to untie me?' Nigel asked. He had been considering this for hours. If he was free, should he help his father?

Father. It was strange to think of him like that. To be in the same room as him. He had imagined their reunion one day, and it was a stilted conversation over a pint or a coffee, maybe a walk in the park around a lake. Not in front of an assassin surrounded by high explosives.

Dreher had thought out the process. At 6.55, he pulled the pistol from his pocket. For the umpteenth time, he checked the barrel and made sure it was loaded and primed. He produced a penknife from the other pocket. With the gun trained on Nigel, he crouched down and cut the bonds attaching his feet to the chair. Nigel flexed them immediately, a sear of pain soaring up his right leg from his ankle.

'Don't do anything stupid. There is a silencer on this gun … I can kill you and then I can kill your father. You may not believe me, but I don't want to harm you in any way. As a baby, I dandled you on my knee. I gave you a bottle. I knew and loved your mother, first as a lover and then like a sister. It would please me if you walked away from here with your life intact.'

6.56.

Nigel felt a sense of rising desperation. 'Is there no other way this can play out, Thomas?' he asked plaintively.

Dreher shook his head dolefully. 'No. I am sorry. It has to be like this. Your father saw fit to betray us and destroy our lives. It must end here.'

6.57.

'But…'

'Save your breath, Christoph. I hope you'll draw many more of them.'

Christoph. Not Nigel. The first time Dreher had used his name.

6.58.

Dreher picked up a small grey box in one hand, still with the gun in the other. Throughout the night he had kept the box next to him at all times. He must have seen Nigel looking at it. 'The detonator,' he explained.

6.59.

All night, time had been elongated, stretched. Now for a few agonising seconds it was suspended altogether. The read-out still said a minute before seven when the buzzer went, jolting Nigel. He'd been wondering throughout the long dark hours that had passed how he would feel when the hour came. He was surprised that he felt almost calm, as if the sequence of events that followed were entirely out of his control.

7.00.

Aiming the gun at Nigel, Dreher edged towards the front door. Nigel thought about making a headlong dash at him like a battering ram. He would have done, had he still been holding only the gun. But the detonator kept him seated. The flats might have been evacuated. They might not. It was not right that innocents should die because of his impetuosity. Dreher reached the intercom on the wall. He said nothing, merely pressed the button, all the time watching Nigel. He waved the detonator, as if reminding him. Nigel could tell him, if his throat had not been so tight, that he would not forget. The bomb was only eight or nine feet from him.

After releasing the door downstairs, Dreher unlocked the entrance to the flat, slowly and methodically. He was now in perfect control of his emotions and actions, not even a sign of any shaking, his earlier nerves gone. The bolts freed, he edged the door slowly open. Nigel felt a gentle draught of cold air from the passageway, and its familiar musty odour trail in with it. He could hear footsteps on the stairs below.

'Hands above your head,' Dreher barked. 'I have the detonator in my hand and a gun.'

With Dreher's attention on the stairs, this was Nigel's chance. To do what? Get the place blown up? He remained sitting. Waiting for his father to appear.

Dreher walked backwards to the entrance of the room, from where he could see the landing below. 'Hands up,' he repeated. The slow footsteps continued, coming nearer.

'Stand up,' Dreher hissed out of the side of his mouth. 'Now!'

Nigel rose. As he got to his feet, he too could see the landing below.

There stood a figure. Hands aloft. His father.

He was tall, with a thatch of thick grey hair and a bushy yet well-trimmed salt-and-pepper beard. He carried on moving forward, his face devoid of emotion, eyes focused only on Dreher. Nigel tried to smile but his face was frozen. The eyes were clear like his. The face worn but still youthful. He was in a knitted jumper and brown cords, and a tweed jacket. He glanced quickly at Nigel, and was he dreaming or did the eyes twinkle with recognition? He was transfixed, unable to take his eyes from him, forgetting he was less than ten feet from a bomb and just a few from an armed terrorist.

Here at last was his dad.

'Keep coming,' Dreher ordered

He was almost at the landing outside the door.

'Let him go, Thomas,' his father said. The voice was warm, rich.

'Keep coming!'

He had reached the entrance. Dreher backed a few feet further into the room, towards the kitchen door.

'Now you can go, Christoph.'

Nigel couldn't move. He stood, gawping at his father. 'Hello,' he said, pathetically.

'Hello. You must go now.'

Nigel nodded. He began to walk, his legs giving way. He passed his father, catching a faint whiff of aftershave. It was then he realised that tears were streaming down his cheek.

'Keep coming, Kris,' Dreher said again. He stepped forward and by now Nigel had passed his father, the door to the hall in front of him. He took a couple more unsteady steps.

'Let the boy go first,' his father snapped back.

Nigel took a few more steps. He was at the top of the stairs.

'I am here. You can put down the detonator, Thomas. We can talk.'

'I didn't bring you here to talk,' he hissed. 'But as I only want you, and have no need to kill anyone else, I will put it down here.' There was a pause.

It was if a fog had cleared from inside Nigel's head. The next few seconds were pure instinct, as if they came from a part he had always kept hidden.

He spun on his feet and raced back into the flat, his head down and forward, heading through the door and the small entrance hall into the sitting room, altering course by a few degrees straight at Dreher.

Dreher was staring at his father. There was a look of bewilderment on his face, not anger.

'You're not...'

He stopped talking when he saw Nigel coming, and pulled the trigger of his gun. There was loud crack that made his ears ring as he launched himself bodily at Dreher, his head plunging into his wiry midriff, knocking him off his feet. The smell of cordite and smoke filled the air. He heard Dreher groan. He got to his feet. The German was winded and writhing, his eyes bulging. Nigel turned. His father was sprawled across the floor, on his back.

Shot.

Nigel dived to the floor, to the gun which had fallen by his side. Dreher was trying to get up, gasping, his gun having fallen from his grasp under contact. But he was reaching for the sofa. There was the detonator.

Nigel, hands still bound, grabbed the gun and juggled it into position. Dreher was on his knees, still struggling for breath, but his hand was reaching for the small grey box, just inches from his grasp.

He could hear footsteps on the stairs. Lots of them.

Without aiming, and off balance, on his knees, he pulled the trigger, just as Dreher grabbed the box. The recoil set him tumbling sideways, and onto his front, just by the prone body of his father, glassy-eyed on the floor. He prepared himself for the blast. Nothing came. He rolled onto his side just as a dozen armed police flooded through. They ran straight to Dreher, slumped sideways also, half kneeling, on the sofa.

The side of his head was missing. The walls sprayed with his blood and brain matter.

'Dad!' Nigel shouted.

Bodies flew in. A few knelt to attend to the body of his father, while others surrounded the box. There were shouts and cries to get back.

'Nigel!' he heard a voice say. It was Foster. He was at his side. 'You OK?'

'I think so.'

'Come on, get out of here. It might go up any second.'

He hauled him to his feet, one arm round him, placing his arm over his shoulder. They headed quickly to the door. Both saw the gory remnants of Dreher's head decorating his wall.

'Going to be a hell of a cleaning bill,' Foster said as he dragged him to the door.

'My father,' he mumbled, feeling faint, nauseous.

'They'll do what they can,' Foster said as they reached the stairs.

It was then that Nigel blacked out.

40

Foster appeared at Heather and Nigel's side and nodded at them both with a tight smile. *At least one person came*, Nigel thought.

They were at a grave in Kensal Green Cemetery, where Nigel had spent a number of days in recent years, but none as bleak as this. The rain had kept off and there was only a gentle wind which made the trees bow gracefully. The empty grave in front of him was in a less tangled and overgrown part of the graveyard. In the distance he could hear the chorus of London going about its business; the blaring sirens, hum of traffic, unaware as always of all the sadness and loss that were part of its daily life. Heather gripped his gloved hand tighter. Once again, the tears flowed. He could only remember crying twice in his life. Once when he was four and stung by a bee. The second when his adopted mother passed away. But in the past week he had wept countless times. Heather said he was grieving for both his father and a life they never shared. As usual, she was right.

It didn't help that with just him and Heather there, and now Foster, it all seemed such a lonely end. Spies and spooks obviously made few friends, but this few?

Then there was the guilt. He couldn't help but feel responsible. Had he not let Dreher into his flat in the first place, this all might not have happened. Then there was the idea of what might have been had he continued down the stairs and not rushed back in to help. His father had been sent in with a gun, hoping to find time to fire off a shot before Dreher did, Foster said. Nigel rushing back in caused Dreher to fire in haste, killing his father before he'd had a chance even to cock his weapon. Foster told him not to give himself a hard time or feel any guilt. His father had walked in knowing it was likely he might die. The odds on him being able to fire first with his hands above his head, while Dreher's finger was on the trigger, were long. Nigel had at least prevented the bomb being detonated, on purpose or by accident, and for that he was a hero. He had killed Dreher and there, hopefully, the matter was ended.

Nigel appreciated the sentiment but knew that he would mull over the events of that morning every day until his own last breath. The meagre comfort he did take came from having been able to look his father in the eye, to have known him for those few precious seconds. It was better than nothing.

He watched numbly as the coffin was lowered into the ground. The priest had finished his recital.

Heather gave him a hug. They stood a few more seconds over the side of the grave.

Then he turned to Foster.

'Can you come in and see me tomorrow? We need your help,' Foster asked.

'What for?'

'I may have some work for the Home Office for you, if you can bear it. Tracing the living relatives of some of those people on the memory stick. We need to keep an eye on them. The aftershocks will rumble on for some time, years perhaps.'

Nigel nodded. It would be good to throw himself into something like that, even if it did provoke mixed feelings. But he wanted to stop other people experiencing an ordeal similar to his.

'Sure.'

'Good man. I appreciate it,' Foster said and shook his hand. Heather said her farewells and hand in hand they walked away from the leafy, dripping sanctuary of the old graveyard towards the teeming bustle of Ladbroke Grove.

It wasn't Nigel's only impending appointment. He was due at Lara Harrison's house later. She was performing some kind of exorcism and wanted him there. The bedroom with the bricked-up nursery had been converted into one room, redecorated and refurnished. Lara said that as soon as India and she had moved back in, the little girl had been having fewer and fewer bad dreams. Now she rarely woke up. When he saw Lara last she had been rejuvenated, completely different to the hollow-eyed wreck who had first approached him. The casting out of any ghosts or restless spirits would end the matter once and for all, she hoped.

Nigel didn't know what to think. He was glad the child slept and the mother had regained a semblance of a life. Maybe one day he might come to revisit the case and see if it had changed his view of psycho-geography and the idea of events leaving imprints on places. But right now he couldn't. He had just buried his father, who had been shot dead in his flat. That might leave a few imprints of its own for him to deal with. If he ever went back home. Right now he was living at Heather's, given new perspective from what had happened. He wanted to have kids himself, to be there every single day as they grew, a constant, stable figure in their lives. For them to stand over his grave knowing a man and a father, not an enigma.

Foster watched Nigel and Heather leave, two people in love, united in grief. He looked at the grave and the coffin within, then shook his head slowly.

In a graveyard in Northumberland they were burying Jackie Corrigan that same day. His funeral would have once attracted thousands, but now it was unlikely to have outnumbered the few who had turned out to bid farewell to Nigel Barnes' dad.

Helen Chester had confessed to the murder of Schofield. In her interviews, she admitted that for years she had been abused as a little girl by her

Uncle Vince, who had since been arrested. There was talk of a plea of diminished responsibility, which he thought nonsense, but recent experiences had warned him against judging cases so quickly. The Chester family was falling apart. Torn asunder by the secrets of the past seeping to the surface like blood through sand.

'What ails you, DCI Foster?' a voice at his shoulder said.

He turned. It was Henry Mann, the deputy chief of MI5, the urbane, well-groomed spook who had come onto the scene in the last few hours of the siege which saw Barnes' father killed.

'I don't like deception, sir.' He had no idea about seniority between the police and security services, but there was something about Mann that encouraged deference. 'It doesn't seem right.'

'It's for the best, believe me,' Mann replied. 'And as I said before, you can call me Henry.'

'Yes, well, I'll take your word for that, Henry. I just think if he ever finds out that he cried over an empty coffin, and discovers that it wasn't his father he saw being shot, it will cripple him.'

'Well, he won't find out, will he? Unless you tell him. His delightful girlfriend isn't aware of the truth, is she?'

'She knows only what he does.'

'He now has closure, as I believe the modern term is. He knows the truth about his father, who he was, what he did, how he came into the world, and a host of research avenues into the past in which to find more. It is more than he had before.'

'I think he actually wanted to have a relationship with his father.'

'Yes, well … he'll be watched over. His father has made several enemies over the years. It is best for his own safety not to become attached. How is the man we sent in?' he asked, switching subjects.

The officer who had been sent into the building in the guise of Nigel's father had been wearing a Kevlar vest. Other than bearing a similarity to Roland Wilkinson in looks, he was a good shot, but more importantly an expert in bomb disposal, should Dreher have triggered the switch and there had been time to defuse it. But that had all come to nought. The bullet had struck his chest, the vest had taken the force of impact, and he had survived.

'Out of hospital. Back at work soon, I heard,' Foster replied. 'Which is exactly where I should be. If you'll excuse me?'

'Of course,' Henry said. 'Thanks for all your help with this matter. I think it worked out as well as we could have hoped. Dreher is dead. No one else is.'

'I suppose so.' With that, Foster left the graveside and the tall grey-haired man with the black umbrella.

Henry Mann watched him lurch off, the large golf umbrella looking small and insignificant in his giant hands. He turned back to the grave, still open but now deserted.

He looked back at DCI Foster. Beyond his hulking form, at the entrance to the graveyard, he could see two figures walking through the old Victorian arch. It was Heather Jenkins and Nigel Barnes. He smiled.

My son, he thought. *A good man.*

His smile faded.

'I hope he carries his sins better than I have,' he said.

Author's note

This book has experienced an interesting life. I started writing it in 2010 but had to put it to one side in favour of other, more urgent projects. Then as *The Blood Detective* and *Blood Atonement* – or *Code 1879* and *Depuis le Temps de vos Pères* as they were renamed – started to enjoy some success in France, my publishers there asked if there were any more books in the series. I had a draft of *Blood Reckoning*, but wasn't sure if it was ready. But my wonderful French translator, Jean-René Dastugue, read it, loved it and said they would publish it. So in 2014 it appeared in French only as *La Moisson des Innocents* where it received another warm reception.

Since then, I've been asked when it would be available in the UK. Now, at last, it is. There are some changes, corrections and additions to the French version, all of which I hope improve the story.

I am certain of one thing, however. Without the gentle encouragement of Jean-René and his wise counsel, this book, and perhaps this series, might never have progressed. Sadly Jean-Rene died last summer, aged just 49. He was funny, intelligent – and clearly an excellent translator. I often joke that, thanks to him, my books might have been a rare example of those which gained in the translation. This book is dedicated to him.

With his voice in my ear urging me on – 'Dan, don't leave these characters gathering dust' – I hope to release more in the Blood Detective series very soon. So please get in touch via Twitter or Facebook and if you enjoyed it, leaving a short review on Amazon is a great way to let other readers know it might be for them – or not!

Printed in Great Britain
by Amazon